Eating Wolves

First published in the UK in 2003 by
Dewi Lewis Publishing
8 Broomfield Road
Heaton Moor
Stockport SK4 4ND
+44 (0)161 442 9450

www.dewilewispublishing.com

ISBN: 1-899235-84-1

Design & artwork production: Dewi Lewis Publishing
Printed and bound in Great Britain by
Biddles Ltd, Guildford and King's Lynn

3   5   7   9   8   6   4   2

First Edition

Eating Wolves

Alexis Scott

DEWI LEWIS
PUBLISHING

With thanks to Sara Howard for reading the manuscript and making helpful comments. Any errors are my own.
Alexis Scott

For Sara and Brendan

This is a right bloody dive, she thinks as she squats in the empty bath with the shower turned off, soaping herself. The shower head in one hand she turns on the water with the other, fiddling until she gets the temperature about right. Jets of water pummel her skin and she sighs. At least she is by herself again, guaranteed a good five minutes peace and quiet. But there's no such thing as enjoying the whole experience. The shower won't stay on unless you hold onto this funny plastic knob, so just to rinse yourself, you have to squat, bent double, one hand on the knob and the other holding the shower head. Not that she should be surprised. Things not going right is the story of her life.

It's just another of the things that isn't working in the apartment. Even if the shower was fixed you couldn't stand up and let the water go where it will because there's no curtain. The last thing she needs is a bill for flooding the folk downstairs. There's no point in complaining because there's nothing to hold a curtain up. A budget hotel, Madge said. She's been to plenty of budget places in her time, but there's always been a bloody curtain in the shower.

It was the evening of the day they moved in before anybody noticed and when people looked at Madge as if to say, You're the one that speaks French, you should be doing the complaining, she just says, There's no point. She doesn't blame Madge. It's too much trouble moving to another apartment (assuming there's one available) and maybe none of them have fixings for a shower curtain (or a shower where you don't have to hold onto the plastic knob, although that seems less likely). How would she know? She has no experience of French showers (or much else that's French, come to that).

We've been to France loads of times, Madge told her. Although just a couple of weeks once a year at the most is hardly enough to keep up. She said nothing. Madge knows fine well this is her and Gavin's first time in France.

All French folk could shower like that all the time for all we know, Gavin goes. He was sloshed, right enough, him and Stuart having gone straight out the minute they got here and returned with a dozen odd bottles of beer but not before, she suspected, they'd had a good few in a bar down the road.

Don't be ridiculous, Madge said. Madge was always one for speaking her mind. This time she couldn't blame her (not that she would ever speak to Stuart like thon). But I mean, for Christ's sake. It was like that was what Gavin's understanding of different cultures amounted to – some notion that they bathed or showered differently from you. Christ. Married fifteen year and before that they lived together for three year and he can still come out with shite like that. It is bloody frightening sometimes. He's done it before, of course, made an arse of himself. Sometimes she thinks he's getting worse. Regressing or something. Or maybe she's the one who made the mistake of thinking she knew him all these years and she doesn't, she doesn't know him at all.

Och, she shouldn't make too much of one wee incident. They're on holiday, for Christ's sake. Although Gavin drinks too much as it is. It is hard to know where to take him on holiday. *Take* being the operative word for if it was left to Gavin to decide it'd be Christmas before he made his mind up.

She could have a bath instead but she doesn't want to set a precedent. If Alan started having baths he'd be in the place all day. She'd go daft stuck in the apartment all day. She'd go daft in the house never mind this place. At least they're getting out and about a bit though, doing a bit of sight-seeing, even if they don't always see eye to eye.

It's funny the things that draw you together. Like differences. Not the ones Gavin maybe imagined but there are differences just the same, differences between them and the French. Here they are, the four (or five) of them, seething with loathing at one another after just three days, blaming one another for everything that has gone wrong or even stuff that just hasn't happened (like the fact that they are wasting too much time and haven't got round to doing X and Y, for example). Not that you say as much. You don't really say very much at all. Only a look says a thousand words and all that. Afraid to fall out, so they are. One fall-out and then where will they be? Up the proverbial shit creek. It's natural for tensions to arise when you're spending all day long in one another's company. That is maybe why they should never've contemplated the idea, coming here thegither, pretending they were all palsy-walsy. At least her and Madge usually get on pretty OK but then they don't see one another that much. Gavin and Stuart and Alan don't really know each other at all. How in the name her and Madge imagined them all having a holiday together…

There were a few wee complaints that drew them thegither right enough. Like the dogshit – the way the wee wummen wi the wee dugs go aboot like they own the place, as Gavin said, the way they hold their noses in the air when the dogs are doing a shite. They don't really, but right enough you never see anybody wi a pooper scooper. You see dogs in cafés with the waiter all over them and wonder if he went to wash his hands when he went back to the kitchen, and wee wifies wi dogs in baskets in supermarkets that folk come over to pat, never knowing or caring where they've been. Then there is the attitude of the receptionists when you went to ask for another toilet roll, for example. You have finished – already?

Aye, we've all got diarrhoea wi the strange food, hen, Gavin said, but only under his breath after she'd went away in the back for another one. At home he'd have bantered wi her, made a joke of it. Only reception were all straight faces, unless they were talking to one another, anyway. They weren't exactly what you'd call straight, as Madge said. Reception smelled of cannabis all the time. It stunk to high heaven in the evening, so it did. Made you think the lazy gits just sat about and got high all the time, they had that little to do. Students, probably, just wanting to eke out the summer.

Maybe we should ask one of them for a drag of the joint, Stuart says. Madge laughed but Gavin and her said nothing. Alan was there, after all.

It was Madge that had the idea about communication – but communication between cultures is something else. She has worked with Asian women, helped them set up community groups, all that. It is not that she is some sort of cultural nationalist but she has a long way to go before she understands the French. Maybe she is getting too old.

The worst was the business about the wolf. That drew them thegither all right. Jesus! It'd be some laugh if it wasnae serious but! Only really you could hardly credit it what with them being a nation of dog lovers.

They maybe would've thought it was all some mistake on Madge's part – Higher French or no – but her own (bang up to date) dictionary translated *loup* as wolf so how could there be any mistake?

She was still pondering over this when Madge read out this column (or translated it, to be accurate) from this French newspaper she'd bought. *Nice Matin* it was called. Something about the problem of the wolves in the Alps. Causing a nuisance, killing thousands of sheep.

Apparently they used to be extinct in France, Madge says. Only then they crossed the border from Italy and started breeding in France. They're allowed to hunt in Italy as well.

But not in France?

I don't think so, says Madge.

Gavin gives her a look. Right enough, Madge, I can just imagine them saying to another, Come on, boys, there's nae hunting in France, let's get ower the border, quick!

Madge gave him an almost friendly smile, for once.

Sheila felt suddenly grateful. There was nothing worse, after all, than other folk – especially professional folk like Madge who could have been colleagues really, if they worked in the same place – thinking your man was an eejit, all the time. I mean, all men have to be eejits, don't they, some of the time? Even smarmy gits like Stuart do, don't they?

Do ye think it's Italian wolves in the cafés, then? she turns to Madge.

Madge shrugs. Could be. No idea.

They could be from Russia or bloody anywhere, Stuart grumbles.

As if it made any difference, she thinks. Honest to God, bloody men.

Jesus Christ! Wait till they hear this at hame! says Gavin. But you should maybe challenge them Madge, seeing as it's you with the Higher French and all.

Madge smiled at him again, a proper smile, not like her usual patronising ones, which are not smiles at all and which she sees now Madge copies from Stuart. That seems to be the extent of Madge's and Stuart's communication – smarmy exchanges. Except they must have sex too. Do they never let it go? She tries to imagine smarmy sex between the two of them. Perhaps it is a kind of play-acting, for all she knows. Only she doubts it. If her and Gavin have normal rows – and Christ knows anybody in their circumstances would row some of the time – there is nothing normal about the moods Madge goes into with Stuart. She always kent Madge was the moody type, thought herself too good for the likes of some (her maybe). Only nothing as bad as this. For the first time she realises Madge and Stuart are on the verge of splitting up. Only Gavin doesn't seem to notice. And how can she say anything when nobody has said anything to her? For all she knows they have been carrying on like this for years, silence speaking volumes. Except it doesn't. It just means you guess volumes. They are over here – some of them anyway – to learn a bit of the language, improve communication with folk from other cultures. That was how Madge persuaded her to come that night they discussed it in the pub. Improve communication. With other cultures. When they cannae talk to one another. What a bloody joke. If it was funny. Ha. ha. Fucking hell.

A bang on the door halts her. Did they no hear her having a shower, for Christ's sake? Except she was finished a couple of minutes ago. Now she is having to struggle in the poky wee bathroom, struggle into the one pair of shorts she's brought that doesn't cleave her stomach in half so she has to wear an extra long T shirt, when Madge who is five years older is wandering about in these skinny midriff tops. Madge always was full of herself anyway.

Wait a minute!

When she's out the door she sees it's Alan. He brushes past her into the toilet and locks the door before she can say a word. He can never wait a minute at home either, but at home he'll start a shouting match but no here. That's the reason, primarily, she thinks, she wanted to come. Nothing to do with self-advancement and even a break (how can you get a break with your son and your man in tow?). It was Alan she'd had in mind all along. Not just the French, although that too. Experiencing different cultures, any culture apart frae just the football and the stuff he does at home. She'd never get him into the Gallery of Modern Art in Glasgow but here it is different, especially with Madge and Gavin here. At least some of the time he is willing to go along with other folk's ideas, compromise. Pity the *Musée d'Art Contemporain*, or whatever it was called, was shite, mostly.

She sees Stuart through in the kitchen eating his breakfast and smiles across to him on her way through to the bedroom. *Bedroom* is a bit of a joke. The proverbial couldn't swing a cat type. Although it is only for the holidays. The excuse she has been making every time somebody complains, for that – between the silences – is what their communication has been this holiday – a catalogue of complaints. Since they set off she has been adopting the role of the compliant, the persuader, the do-gooder even. Not the role she takes on at home. Well, holidays are about change, aren't they?

A moment before Gavin was lying sleeping peacefully enough. Now he has opened his mouth and is snoring loudly. She can't stand snoring. Especially at nine o'clock in the bloody morning. She shoves his foot gently under the covers and she can see the familiar signs of him waking up. Some things don't change. She gives him another shove, marginally less gentle, and he starts to wake up properly.

Gavin

The shaft of sunlight strikes his face and makes him want to smile with pleasure. Only there is this thing at the bottom of the bed, jabbing his toes. Nearly shoving him off the bed. For fuck's sake. That bloody son of his again. You would think a bloody fourteen year old could gie you peace in your holidays. Sheila has the wee bugger spoilt rotten. Nearly as big as he is now and still coming in annoying him in the mornings. If it wasn't for the fact that the sun is shining he'd be cracking up.

It was the sun that gave away where they were. Their north facing flat never gets the sun. You only get the sun in Scotland once in a blue moon anyway but here it shines all the time. It is incredible, right enough. If it wasn't for the fact that the sun is shining he would ask the wee bugger what the fuck is he doing at this time of the morning annoying his da and could he not give him five minutes peace? If it wasn't for the fact that he doesn't say fuck, at least not to Alan, at least not when they are on holiday. If it wasn't for the fact that they are on their holidays and that he is a parent and the sun is shining so you cannae justify going around swearing, not even if you are jumped on at the crack of dawn for nothing, he'd definitely speak to him so he would. He'd say hell or something only the look would say fuck or at least be interpreted as fuck. He might as well say fuck for all Alan cares except he still has a responsibility as a parent even if Alan doesn't (or doesn't appear to) give a fuck about that. He has a responsibility not to say fuck. Sometimes he thinks that is all being a parent amounts to, a responsibility not to say fuck. Not in front of the weans anyhow. If it wasn't for the sun and Stuart and Madge being here too. Only when he at last manages to get his eyes open it is Sheila standing at the bottom of the bed.

Was Alan in a minute ago? he asks, puzzled.

Naw, he's in the bathroom. Having a shower. Time to get up!

He starts to tell her about the sensation in his foot a minute ago, then decides to forget it. Although for a minute he could have sworn someone kicked him. He must be imagining things. Christ, he knows his brain isn't as zappy as it used to be but he never used to imagine things.

Right, he says, trying to push the thought out of his head. Breakfast, eh?

But Sheila is already gone. It is like he is seeing, and maybe doing, things in slow motion. He could see into it if it was just the holidays but he had this sensation before they came away. Not that there's anything wrong with winding down, slowing your pace. He is forty one, after all. Time to slow the pace anyway. He is over here to slow the pace, have a break, get a bit of sun for a change. Meantime the rest of them want to go haring off all the time. All he wants mostly is to go to the beach, relax, get a suntan. What's wrong wi that?

Alan nearly knocks him over coming out the bathroom.

Jesus Christ, can you no watch where you're going?

Watch where you're fucking going yourself.

Christ, if he spoke to his old man like thon when he was that age – or any age come to that – he'd have bloody hammered him. He said that once to Sheila and she nearly went down his throat. He has to watch what he says more than Alan does these days. It is bloody ridiculous really.

What are you saying? Are you trying to justify violence against children or something?

Naw, that's no what I'm saying. That's no it at all. You're taking me the wrong way.

She always takes him the wrong way when it suits her. She is always making out he is out of touch, out of the way of how things are these days, the way folk speak to one another even. Offski. Maybe it is her that is out of touch for all he kens. Just because she has this poxy job as a social worker Sheila thinks she knows all the ins and outs about how society operates and he doesnae. And she can be a hypocrite as well. When Alan was wee she gave him a good slap now and again when it suited her. Apologising afterwards. Making out it was her nerves. Men couldn't give excuses like that. Couldn't get away wi them. Men aren't supposed to have nerves.

Hi.

At least Stuart is being civil. Offering him a croissant.

Christ, is that all there is to eat in this place? Bloody croissants.

There's baguettes as well.

Madge. Could never stay out of it, even a wee blether between blokes. A wee joke.

Aye, that's what I mean, bloody French stuff.

Stuart is grinning away. At least somebody has a sense of humour.

I like croissants anyway. What's wrong with croissants?

Alan, sitting down to eat at the table, the way Sheila likes him to.

Nothing wrong wi them at all. Just a joke. Just a joke.

13

Some bloody joke.

Christ. No wonder he tries to ignore him most of the time. You cannae win. If you try to crack a joke they are on top of you. If you ignore them she – Sheila – complains you never give him any attention. Attention, aye, he'd've got attention all right in his day. A slap across the lugs, a sear face is what he'd've got all right. And more. His auld man might have mellowed now he has nothing better to do but sit about the house all day, but thirty year ago he was a right auld bastard. Although they all were, right enough. A good hammering was something every wean was afeard of in they days. It was not as if his auld man was any worse than any of the rest of them, when it came down to it.

Boys that age are supposed to start identifying wi being men. You could understand when they're wee how they defer to their mothers, seeing that their mothers take more to do with them. When Alan was wee Sheila only worked part-time. Now Sheila is full-time – has been full-time for the past four or five year – and he is on the scrap heap.

Stuart is looking at him in a pitying sort of way as he offers the plate of croissants. Normally he would go and put one in the microwave but he cannae be bothered. He nibbles at it cold while he pours the coffee. Madge must've made it. She is the best coffee-maker he's ever come across, for all her faults. It is a sophisticated kind of thing to do, making real coffee. Like walking about quaint auld streets like *Vieux Nice*. Very nice. But then it is all right for some. She's never had anything else to do, apart from her job, anyway. Make fancy coffee and go away gallivanting. Stuart and Madge have no weans. Never wanted them, presumably. He never asked. It isnae the kind o thing men discuss wi one another. It is the sort of thing you could imagine Sheila discussing wi folk, sympathising but no Madge. Somehow he cannae imagine Madge a mother – there are too many hard edges to her.

So, plans for the day? Here she is, sharp as a knife, butting in.

Erm, I was just wondering where Sheila was.

She's away to the shop.

Serrated voice. There was no call for that. He only asked. Didn't even mean to speak his thoughts aloud.

He is tempted to say, Lovely day for the beach. I mean, Christ, what is wrong wi going to the beach? It isn't as if he is talking about going to the bookies or the pub. I mean, he can see into it how women get fed up wi that kinda carry-on. Going over the score too many times. Drinking at all hours of the day. He kens he went over the score himself when he got here. Letting Stuart buy him all that drink. Couldnae carry it. No used tae it. It was the excitement, right enough. Two year since they'd had a holiday. But the fucking beach. I mean, for Christ's sake.

It was the beach that persuaded them, persuaded the boy – Alan – to come. He wasn't even that bothered for going abroad this year, especially with the financial matters. The financial matters were not to be ignored. Precarious was the word for it. Precarious. But it wasn't just the financial matters. He was beginning to lose the kind of confidence you need for going abroad. Not just the passports and all that carry-on. All the wee things they do differently in other countries. Even the times of day they eat. Getting used to the different culture. Adjusting yourself.

For once he fancied a trip to Largs or Rothesay or some place. Somewhere he could reminisce, maybe. He only remembers the two holidays when he was a kid. Camping. He thinks it was Rothesay but he isn't sure. He minds going on the big boat but maybe that was only for the day. But they definitely went camping the once. It poured the whole week. Imagine wanting to reminisce about that.

Aye, reminisce about his sweet fucking childhood. Reminisce about getting battered tae fuck for doing sweet FA. Who is he kidding?

When Sheila came home talking about cheap EasyJet fares and a flatshare so they didn't have to eat out all the time he jumped at the chance. Only they all had different ideas about a holiday. He must've imagined spending the whole time on the beach. It wouldn't even have to cost much. You could make up picnics. Only Madge and Stuart didn't want picnics. They had different ideas.

Aye, different ideas. I mean, fancy spending time in museums when you could be outside in that lovely weather.

I was thinking of the *Musée Matisse* but I can always go myself. I mean, we don't have to hang around together all the time. We've got the two keys between us, after all.

It was Madge, right enough, that arranged the two keys. Asked in French. Although, as it turned out, the guy spoke English anyway. Madge made you feel a right arsehole because you didn't know French and she did. No that he doesn't know any – he was taught it a couple o year at the school after all, but he doesn't have the right accent, can't speak it at all really. The time he learned it at the school you'd have looked a right numpty putting on the accent. It was like putting on airs, trying to speak the way the teacher did. You'd've been called a poof and all sorts, speaking thon way. Even doing well at the school you were thought a right nancy boy (them that did well, no him). No wonder the teachers looked that fed up all the time, a class like his.

15

He knows Sheila wants the boy to get something out of this holiday apart frae a break frae Glasgow, a break frae the school. If Sheila had her way he'd be going to the school twenty four hour a day, seven days a week. Before she went to the college and sat her Highers and then the degree and the rest she was always going on about lack of opportunities, how she'd never got any decent qualifications at the school. Now it's the boy she goes on about. Like now she's got so far she's transferred all her ambitions to him. She never cared about *his* education, never assumed he'd want to do anything, go anywhere. Painting for years wi the bloody council. He was supposed to be lucky to have a job to go to. Never mind how the paint went for his chest, that bloody paint they used for donkeys' years and only now they say it's toxic. And the bloody union's lawyers say they've no case because nobody could've been expected to know in they days it was toxic. Bloody shite.

I wouldn't mind going to this *Musée Matisse*, he hears his son say. For a split second he is astounded, even a wee bit angry that his son has the nerve to speak French like that, the way he never could when he was his age – still couldn't because he's left it too late. Then he feels this warm, strange sensation come over him – pride, that is what it is, pride, that his ain son, frae a working class background wi a da that never had any opportunities, wants tae better hissell, tae speak French properly, tae go tae museums and art galleries and places tae improve his mind the way his da never could.

Right, he says. If that's what ye want, that's what we'll dae. And then we'll go to the beach this afternoon.

You don't have to come, Alan goes, no even calling him dad, the cheeky wee bastard. I can just go wi Madge. I'm free anyway.

He is speechless. He never even mentioned Stuart. So that's his game, is it? Thinking of gallivanting off wi a woman in her late thirties if she's a day. Pushing forty. Dirty wee tyke.

Maybe your dad wants to come as well. It is Sheila, smiling, her arms cradling two big French loaves – bigger than they baguettes that hardly fill ye anyway. He never even heard her come in. I quite fancy going myself. Are we all going then?

Aye, we're all going, he says, but not too loudly in case Alan starts a shouting match the way he does at home. He doesn't want a showing up. There's been disagreements this holiday, sure, but nothing worse than that. But he'll remember to speak to Sheila later about this carry-on. She heard it right enough but maybe she doesnae realise the

16

implications. Although maybe, right enough, as long as Madge doesnae encourage it, there's nothing wrong wi the odd sexual fantasy. He has them hisself, after all. At least Madge isnae wearing that sexy top that shows her bare midriff. If Alan wants to look at half-naked women all he has to do is go to the beach, for fuck's sake. All they topless women, ancient ones as well wi their tits hanging all over the place, you'd think they'd be ashamed. At least Madge and Sheila have some modesty, decent married Scotswomen.

On the bus Alan lets it out about this other museum place. Apparently it is right next to the Matisse place.

Only it shuts for lunch but the Archaeological one doesn't. Would you mind if we went there first?

He is turning to Madge as if she is the only one that matters, as if none of the rest of them have any opinions, as if they just came along to please him or something (which maybe they did, right enough).

Well, Madge hesitates, recognising it is not just her province, at least. Only he is at a loss what to say. Should he come down the heavy parent, say, look here, boy, you cannae tell folk one thing and then change your mind, it's no fair. Besides which it was Alan's idea to go to this crappy place the other day, this really shite museum – the kind that looked like it hadnae been done up – or hardly – since you were a wean yourself. Only he doesn't want a scene, has been trying to avoid one since they came away. And what is this archaeological place anyway? Maybe the boy should get another chance to pick.

Sheila saves the day (maybe). Now that sounds interesting, let's have a look, will we?

Folk are already tired of making decisions – that is what all this gallivanting is about, isn't it, after all? It's all right for folk like Madge and Stuart and even Sheila that make decisions in their workplace, every day of the working week. Folk wi their middle class jobs that go about telling other folk what to do. He has always been the one to get told what to do. Och, what the hell, the rest of them are nodding their heads. He might as well go along wi it.

* * *

The museum Alan took them to the other day was called the *Terra Amata* – something like that but longer – that long you could never remember all the words even if you knew French. Unless you were Madge and made a point of remembering everything, to show other folk

17

up, probably. The worst thing about it was not just that it was boring shite but that he encouraged Alan in the idea. Alan is right into the history and geography at school, only mainly it is ancient history and oceans and plants and animals and all that stuff. If the boy wants to get into history he would rather it was Culloden and Stirling Bridge and John MacLean and the Red Clydesiders, but maybe all that will come later. Rome wasnae built in a day, nor Scotland either. Together him and Alan had looked the museum up on one of the free maps of Nice Sheila had found for them at the airport. Reconstruction of a Paleolithic site, it said. The picture looked good too. He wasn't sure what he – still less Alan – had imagined, but something bigger, grander, than what this was. They thought they would be late and Alan was rushing them, getting at them. Then when they got there they spent barely half an hour in the place and that was them pacing themselves.

It was Madge had complained the most, even though she was the one knew French. She had spoke to the guy in French but he had caught the word *Anglais* and the next thing Madge was handing out these leaflets.

He says if we wait here there'll be a sound recording in English, Madge said, sounding pleased with herself, as if she'd arranged it or something. So there's the five of them hanging about like lemons, trying to match up this leaflet with the pictures on the walls. Right enough it was worse for Madge because she was trying to match up the two different writings – the French on the wall and the English on the leaflet. When the sound recording started they thought it was all right – at least for the first minute or so. Only after the first minute or so it gets to be really boring. Stuart was glancing at him and he was glancing at Stuart. Sheila and Madge tried harder for that little bit longer but then Madge starts wandering off and Sheila starts following her.

Alan was still interested, that was the funny thing. Even though the place was crap, and not designed for kids or teenagers at all as far as he could see really, Alan was far more interested than the adults were. It was not as if he was putting on an act, the way adults do when they feel they have to be polite in company or in a strange town and especially when it's a foreign country. Alan never felt he had to be polite, no the way he did when he was a kid. He just went all quiet and looked bored if he couldn't relate to something or he wandered off or, worse, he got mad and just wouldn't put up with whatever it was he couldn't stand. Only here was Alan more interested in these artefacts and what have you than the rest of them.

Madge had started giggling. A grown woman, a social worker as well, and no even had a drop to drink (well, it was only eleven in the morning right enough) and here she was grinning all over her face. Trying to control it right enough (he had never seen Madge out of control, never seen her drunk, come to that – the woman, he always thought, was something of a control freak so she was hardly going to lose control in a place like this, was she?) Only he had to laugh himself. Controlling it as well, right enough, not wanting to appear pig-ignorant, like, in front of these French folk. Show up the Scots.

Look at that footprint, Alan goes.

He stares at the reconstructed footprint. Interesting in a way, as all ancient things are. Only there again, it is only a footprint, it is nothing special. It doesn't look any different from a twenty first century footprint except its outline is vague, you cannot see the toes. For all he knows they could have made it up, concocted the whole shebang. Madge had bought this guide – the *Rough Guide* it was called – to the area. There was this bit at the back that went on about corruption in Nice, in the local government and all that, about what a right-wing place it was.

Maybe we should've gone somewhere else, he says.

We never bothered about that before, did we, though? Sheila says. I mean, isn't Majorca right-wing as well and we went there, didn't we?

Aye, he says.

He is thinking about the wolf now. Wondering if there is a connection. Fascists eating dogs.

Alan is calling him over. Amazing how a place like this can hold the boy's interest. They've all moved away from the speakers broadcasting the droning voice boring into your ears. They are all up the stairs, looking at the wee bits and pieces in glass cases. A security guy is following them about, watching them. There's nothing to steal anyway, is there? It's all in glass cases. Although you could break the glass, maybe, if you were mad enough. Protesting about the wolves or something.

Suddenly he feels more relaxed. If this is what Alan is into he can't be that bad. Wee bits of flint and stuff they used for their hunting. Hunters and gatherers. He minds some of the stuff now he was taught at the school, thank Christ. Only, he only learnt it because he had to. Never went into a museum in his life until Sheila took him to the Kelvingrove. Sheila was the sophisticated city kid from the south side while he was a schemie frae Easterhouse. What was he into at Alan's age? Football, football and football. He liked painting and drawing too, of course. You could only paint at the school but he has always liked the drawing. Still sketches now and again. He minds when he was asked at school what he wanted to be when he was older and he said a painter, and the teacher just assumed he meant a house painter, and sure enough that's what he ended up doing. If he had lived in Bearsden and went to a different school maybe people would have took him seriously but you never got landscape painters in a place like Easterhouse, did you? In a place like Easterhouse people weren't supposed to have heard of Dufy and Pissaro and all they artists. Leonardo da Vinci and Van Gogh and your Monet maybe but that was about the height of it. Even though there was countryside round about Easterhouse too – cornfields and all that – the teachers never lived there and they would have assumed it was just houses. So if you were from Easterhouse and you wanted to paint, naturally it would be just houses, wouldn't it?

Here they are at the *Musée Archaeologique de Nice-Cimiez*. Christ, what a mouthful. They can see straight away this one is a real archeological site – not some reconstruction, the way the other one was. Only they have to go inside to pay first. They will come out and see this stuff later. Aye, this stuff looks pretty amazing right enough. Trust his son to pick a good yin.

This lassie hands him a couple of pieces of paper. Speaks to him in English. Maybe heard them talking, right enough. A lot of people just speak English, right enough. But no Scots, ha ha. He imagines replying to the lassie in broad Scots just to see her face. Only he widnae be that cruel.

Thanks, he says. Thanks very much. Maybe he should've said *merci*. Anybody can say *merci*. It's a bit pathetic to say *merci* in English when you're in France.

I would be very grateful if you would take some time to fill this in, the lassie says. After your visit. Her English is very stilted considering this job she has. Some of the waiters speak better English, he thinks. He smiles at her and stuffs the paper into his pocket. Madge looks enquiringly at him but says nothing. Wanting to fill it in herself, no doubt. Well, it's no big deal. Maybe they can all do it after.

More artefacts only this is the Romans. It is sort of coming together now, though. The *Terra Amata* was pre-history whereas this is the Romans. Everybody knows about the Romans whereas pre-history you just tend to associate with dinosaurs. At the *Terra Amata* Sheila remarked they could be making it all up. The worst bit – the bit you expected to be the best, maybe because they had a seen a photo on the map and it looked – well, vibrant – only it turned out to be these wooden-looking models wi faces resembling apes – early man – thickos by anybody's standards. Anyway the worst bit was these models because you felt the curator – or whoever it was that put all this stuff together – had just overused his imagination. Putting these savage expressions on these folk just because they were prehistoric. Who's to say they were that thick? They made tools, they could build fires. They built a primitive society, maybe better than the one they have now.

He should concentrate more on the moment instead of thinking too much or he will be missing things. Already Alan is looking a bit fed up. He doesn't understand it because there are real, big Roman remains here (is that what they call them – remains?). Statues and stuff like that. Statues of their Gods. Madge is translating because Madge knows her Latin as well as French. They never did Latin at the school he went to. Never did fuck all. Although Alan doesnae do Latin either, nobody does any more. Except at the private schools. They bring in comprehensive education and still kids are being deprived. Still the middle classes send their weans to private schools or Jordanhill if they can afford to live there. Some fucking socialism the Labour Government's – the Scottish Parliament's – brought.

They troop outside and Alan is leading the way again. Going to be a right bossy boots when he's older. A manager or something maybe. No that you need an education for that. Just a hard neck. You get some wankers in some fancy jobs whereas there's graduates on the dole. Would he rather see his son with a degree on the dole or an ignorant prick like hisself in some fancy job wi loads of money? Except he doesnae have the fancy job, o course. Never did have. Except plenty do. He doesn't know the answer really. He'd like him to be happy. Wi a house of course. You cannae get a decent house these days if you've no got a decent job. No such thing as getting your name down on the list the way his ma and da did. They were in a room and kitchen when he was wee. He minds the day they got the front and back door. His granny was looking after him to keep him out the way when they were flitting. No that they had much to flit wi.

They leave behind the statues and go outside to see the big stuff. The history beneath them, as it were. Brings it to life, this stuff, so it does. Walking next to real Roman buildings.

Sheila points out the sign warning them where they can and can't go. The instructions are not clear, not at all. Well, it's unlikely they'll do anything that'll get them arrested, he says, laughing, but no-one else laughs. He wishes they would all lighten up, for Christ's sake. Learning is supposed to be fun these days, isn't it?

Alan is reading off the leaflet which is only a wee bit easier to follow than the one at the *Terra Amata*. There is a map on the leaflet too. The first ruins they have come to apparently date from 1 AD (*après Jesus-Christ* – even he can understand what that means – he's no that ignorant). This is apparently some sort of church. They carry on and come to the bit that shows (sort of because you have to imagine most of it – it is all but all away – this is merely a representation, after all) where the central heating was and everything.

It's like the model inside, see, Alan says to him. He never calls him dad, or da, any more. Still, at least he's talking to him, not Madge or Sheila who are talking together, wandering on ahead.

The slaves must have had to crawl, Alan says.

Slaves, aye. Jesus Christ. Some civilization, he says. Bloody terrible.

He feels there should have been more acknowledgment of the slaves, somehow, but this is all there is. He doesn't even know how to express what he means. How could they represent people who were made to look invisible? In a way it is terrible that the rich folk's possessions have survived – their silly wee bits of gold jewellery, their statues and stuff – and there is nothing to tell you about how the slaves lived and died.

Sheila is coming towards him. What is it? she asks, as if there is something wrong.

The slaves, he says, I was thinking about the slaves.

She doesn't reply but he thinks she knows what he means.

Afterwards she says, What you were saying about the slaves (although he didn't actually say anything, apart from uttering the word) – I mean, their very existence speaks for itself, how it was for them, doesn't it? I mean, the fact of the low ceilings in the basement, where they had to light the fires. It doesn't need another statement, does it?

I see what you mean, he said slowly, but I still think we cannae let the Romans speak for them. As if they were illiterate.

Well, probably they were.

Well, maybe not all of them. He thinks he has heard of at least one who wasn't and anyway don't people sometimes teach themselves? No, no they don't if they don't have the opportunities. He is ashamed for a moment to have ever thought he had none himself. Him that had a half-decent education. He should shut up moaning sometimes, be grateful for what he has. Try and make more of his life. There isn't that much of it left maybe. Need to start making each day count.

There are only nine days of the holiday left. They have had four full days here. Three museums and two mornings and three afternoons at the beach. Maybe it wouldn't matter if he never got to the beach again. Or maybe if he only went the once more. Only Alan is talking about going to the beach tomorrow.

Aye, all right, he says. He is glad to be asked. It makes a difference when you are asked.

Madge

She is lying on the beach by herself. Not by herself, of course – there are hundreds of other people too, some of them only a couple of metres away, but the men are in the water and Sheila is away to the shops. Away to buy presents or something. They agreed the first day the easiest thing would be for one of them to stay and look after the stuff. Maybe at home you would trust people – it is not as if they were going that far out in the water – they can still see their stuff – but here you have passports and insurance documents as well as loads of cash you normally never carry. She has left hers and Stuart's in the apartment today but Sheila and Gavin are too paranoid to do that.

She turns over carefully because it's uncomfortable if you move yourself too quickly on pebbles. Not as bad as walking on them though. They could have got beach mats but thought they were too much trouble to take home and maybe they'd never need them again. Although there is something she loves in the place it is perfectly possible – likely even – she will not return, with or without Stuart. The world is a big place, after all. Plenty of other places to speak French, plenty of other places to see, plenty of other cultures to learn about.

She has brought a book but today she cannot concentrate. Maybe because the boys, as she has come to think of them – including her husband of eighteen years – will be out of the water any minute and there is not enough time. That is the trouble with holidays. Absurdly, paradoxically, there is not enough time. Not enough time to do things properly, learn about places, about the people who lived here – the artists, Dufy, Matisse. That bloody Yves Klein who caused so much of a stir between them this morning.

At first she had laughed. Laughed at the pool of pigment. Delighted because it was such a puzzle. To start with you would never have guessed, thinking it was some material or something with more substance. Then, after you had seen, not even the video, but the photo of the women getting dragged round the floor, not just smeared in paint but spread with it, like thick paste or peanut butter on bread, then you made up your mind. The women were not just getting dragged round, but dragged along to the orchestra of men sitting there, apparently oblivious yet also complicit in this attack on femaleness. She is ignorant about art, she knows. Maybe not as ignorant as your average

Scot for she has art books in the house she dips into now and again but she is still ignorant. Never studied the history of art or anything. The art teacher at school was crap. In some ways the school she went to was crap although everybody used to say what a good school it was. There was all this emphasis on science and a wee bit on languages but art got sort of left by the wayside, as if it was not really a truly academic subject. As if representation did not matter, only facts. When you cannot have the one without the other. Aye, she was, is, ignorant, still. For that reason (because she is educated, after all – she is not ignorant about everything) she was prepared to give artists the benefit of the doubt. Until now. She thinks she may have heard of Yves Klein before but is not sure. Certainly not in the same league as Warhol whose Campbell's soup tin she much admired, at least because of its 3Dness. Was Klein ever as big as Warhol? Did feminists ever dare to spoil his work the way they attacked Warhol's? Did Warhol treat women like shit too? She has only the haziest recollection about the attack on Warhol's work or was it on him? Some sort of feminist protest. The kind she normally supports in principle only can you justify destroying art? Can you not draw a distinction between the man and his art (if it is art)? She should find out more. This, being a tourist business, is just skimming over the surface, pretending to want to find out things when really it is just being lazy. Coming here in a group does not help matters. They all have their own motives. All Sheila and Gavin think about is Alan and all he thinks about is himself. Like all kids, she supposes. Once upon a time she wanted kids. For years she wanted kids. For years they tried to adopt. At one point they even considered older kids when they realised babies available for adoption were like gold dust. Then they tried IVF but had to give that up too. Now, at forty-one, there is no chance. Even though the doctors couldn't find anything specific there has to be no chance at forty one. And at forty one she no longer wants kids. It has taken her eighteen years – the length of her marriage – to appreciate being by herself, appreciate the freedom parents don't have.

When she asked Sheila about coming here she assumed Sheila knew she meant just her and Gavin. By the time Alan was mentioned the accommodation arrangements had already been made and it was too late to back out. It was only when they were discussing flights that she twigged. If she'd said something then Sheila would've just backed out. You could see by her face that Alan was a major reason for her coming. He'll be doing his Standard grades in a couple of years. Needing to improve his French. The lion's share of the holiday, as far as Sheila was concerned, was for Alan while her and Gavin would just have the left-overs.

Some things she can talk about, quite intimately, with Sheila. Womanly stuff – periods, their men (up to a point), sex even. But not kids. Not beyond the usual sugar-coated lies people perpetuate about their family relationships.

She has known Sheila for years but she didn't really know anything of Sheila's relationship with her kid. Not until this summer anyway. She knows Sheila thinks a lot of her son but what mother doesn't? She has always seen Sheila as an independent sort of woman who does her own thing. Now she knows different. Sheila was the one who would go on about men holding you back and she always saw Sheila as somehow more independent from her man than she ever was. Sheila is five years younger, after all. Five years can make a lot of difference to a woman's attitudes.

She wishes now she had asked someone else. Someone who spoke better French, for a start. Although there are advantages to being the only one who does, reasonably well. She has never thought learning the language was just for going into restaurants and ordering things to eat. Showing off in other words, for most of the waiters and waitresses seem to speak English. She has been attending an A level class for the past year as well as reading loads of stuff at home, watching French cable TV. During the brief holidays she spends over here she has been trying to pick it up again, trying to pick up all the nuances she missed when she was at school. There is more to a language than the grammar, there is the whole expression of a culture, of yourself. There was that time, when they arrived at the *résidences* and the guy was distinctly blasé, no doubt about it. Bloody cheeky, he was (or maybe just funny) – asking if they had a cat or a dog with them. As if! Still, she spoke away in French there and no-one corrected her. Whenever Stuart tries to speak French people generally answer him in English so he gives up the way he gives up on everything. Stuart got his French Higher too, years ago, round about the same time she did, but only a C so he doesn't like to mention it hardly. No wonder. Stuart would never in a million years manage the nuances, she thinks. The guy at reception had spoken to her (all this in French) about whether they needed sheets. He said he would bring them up. By eight o'clock or something that evening they were all ready to go out and still no sheets to make the beds. She phoned up reception and he goes, dead snappy, *Oui, ils sont là*. You could just about hear the yap in his voice. She snapped back but agreed to come and get them. She isn't used to people waiting on her anyway.

Paradoxically, she uses her knowledge of French to hide her own identity, to pretend she is one of them. Occasionally, it works. Like when she asked for a *pizza carrée à emporter* at the market the other day. Saving a bit of money not eating out all the time, the way you do at home. It was just 10 francs or something only the woman gave it her half price. Asked her first if she was going to eat it *à la maison*, and she said *oui*, without thinking, not meaning to deceive but chuffed nevertheless at getting away with it, whereupon the woman goes and wraps it up. She had never heard of a *pizza carrée* in her puff, would never have been able to translate a pizza slice into French but there it was, written on this notice, staring her in the face. That is where the good accent comes in. Even though hers is Parisian and therefore obviously identifiable as non-local — still French, though, which is what she wants. And in the Galeries Lafayette, in looking for bargains, she is sure she was taken for French again. Although these are only the briefest of moments. Two minutes (or less) into conversation with anybody and she would let herself down, be revealed for the trickster that she is. It's not that she cannot hold a conversation. She could, oh, she could, given the chance, but where are the opportunities? There is no opportunity really for intellectual, meaningful conversation with the folk she has brought with her on holiday (even Sheila who has turned back into the mammy), so she can hardly expect to have meaningful communication with strangers in a foreign language. She never meets anyone new at home these days. She just spends her life working and learning French and thinking about travelling. Her and Stuart hardly go out thegither anymore. They don't even sit and talk to one another that much. They don't even go out much to the cinema or the theatre. If there is something she is really enthusiastic about sure Stuart will come but she would rather he wanted to go rather than being badgered into it. As though he has no intellectual life of his own. Even watching TV Stuart will prefer a thriller or murder mystery or whatever. He'll hardly even sit and watch *Question Time* these days. When the two of them met, donkeys years ago at uni, Stuart was right into his politics. Still is, he would say. Times have changed, that is all. In his more honest moments he'll admit maybe he has changed a wee bit too. He has more sense. Then if she doesn't watch out he'll start one of his diatribes, like he's giving one of his talks at work (she doesn't really know these days what he does at work but she imagines he goes around giving talks). He could always talk, Stuart, when it suited him. Talk the hind leg off a donkey, her mum used to say, God rest her. Not that he talks so much these days. At least not to her he doesn't.

You have to have sense in your forties, for Christ's sake, Stuart will say. He hasn't sold out. Not a bit of it. He's a union man, isn't he? There's them that were revolutionary socialists at uni – the ones just about as far left as you could get – loonies, really, although you couldn't say it in those days – they're the ones that sold out, got jobs in MI5 and whatnot (Stuart would say – she doesn't agree they were all loonies – she went out with one once, before she met Stuart but he doesn't know that. As for the remark about MI5 that is just Stuart's paranoia). Stuart was part of what they called the Broad Left. In those days the right – the Tories – were considered the loonies really, not the revolutionary socialists. Nobody ever took the Tories seriously. Nobody she knew anyway. Knowing Tories was unthinkable. Knowing them personally anyway.

They should get out more. It is ironic that at a time of her life when she is more comfortable than she ever was – than ever her parents could have hoped to be in a million years – she feels more socially isolated than ever. Intellectually too, although maybe the one follows the other. Even if they travelled more. In recent years the more she has hankered after France the more Stuart has resisted. He always wants to go somewhere in the States – Florida, usually. This is the first time in ages she has got her way without a huge argument. She always puts the case for culture – for expanding their consciousness – whereas Stuart doesn't seem to care anymore. Perhaps he never did. Although sometimes she tells herself it doesn't make any difference – it's all tourism anyway. You can't really call a couple of weeks a year travelling.

When she was seventeen and went away to university, escaping her ma and da's clutches at long last, she met new folk all the time. It was like paradise. You spent the whole night sometimes sitting in smoky rooms, talking about the state of the world, about literature, about the meaning of life. Not that Stuart ever had a lot of time for the meaning of life. Used to say it was only the middle classes could afford to sit on their arses and contemplate the world – other folk just had to live their lives. Although as far as she remembers Stuart's life has consisted of precisely that – sitting on his arse. And what are they now if not middle class? There is less of the contemplation, certainly.

Stuart goes away travelling, right enough. Only for his work. A lot of it down the south coast. Once she asked if she could come with him. He just told her she wouldn't like it. Wouldn't like the company. All men.

That was a good few years ago. She has never really asked since. Only surely these days it is different? There are plenty of women in good jobs all over the place. The unions must reflect the changes in society over the last few decades. Maybe she will speak to Stuart again about going away with him. Only if she cannot talk to him here (or, rather, he cannot talk to her) what would be the point? She does not want to be some sort of hanger-on, to be treated as some appendage of Stuart. She wants to be treated as an intelligent woman in her own right. She has earned it, after all. She has sweated blood and tears to get where she is although sometimes she wonders, for what? Stuart has a general degree whereas hers is honours. Stuart still earns twice what she gets and has half the stress. Her own fault right enough for going into social work. Who in their right mind would choose social work as a career these days?

If she had her life to lead over again. She remembers her mother talking like this, when she was younger than she is now even. A terrible thing to say, she used to think, at the age of ten or eleven. A disgrace, for your own mother to be regretting marrying your father and having children and all that. And her supposed to be a good-living Christian as well. It was only years later, when it was too late, that she forgave her mother. When she understood. Her mother had more to complain about than her. Her mother had no opportunities. Her mother had never stayed on at the school, never mind getting to university. In her mother's day women stayed in the home and all men were bastards. OK so men are still bastards but not as much. At least women don't let them away with as much.

Her mother would have hated coming to a place like this. Seeing all these topless women. She is a wee bit shocked herself although she would never admit it. She is not shocked at young, beautiful women with their firm, high tits – big and small. There is a code, of course. You only sunbathe or swim bare-breasted. You do not run or walk up and down the beach showing off your tits. You pretend you are not showing them off. No, the young beauties whom she assumes are showing off do not shock her in the least. She has seen them before, anyway. Rather, it is the auld ones – Christ, there is an auld biddy of about seventy – wandering (and wandering is the word – she can hardly walk in a straight line) along the water's edge. Her man is holding onto her, trying to get her in the water. He looks nearly as bad as her, with this collar clamped round his neck. No, she is far more than seventy, she must be nearer eighty. More even. Him as well. A couple of geriatrics, you would think. Social work clients. Some of her clients that are half doolally don't look as far gone as this old couple. Twenty years ago they'd have been in a home (assuming French social policy in this area to be the same as British – which it won't be). Nope, this old biddy can't be showing off. There must be another reason for baring her breasts then. Maybe she has always done it. Maybe it feels more natural. Maybe she should try it herself. Maybe she would if it wasn't for the fact that Sheila and Gavin brought Alan. Maybe Sheila would too. Her and Sheila topless. She can't imagine either Stuart or Gavin liking that. Probably they think their wives' tits are for their eyes only, something like that. Alan has been OK, right enough, for a boy. Maybe her and Sheila should show him Scottish women can be assertive about their bodies too, for that is what it is about, isn't it? About not being ashamed. Nothing to do with showing off. Like rape has nothing to do with sex.

If she'd had a kid she would have spent the whole time trying to be the good parent. She would never have had a life of her own, she can see that now the way she never could when she (and maybe Stuart too although he would never admit it) thought about nothing else. She has always despised people who let their kids lie around watching TV all day. Alan probably isn't the worst. She has been getting to know him a wee bit, helping him with his French, stuff like that.

She takes out the book again, tossing a last glance at the sea. The auld yins have moved on. Two young girls – about seventeen years of age or so, they would be – have taken their place. Topless. Great they have that kind of confidence at that age, although in a way she did too. God, if she'd had the money to come over here when she was that age she'd have probably done it and all. Maybe the French kids aren't that different, really. It's the men that are maybe different. She can't imagine the Scots boys she knew in those days dealing with their friends being topless. One peek at your tits and they'd think you should be in bed with them. Aye, and then they didnae know what to do. She smirks at the memory. Christ, it was awful being young in some ways. She'd never have had the nerve to go topless at that age, here or anywhere else. Never.

God, it's gorgeous.

She looks up. Her reprieve is over and she has done nothing. Wasted all that precious time.

It is Gavin, not Stuart, speaking. Stuart never calls anything gorgeous, never mind the sea.

Gorgeous, she repeats. It seems funny to call the sea – or the experience of swimming – gorgeous. It's a word she associates with human beauty, not the natural world. But maybe there is something about Gavin she hasn't appreciated. Or maybe it is just a word he has picked. Out of context.

Aye, gorgeous. Heaven on earth. Fantastic.

She smiles. Puts the book away. Right, my turn. Anybody coming in again?

They all shake their heads, the three of them. Really, she just meant Stuart. She was just being polite. Swimming in the sea in a bikini is something sexy to do with your husband. Only he doesn't seem to see it like that.

Had enough, he is saying. Maybe Sheila'll join you when she comes back.

It's OK, I'll go myself.

Maybe he is getting into this male bonding thing, she wonders, as she steps clumsily towards the water's edge. The holiday was supposed to have brought them closer but they have hardly had any time by themselves. If it was just Sheila there she'd've said something. Oh, come on, whatever, but she cannot talk to him when he is wanting to be one of the lads. What can she do? Maybe she could discuss the business with Sheila afterwards, when they can get a minute. They have discussed the subject, in an abstract way, often enough before. Only abstract is not the same. She doesn't want Sheila thinking her and Stuart don't get on or something. That would be too much like disloyalty.

The water is lovely, right enough. There is no chill the way there is on the south coast or even in the north of France. You melt into the liquidness of it, let it carry you away, soothe away all your worries and troubles. And Gavin was right. In a way it is gorgeous – there is beauty in the experience of being out here, alone with nature (not exactly alone, right enough). And maybe it will do Stuart no harm to get friendly with Gavin and Alan. See how the other half lives, for a change. She casts a glance at the wee group on the beach, half-hoping to see the three of them in animated conversation but Alan is buried in a book and Gavin and Stuart are conked out on the pebbles. Oblivious. Aye, well. We all need oblivion from time to time.

Stuart

God, he needs to lie down and just do nothing but think of her. Gavin was dead right about the beach. It is just glorious, all this sun and swimming. He is randy as fuck, thinking about her. Although if he thinks too long about her, Jesus, he will start having an erection. Worse, he will want to go off and masturbate. Or want to go and relieve himself with those prostitutes he has seen hanging about not far from where they are staying. Ha ha, trust Madge to find them an apartment in the bloody red light district. They hadn't even properly discussed it, mainly because of the boy. The boy that Sheila and Gavin spoil rotten. Although if him and Madge had had a kid maybe they'd've done the same. Who knows? Too late now. To adopt or anything. Foster even. Too late for him and Madge even. He wouldn't admit it to himself until they came away. No even then. Until the day. Him and Madge no longer an item. Water under the bridge.

Aye, bloody red light district. Serve her right. Always thought she was on top of everything. If it hadn't been for the boy he'd've said something, some snidy remark. She shouldn't get away with it. Although him and Gavin had a few laughs that first night they went out and had a tankful. Maybe that is what he should be doing, going and having a tankful. Although not yet, not yet. It is still too early and it is too hot.

After the laugh about the red light district Gavin went all serious right enough.

It's because it's cheap. That's why she got it, Gavin explained, as if he knew his wife better than he did.

He cast him a look but Gavin didn't seem to notice. I mean, he went on, I mean, she understands me and Sheila don't have the money. What with me being made redundant, like.

Aye. What else could he say? Christ, he felt for the bugger. Only when he starts on about the union, making out it was union's fault, he soon shut him up. Put him right there. Got to stand up for your own.

It was ridiculous in a way him and Madge spending their annual holiday coming and staying in cheapsville like this when they could afford better. There's plenty of nice looking hotels right on the *Promenade des Anglais*. Dozens of hotels, so there are. And they have to wind up in the fucking red light district. Although if Karen left her man there'd be a divorce on the cards and divorce is expensive. He couldn't get the union to help him out there, ha. Still, Karen is an independent woman, same as Madge. No – correction – not the same as Madge. Karen isn't opinionated the way Madge is. Karen can look after herself financially, but you still feel she needs you. Not just in bed but generally. She asks what you think of this or that. She values your opinion. Once Madge did too. Ironically, the more he grew in status (at work anyway), the less Madge seemed to care for his opinion – or for him, maybe. Madge likes to take the lead and as she grows older she is getting worse. It is partly his fault, he is forced to acknowledge. He left the house, all the domestic stuff, to her. Thinking maybe, obviously wrongly, that that was what men did. They have no kids, so apart from her job (and him of course) what else does she have? He is all for equality of the sexes, always has been. If women want to throw themselves into their work – especially if they have no kids – that is fine by him. Only Madge was never contented in her career but still never had the nerve to clear out. Not that he wants her leaving without having another job to go to – Christ, she'd be financially dependent on him then and that would never do – but people can retrain. He is always telling that to people who've been made redundant. You can retrain. There's no need to go on the scrap heap at forty, forty five, whatever (granted, at fifty it is getting that bit harder).

Sometimes Madge makes out he's had it easy. He's never let her away wi that one. No way has he had it easy. The competition fifteen, twenty years ago was as fierce then as it is now. Now he can maybe sit back a wee bit, but only a wee bit, now he has made it. Is it his fault if Madge chose the wrong career?

Karen now, Karen never moans like that. Karen is only thirty right enough but Madge was moaning long before she was thirty if he remembers correctly. He doesn't know how he put up with it really, when he thinks about it. He used to think it was because they couldn't have kids. Really, it was because they couldn't have kids. He can acknowledge that, quite freely. There was more to it than moaning, right enough, there was real suffering there. There is still, is or would be, if he and Madge were still an item. Only the suffering with Madge has turned into moaning, pure and simple. Now it's Madge being insufferable, pure and simple. The kids issue is water under the bridge.

At least it is for him and Madge. Not necessarily for him and Karen. Him and Karen have discussed kids. It was her brought it up. Her man doesn't want them. Never did. A right prick by the sounds of it. Karen said she wasn't bothered at the beginning but now she is thirty she is having second thoughts.

They were at Southampton. About six months ago. This course. He was taking just the one workshop. One workshop on the Friday. They decided to stay the whole weekend. Just the two of them. They didn't really know the other folk at the conference anyway. Maybe he wouldn't've cared if they had. The relationship was becoming like that, devil-may-care.

After the conference they decided they were going to go somewhere together. It was easy enough spinning stories at home. Presumably for Karen it was easy too. She never said much. That was the thing about Karen, she never made excuses. She was a can-doer – a phrase he was fond of using in his workshops. No such thing as can't, he snapped at a young woman who protested once that she just didn't have time to go to any training sessions to improve her chances of promotion. Most folk (thank Christ) had laughed. One guy warned him once about going over the score. Need to take account of the Equal Opportunities policy, all that. Women wi weans needing special treatment, special conditions, part-time and all that. He was on the ball about part-time working but the law never said anything about special conditions. He knew, he had done all the courses. He was no workaholic but you didnae need to be a workaholic to pick up on stuff. That was how he kept on the ball, updating himself all the time. The one thing he had never updated was Madge. Well, now it is about time. Time to take the plunge.

At the beginning it was all casual-like. Great fun, so it was, all the sneaky stuff. Her place usually, for her man was always away whereas he couldn't guarantee Madge wouldn't be dropping in for a cup of coffee in the middle of the day even. She drove all over the south side and did that when she was passing the house sometimes, she said. So he had to be careful. Then he got more sneaky and started making sure Karen could come to the same conferences, same courses, that kind of thing. It wasnae easy, Christ – it wasn't as if she was his secretary or anything – and she had her own boss but he was her boss's boss, after all, so he had the final say. Although the mechanics of it could be awkward.

So it was hotel rooms at conferences and everything for a good while. Bloody brilliant it was, right enough. Bloody best sex he'd ever had in his puff. And she'd come in no time, like she was desperate for him. None of this farting around wanting you to suck them for fucking ages and you end up coming all over their stomachs or something

34

because they kept you waiting too long..

At the beginning he had no idea women who dressed as smart as Karen – power dressing, some called it – were into casual sex. Because it was definitely casual for a good few months. Women who were as good as men at their job and yet could just switch off and have a good fuck, without wanting to drag you to the altar. The way it was supposed to be back in the seventies when he was at uni, although if he remembers correctly there were a fair few thought that one fuck meant an engagement or something ridiculous like that. There were a fair few not even on the pill as well. Before all the scares and everything too so there was no excuse, really.

He doesnae really remember when the casual turned into something else. Except that if the sex is that good wi somebody you just want them there in your bed every night. Plus the woman had a brain. Otherwise he'd never have taken her on, obviously. If it was just pure sex you'd just keep it casual and when you couldn't keep it casual anymore you'd go to prostitutes. He's had prostitutes a fair few times. Amsterdam, mainly. London as well. Always far away from home. Always be discreet. They cost a bloody fortune right enough. He's never been with a prostitute since that first time with Karen. Although he's wondered, right enough, about the ones here. Only wondered but. He's no interested, no really. He just wants to fuck Karen these days.

It is a good working relationship he has with Karen as well. No that they talk about work much, no really. But they are on the same wavelength, so to speak. Have their priorities right. A good job, doing good for the workers, taking a stand without letting folk shit all over you, all that. A pragmatist, Karen is, like himself. As for Madge, she still fancies herself as some idealist. Sometimes she makes out that is how she is still in that rotten job. Dealing wi the dregs o society.

He said that to her once, out loud. Dealing wi the dregs. Although it never occurred to him it was the first time. She sat there, like she was genuinely shocked and maybe she was, right enough, for doesn't Madge live in cloud cuckoo land, wi no idea about him and Karen whatsoever? Tunnel vision, that is what it is. Madge likes to think that Tories, or sexist men, or her bosses, or maybe just people she doesn't like, have tunnel vision but there is none so blind as them who can't see (or don't look).

Aye, the day came when the casual aspect was definitely at an end. He had to decide and so had she. About the future. At forty one all some folk think about is the past, but much of the time he cannot remember the past. Madge will say, Do you remember this or that? Talking about uni or the early days or the first time she went for the IVF? Talking about stuff when for all he knows he wasnae even there. Like her mother. Her mother. For God's sake.

He sits up, realising he is burning. Madge is back. Never stays long in the water. Afraid to try anything different when it comes down to it. And there she is, ignoring him but helping the boy, Alan, handing him the suncream. Next she'll be bloody putting it on for him, for Christ's sake. Like some bloody paedophile. He checks himself. That is not fair. Just because they are going to part there is no need for anything nasty. Alan could have been her – their – son, after all. That is what she is being – motherly. Except it is too late for all that. But there will be no bitter divorce, not as far as he is concerned, anyway. What he would like is a clean break. The only question is when. Karen has a right to know. He does not want to spoil the rest of the holiday though. Not just for him and Madge but for Gavin, the poor bugger. And Sheila and the boy. They hardly ever get away, do they, and this will be the last time for a while, by the sounds of it. He wouldn't be surprised if Gavin never works again, the state of him. He is coughing again. He sounds like he needs antibiotics or something. Only they never took out insurance, he says. Couldn't afford it. Thought the E111s would do. Insurance maybe wouldn't have covered it anyway. Pre-existing condition, all that.

Madge is sidling up to him, having done her paternal bit.

Wanting some? she asks, holding out the suncream.

Aye, he says, taking it off her.

He knows fine that is not what she meant. She was going to put it on for him. He used to ask her to. Time was he enjoyed doing her, giving her a good massage with the stuff. They always buy factor 12 or something so it's quite creamy. Needs a lot of rubbing in. They've always been very careful about sunburn, always looked after themselves, not like Sheila and Gavin who both look sunburnt which is ridiculous at their age. They should know better. The boy is more careful than what they are.

Thank Christ Sheila is back anyway. Now he has made his decision he has eight days left to say nothing, to avoid the subject of *them*. An impossible task, really. Maybe if he was at home he could do it easier, keep out the way. He'd be at work anyway. Still, he can hardly keep out the way for eight days and then just announce it, can he? At least here he has the excuse (thank fuck) he couldn't get her on her own, didn't want to spoil the holiday. Not that you should need an excuse when you're in love with someone else. That is what it is, isn't it? He was in love with Madge once too, years ago. Anyway, even if you're not in love, if your relationship has gone stale — has withered the way his and Madge's has — then you should be able to just let go. Marriage isn't slavery, after all. Especially in this day and age.

Sheila is showing Madge her shopping. Gavin is complaining. If he wasn't worried about sunburn he'd lie down again, try not to hear.

Jesus, Sheila, did you rob a bank or what?

I've still got a job, you know, Sheila is muttering. He can hear the tension in the voices. Maybe she doesnae mean to hurt Gavin's feelings, isnae making any reference to the fact that he's got no job but a sidelong glance at Gavin's face shows how hurt he is. Women can be so bloody insensitive.

How about a nice refreshment? he asks pleasantly. I think we all need to get out the sun. Drinks on me.

Not at all. We're going Dutch. Gavin again. He can be a right pain in the arse sometimes. Him and his stupid pride.

Listen, he goes, grabbing Gavin's elbow — something he has never done before, for they are not great friends really. Not friends at all, come to that. Sheila is Madge's friend and Gavin, well, he supposes, Gavin sort of just came along for the ride. Hubbie and child in tow as it were. God, he'd never stand being treated like that. But he doesn't dislike the guy and, besides, he is used to dealing with people, isn't he? His job is all about dealing with people. Sure he needs to know the law and whatnot but at the end of the day what he has are people skills. He spent his early days dealing with the likes of manual workers like Gavin. The world is full of Gavins. Folk who don't know their arse from their elbow half the time. He is no elitist, he can get on with any man — or woman.

Listen, he goes, when you get another job you can pay me back. Meantime it's my treat. And I'm paying for the dinner as well. We're having our dinner out the night as well. Somewhere posh.

Nobody is saying anything so he looks at his wife for approbation. Right, Madge?

Madge nods, smiling. It's not that he needs her approval, he's just trying to make it easier for Gavin. For Sheila too. Or maybe he does need Madge's approval. For the rest of the holiday anyway. For the rest of the holiday, he decides, he is going to be the Archangel Gabriel. He catches the boy Alan looking at him now and smiles at him. You can do the ordering the night, Alan. Give you a chance to use your French, eh? He turns to the rest of them. Right?

37

Fine by me, Madge says, still smiling. He's going to keep her smiling right till the last minute. Nobody'll be able to say he didn't treat her right.

Gavin and Sheila just look embarrassed. The boy gives him an embarrassed smile. All right, he says. Thanks.

Alan

They are at this posh restaurant. He isn't sure how posh. The waiters aren't really that dressed up. No bow ties or anything like that. Apart from the bow ties business he couldn't really tell the difference between a posh restaurant and a non-posh one (McDonalds and the like apart).

He never eats out when they're home in Glasgow. Neither do his mum or dad. If they go out together – which is hardly ever now – it's to the pictures or the theatre or something. Even when his dad was working they never really went out for a meal. His dad likes to cook. Is a better cook than his mum. Likes doing Chinese and all that. Except recently there's been more beans on toast type stuff than stir-fried king prawns. Stir-fried king prawns are really expensive, even when you do them yourself.

In a way he doesn't know where the money is coming from for this holiday, never mind the meals they've been having out. Stuart might be paying for this one but his mum and dad have paid their own way for the others. He never used to think about where money came from because there was usually enough. It was just that you couldn't be greedy. You should only have what you need, his dad always said. His dad hardly ever buys new stuff for himself. He's been wearing the same old jacket for years. Says there's nothing wrong with it. Aye, but it's not going to last forever, and now his dad has no job, just the Sick.

The last couple of months have been hell. It wasn't that there were rows. Not exactly. It would have been better if they did row. Bottling things up just causes tension. He can sense the tension between them all the time. Has felt it ever since his dad got made redundant. It is fucking awful, so it is. There are kids at school whose parents are divorced. You can always tell, not just because they never mention their dad but because they always go quiet when certain subjects are mentioned, like getting new trainers and stuff. All the ones whose parents are divorced have no money. Like them. Until a matter of months ago he was the same as everybody else, apart from the ones whose parents are divorced, or the ones from single parent families (he just means financially, of course – he isn't prejudiced or anything like that. Poverty can happen to anybody, good or bad, thick or clever). He was stupid, sometimes, right enough, wanting too much. Stupid labels. Reebok and Adidas. Mean fuck all. He never listened when his mum said money doesn't grow on trees and his dad would just grin and hand him over what he wanted even though he wore that stupid ancient jacket himself. Now he never asks for anything.

The other day he started worrying about the mortgage. When people are hard up they always worry about the mortgage. He heard the two of them on about it before they came away. He was in the kitchen and they were in the living room.

The mortgage has to come first, his mum was saying.

He never heard what his dad said. Sometimes he doesn't want to hear. He has his own life to lead. That is what his dad is always telling him, but it isn't as easy as that. His dad gets on his nerves more often than his mum. It's worse now he is in the house all the time. He's been coming home to the house himself since he was twelve. Before that, after his mum started full-time, which seems like ages ago now, he went to a childminder's. It was all right. Lots of kids go these days. At first he didn't like it but he got used to it. When he started coming home to the empty house with his own key he wasn't sure about it to begin with, even though it had been his own idea. It was quite exciting but. His mum even said he could bring his pals home as long as they didn't wreck the place. His dad wasn't so sure but he still let him. Now he doesn't really want to bring his pals back because his dad's in the house all the time. Your dad isn't supposed to be in the house all the time. It looks like he's unemployed. Like some lazy arse or like he got the sack or something.

When he says this to his mum the other week she nearly went off her head.

That's just rubbish, Alan, she goes. There's plenty of folk work at home. If you don't want to tell folk your dad's on the Sick just say he works at home.

That's a lie but, he says.

She just shrugs, even though she's always told him not to tell lies.

His dad has been painting lately. Getting a bit carried away. Not just DIY stuff. More like *Changing Rooms*. He's no good at the joinery bits but he's started this mural in the kitchen. Lots of fruit and flowers and everything. His mum wasn't too keen to start with, as you can imagine, but he thinks it's growing on her. He'll maybe ask him to start on his room next. Only no flowers and stuff. Folk'd think he was a poof if his dad did that – or that his dad is a poof which is almost worse. He's not supposed to say poof but that doesn't stop people thinking stuff. All the guys at school who think they're wee hard men. Maybe they're poofs themselves. Doesn't mean they cannae stick the heid on you but. No, what he would like his dad to do is a map of the world. All the way round the room. It'd be awfully difficult, right enough, trying to do it to scale and everything. He knows what his dad would say. It isn't art but. Art is a representation. That was the way he kept going on in the Matisse place. He was really surprised at his old man. He seemed to like it more than Madge, even though it had been Madge's idea. He reckons Madge and his old man have more in common than they'd care to admit. Not that he thinks they fancy one another or anything like that. His parents aren't like that.

He has been reconsidering his parents since he came over here. He only met Madge a few times before, when his mum had brought her round to the house, but he could tell his mum thought Madge was the fount of all knowledge or something, and his dad was even worse. Always going on about how ignorant he was. Even if he wasn't going on about it you could sense his embarrassment all the time. When he went to the school meeting with the teachers, making out he didn't understand the subjects, stuff like that. He was especially embarrassed about the French even though he knew a few words. His dad had went to the library and borrowed tapes. French for beginners.

Still he practically believed his dad until he came here. His dad has been more interested in the museums and stuff than Madge's man Stuart who has a good, well-paid job. A union man, his dad said. Stuart just goes about making snidy remarks about everything at the museums. Like he knows it all already. Like at the Matisse he just went about shrugging, like he wasn't interested. Whereas his dad, his dad was right into the tapestries. Even if they weren't woven by this Matisse fellow they were based on his design. He was a bit sceptical himself, he had to admit, until he saw the sculptures. It was the sculptures made him realise the guy was an artist. He got a print of one of the collages for fifty francs.

He never told his dad what Stuart whispered to him when he saw it. Like the naked women, eh? You'll have to wait till you're sixteen, I'm afraid, son.

He was raging, so he was. Only he didn't want to spoil things so he never told anybody. He didn't think his dad would've been too chuffed though if he knew what Stuart says to him. At least he had his answer for him.

It's not like naked women, he said, not knowing where the words had come from even. It's a – a representation.

The picture didn't even show breasts and all that. It was more of a silhouette. That was partly how he felt it was OK to buy it. Nobody in their right mind could've called it a dirty picture. Except dirty-minded bastards.

His mum made out this guy Stuart had been to loads of places. America even. He has always wanted to travel, see the world. At home he is always looking up atlases and encyclopaedias. He could spend hours and hours doing it and just forget about the time. He wants to know about the weather, about the mountains and lakes, the wildlife, all that there is to know about the geography of the places. Geography is his favourite subject at school. His teacher was amazed about things he knows that they have never covered in class. He doesn't just want to know about the physical geography but about the peoples as well. He knows bits about the aborigines in Australia, about how their way of life has been devastated.

He never really thought before that people could go to all these places and not really want to find out things. Like they could go to America and just stay in their hotel or something. Probably that is what Stuart does. Goes all that distance just to stay in some posh hotel. Probably reads dirty magazines too. He's just the type.

Just because this fellow Stuart is paying for his dinner doesn't mean he has to feel grateful or anything. He can afford it, after all. Just because he has some fancy job doesn't mean he isn't an ignorant bastard.

We'll just go for the hundred franc menu, his mum is saying. Right? Cheaper than *à la carte*.

Fine by me, says his dad.

A glance at the card tells him it is the cheapest *table d'hôte* menu available although a hundred francs doesn't sound exactly cheap.

It looks very nice anyway, Madge goes.

Bonsoir, he says to the waiter when he comes over.

Bonsoir mesdames, messieurs, says the waiter, turning to each of them.

Good evening, says Stuart.

Good evening, sir, says the waiter.

See, they all speak English here anyway, Stuart smiles.

He ignores him. Is that why the bastard picked this place then? So that he didn't get to speak French after all?

Une table pour cinq personnes, he persists. He went over it in the phrase book before he came in. He went over some stuff with Madge as well. Madge is really decent, he has decided. It is not every adult can be bothered helping some kid with their French.

42

Your accent is really good, Madge told him. The accent is the most important thing. It's how you get taken seriously.

That is why he persisted. Because Madge encouraged him. And now the guy is speaking in French.

Bien, une table pour cinq personnes.

On voudrait le menu à cent francs, s'il vous plaît, he remembers to add. It was Madge told him about saying *on voudrait.* He hasn't learned that much French at school, not really. If it wasn't for Madge he'd be able to say fuck all really.

He flushes with pleasure as he accepts the menu from the waiter. He is a wee bit disconcerted to find the menu is in English as well as French but he is determined to do the ordering.

I'll have the menu at a hundred and eighty francs, Stuart goes.

Madge gives him a look.

Anybody else want the menu at a hundred and eighty francs? Anybody fancy lobster, that kind of thing?

His mum shakes her head, his dad too. It was the way Stuart asked it like it was something special. Something expensive too. Like you'd be taking advantage if you asked for it.

Even though he doesn't see why lobster should be that dear. They are near the sea, after all. They catch lobsters in Scotland as well. It is not as if they are that rare. He minds they were in Crail harbour once. They were just away for the day. The fishing boats were in and they were unloading these lobster pots and crab pots. They went and bought a dressed crab at the wee hut. They were selling lobster too, he minds, only they were dearer. Not that dear but.

The hundred francs is fine. I fancy a steak, his dad goes. What about you, Alan?

He shakes his head. He thinks he'll go for the fish. Ordinary fish. Not lobster, which he has never tasted before and doesn't even know if he likes. He doesn't like meat that much. He tried being vegetarian for a while but the smell of his mum's bacon was too much. He thinks he could maybe give up meat though if he could still eat fish. He doesn't think it's the same as eating animals really.

He has started thinking about the wolf for some reason but he doesn't want to mention it. Doesn't want to spoil anybody's appetite (apart from Stuart's maybe). Maybe they are all being hypocrites, after all, making all this fuss about wolves that are wild animals after all and no fuss at all about poor cows and pigs. Especially French pigs that might not even be able to turn round in their pens. He saw this TV

43

programme once about these pigs and the terrible life they had in these toty wee pens. That was even before all the fuss they made about lambs and other animals being transported for days in Europe without any water or anything. Still, chicken is different, isn't it? (Isn't it?) He'll just go for the chicken.

When the waiter guy returns he orders the *poulet* and asks for *les beefsteaks* without a murmur. Then Stuart butts in to give his own order in English. He's not having the lobster after all. For a split second the waiter looks put out, then he smiles at both of them and goes, *Merci*, to him as he hands back the menus and, *Thankyou*, to Stuart. When he returns with the food he says, *Bon Appetit*.

Well, that's English anyway, Stuart goes, grinning.

Don't be ridiculous, Stuart, Madge says.

Everybody knows what it means, Stuart goes, still grinning but underneath you know he is really glaring at her.

I suppose it's so common it's been sort of incorporated into the English language, his mum says.

He looks at his dad but his dad is saying nothing.

Aye, that's it, Stuart says.

He relaxes a bit. Starts to eat his chicken. It is lovely, right enough. Maybe he'll never eat anything like this again. Not until he's grown up and has a good job anyway. His dad never had a meal out in his life until he was eighteen, he always used to say.

Not even McDonalds?

There was no McDonalds in they days, his dad would say, avoiding the question for there must've been McDonalds-type places.

He doesn't really think McDonalds counts as eating out. Not to people like Madge and Stuart. Nor even his mum. Even his dad really. His dad might never have had a meal out till he was eighteen but he isn't stupid.

The meal is pleasant right until the very last moment, right up until Stuart is asking for the bill. Madge is asking him about what he has learnt in French and his mum looks as pleased as punch, for once. His mum always looks happier after she has had a wee drink. As long as she doesn't need it to make her happy. That would be a terrible thought, his mum an alkie. He knows there are female alkies that sit in the house with their gin bottles and dress up when they go out and keep themselves clean as well as the ones that lie on street corners and ask you if you've any spare change. He went to this boy's house once and the house was dead posh. The boy thought his mum was away out or asleep or something. Only then she comes down the stairs with this bottle in her hand. You could smell the drink a mile off. He pretended not to notice but anybody would've noticed. The poor kid, he thought, having a mother like that. They could keep their fancy house as far as he was concerned.

But his mum doesn't have bottles of gin lying about the house. They don't even keep beer in the fridge, so they don't.

He understands for the first time what being tipsy is. He has had two glasses of wine. He has never had more than about half a glass in the house and then it was just wee toty ones whereas these are quite big. It was the waiter who offered to pour it and he looked at his mum before he nodded. Stuart ordered the wine too. It is about all he knows in French, how to order stuff. Not that he can talk, but he has only been learning it for three years after all (and not that much till this year). By the time he is Stuart's age – or his dad's age – he would like to think he would not be that ignorant.

It's all right son, I'll no get you to ask for the bill, Stuart goes. He is grinning all over his face.

He glares at him. Not meaning to, but it's not as if it's funny. You don't go taking people out for their dinner and then making snidy remarks about the money. It isn't right. His mum would say he's being oversensitive but he's knows he's not. Except his mum's saying nothing. She knows fine well he's not being oversensitive at all. Stuart is just a prick and that's all there is to it. Just because he's a toty wee bit tipsy doesn't mean he doesn't recognise a prick when he sees one. He'd like to fucking say something, so he would. Tell the bastard to go and fuck himself. The insensitive fucker wouldn't turn a hair anyway, no matter what he said to him.

His mum is giving him a warning look. It used to be she gave him these looks that meant, Watch it, Alan, don't go too far now or else. No that she ever really hit him, no really. Even if she used to give him the odd skelp she wouldn't dare now. She wouldn't know what to do if he went over the score, started telling that Stuart to his face just what he thinks of him. Wouldnae have a clue. And it shows. He never really realised it before but she's frightened he's going to show her and his old man up. That's the way he thinks about them a lot of the time, worried they're going to show him up. He never realised till now they felt like that too.

I've got a surprise for yous. I want yous to know something. I cannae keep it to myself any longer. Stuart has gone all serious even though he is obviously half-cut. He only speaks Scots when he is half-cut. What the fuck is he up to but? He doesnae trust the bugger. He's playing some sick game or something. Fucking mind games, that is what he's up to. There's a teacher at school like him. Always playing fucking mind games. Never know what he's going to say or do next. Into stupid fucking surprises. Always trying to freak somebody out. See if you're man enough to take it. He doesn't do it to the girls, just the boys. Stupid fucking wanker, so he is.

What is it? It's his mum. She's still giving him that look. She cares more about this stupid wanker than about her own son. She shouldn't be letting the bastard away with it.

I'll no be a minute. Got to get something first.

He is away over asking the waiter for something. Showing off that he doesn't need to speak French, that if you've money you can go anywhere, speak any old way, and you'll get what you want. He doesn't get it, does he, this guy Stuart. He doesn't get it that that isn't really what it's all about. That Madge has been learning French and even his mum – Christ, even his dad – they have been learning wee bits, no to the same extent as Madge but still they try a wee bit – not to put one over on somebody but to try and meet them on their terms. The whole point of coming here, after all. Apart from the sunshine and the geography and history and stuff.

Only he has only got a menu. Like his mum is always saying he should calm down. The daft bugger just wants to make some point or other about the menu. Maybe he is even going to get a bottle of wine to take home or something and is asking them what they'd like. It was his dad bought the beer the other night, after all. His dad has been keeping them all on beer as far as he can see.

See this.

It's the menu at a hundred and eighty francs.

Hurry up, Stuart, Madge looks annoyed. Worried Stuart is going to give her a showing up. The waiter is hovering in the background.

Just wait a wee minute, just wait a wee minute. He flicks over the pages because the one hundred and eighty franc menu is bigger than the hundred franc one. They should all have had it if Stuart has that much money. His mum should've kept her mouth shut. Always trying to please everybody. Gets you nowhere.

Here it is. This is what I had for my dinner. This is it here. Will I say it in French? He looks round at the company. His speech is definitely slurred. He is pointing, pointing at him now. His mum puts her arm round him protectively. Part of him wants to shake her off, part of him wants to cry. Who does this bastard think he is, trying to make fun of his French?

Le loup, Stuart giggles. I had the *loup* for my dinner. Yous didnae realise. Did yous?

He isn't pronouncing it properly. He makes it sound more like loo—oo. A heavy, English sound. Like the toilet. But he knows what he is getting at all right.

You had fish, he says. I saw it. But he knows there is still something up. Stuart might be half-cut but he has the quiet confidence of someone who knows he is right.

Aye, that's right. I had the fish. Sea bass it's called as a matter of fact. Sea fucking bass, son.

Let me see, Madge grabs the menu which is, of course, in English as well.

Jesus Christ, so it is. Sea bass. Bloody hell.

And now his mum and his dad are looking as well.

God, imagine us thinking they ate wolves, actually ate wolves, his da is saying, whispering really. Imagine being that daft.

I feel such an eejit, Madge is saying.

Tell me about it, his mum says as they get up to go.

They all kill themselves laughing in the middle of the street.

Jesus, his da goes. Imagine thinking they ate wolves. They're like dogs, so they are. It's just like eating dogs.

They love their wee dogs too, so they do, don't they? Madge goes, sounding more Scottish than he has ever heard her. God, they're mad about their wee dogs. That wee woman in the supermarket wi the wee dog in the basket and a ribbon round its neck and everything. God, they'd go daft if they thought we'd been thinking that.

Stuart is quite friendly going up the road. Maybe he's not such a bad guy after all. He fairly spun it out right enough about the *loup*. Only he was just making entertainment. That was what he was doing, just making entertainment.

I tell you what, Stuart is saying. See the night before we leave, we'll go out for another meal. We'll all have the *loup*. You can get it cheaper than this as well. You don't have to pay a hundred and eighty francs for it. Right, folks?

We'll see, says his mum.

Aye, it's ages till we're leaving, says Madge.

The joke's over, he thinks. Why does Stuart want to keep on about

47

it? And they could have all tried it the night if they wanted. If Stuart hadn't made such a big deal about it, keeping it a secret and all that. It would be nice to go out on the last night, right enough. It'll probably be the last meal out they'll have in a long time, him and his mum and dad. Only Stuart never mentioned about paying for it. Probably his mum and dad can't afford it. Probably that's why his mum said, We'll see.

Still, the holiday's getting a bit better. Stuart's not that bad after all, maybe. Like his mum is always saying, it takes all kinds.

Aye, thon was a right laugh about the *loup*, right enough. You could see Madge was embarrassed, right enough. After all, she's supposed to be the one that speaks French. She was dead adamant it meant wolf and so it does, it seems, but everybody knows words can have many meanings. Alan was dead adamant too but then he is a bit like that with everything. It is just his age. Although she still worries he's going to be a right dead arrogant huffy bugger when he's grown up. Well, you can't mould them to your way of thinking. You can only set an example.

He didn't take it too bad about the wolf, considering. Especially after him giving Stuart the daggers half the night. Thank Christ Stuart was too pissed to notice. He maybe wouldn't've noticed anyway. He's not exactly the sensitive type. Gavin may have his faults but at the end of the day he's a sensitive soul. Wouldn't hurt a fly. She couldn't say the same for Stuart. There's something of the fly customer about him. He's full of himself as well. She doesn't know how Madge puts up with him.

She can see why Madge asked her to come up the town.

Just the two of us, Madge says. Give us a break from the men.

Give her a break, she meant. From Stuart. She has been getting on a lot better these past few days with Alan and with Gavin too. They came away with Madge and Stuart, if they are honest, because for the last few years holidays haven't been great with Alan. As he gets older he wants to do his own thing and usually he never wants to do what you want so life is just the one constant battle. This year he was like that at home, never mind on holiday. It's like when it's just the three of them he has no inhibitions. Fair enough, so they are a close family, but you need to exercise restraint. I mean, for Christ's sake, you cannae go losing your temper all the time just because life doesn't work out the way you thought it would.

She was worried, fundamentally, she sees now, about their relationship with Alan. That he was beginning to hate them or something. Only suddenly – after that meal when Stuart never let on he was eating the *loup* – they have sort of bonded together again. He is getting on quite well with his dad now. He was getting on fairly well with Madge anyway. As for Stuart, the way Alan looked at him you would have thought he was wanting to stick the heid on him or something but suddenly it was all right. Suddenly he calmed down. It must be his hormones or something. That, and it has maybe been a bit much, going away on holiday with strangers. She thought it would mature him or something, but maybe she was avoiding spending time with him. Well, she's taking him out tomorrow and this afternoon Gavin is taking him to this *Parc Floral* place. It was Alan's idea. Although he wasn't being awkward about it, demanding that they go or anything. Quite the opposite.

If you're sure you want to go, because I don't mind. If there's somewhere you wanted to go just say.

Gavin shook his head. Nup. Sounds fine by me.

At the end of the day the two of them just want the best for Alan. The problem is deciding just how to achieve that. Plus a lot of it is down to Alan, now he is getting that bit older. You can't coddle them forever.

They are in this bar in *Vieux Nice*. They decided to go inside, for a change. Get out the sun. It is not a particularly olde-worlde place (is that the right expression? Probably not – too English.) Definitely not quite in keeping with the rest of *Vieux Nice*, anyway. A bit too seedy. Or maybe she has got it wrong. It is easier to get these things wrong when you are abroad. It's not even the language she has difficulties with, it's her whole perception of things, of reality. Maybe everybody feels like this. She thinks Alan especially does. That is why he takes so long to adjust. They are just beginning to fine tune their perception of the place and it is nearly bloody time to go. Bloody terrible really.

Madge is back already. She was away at the toilet.

God, I'm bloody desperate, she says. Right enough, she needs to go as well. The French toilets are mostly terrible. Either non-existent or bloody filthy or they cost you an arm and a leg. Yesterday Gavin was trying to persuade her otherwise.

We're too Britocentric, he was saying. It's just a question of perception.

Bloody shite, she laughed at him and he had to laugh as well.

I need two francs, Madge is saying. Two bloody francs for a pee and the beer costs an arm and a leg as well.

They both laugh. They are more relaxed with one another the day than they have been the rest of the holiday. They should have done this before. Women never set aside enough time for themselves. She always says that to her female clients and most of her clients are female. (Let's face it, the last thing most men feel they need is a social worker.) She says it to the Asian women, the women with the unemployed husbands from the schemes, the single parents worn out with their hyperactive toddlers, the grandmothers, the women with disabilities or the ones looking after an elderly relative with a disability. She tells them all they have to set time aside for themselves and yet she doesn't set aside enough time for herself. She spends her life worrying about other people. Her mother would say it's second nature but that is rubbish. It is brainwashing. Pure and simple.

Madge is back from the bog. The two of them take out their shopping and compare bargains. They have been to the *Soldes* in the *Galeries Lafayette*. Maybe she will regret the spending tomorrow but meantime she is having a ball.

As long as you wear the stuff it's never money wasted, is it? Madge says, as if she can read her mind. Well, she knows Gavin's not working any more.

They have both bought their men something.

Stuart'll normally never buy himself clothes unless I persuade him. He's always been the unfashionable type. But lately he's been splashing out a bit. The last time he was in London he came back with this fancy jacket. I asked him how much it was and he said he didn't know. Can you imagine not knowing what you pay for something?

The waiter is round. Madge is just having mineral water, she notices.

What's got into you? she asks. I thought we were going to have a booze up, just the two of us.

Och, changed my mind. I feel a bit dehydrated to tell you the truth.

Have you got cystitis as well? Because Madge has been in and out of the toilets all day as far as she can see. There must be something up with her.

Madge nods. Aye, that's it. Cystitis.

I always find cranberry juice helps. You can get it in the *Casino*. We can call in there on the way back.

Aye, all right.

I suppose you're as well staying off the drink.

Aye.

That and sex.

Madge laughs out loud this time and so does she.

Christ, since you're in such a good mood I don't suppose you need the drink anyway.

Madge shrugs. Och, I can take it or leave it.

She says nothing. It's not the same drinking when you're not in drinking company, although she would never force drink on anyone. Not like some. And it's not like Madge to say no to a drink, cystitis or no. Maybe she's trying to set a good example to Stuart. He could do with it, right enough. He drinks more than the rest of them put together.

Just seems a pity not to try all this lovely wine, that's all.

Aye, well. There's more to a holiday than drinking, right enough.

You mean Stuart. She didn't mean to be that direct but it sort of slipped out. A mistake for a shadow of anger crosses Madge's face.

He doesn't drink like that at home. He works too hard. Plus I think he's been sort of uncomfortable in the group, you know. And he's not used to teenagers. Well, he's not used to kids full stop.

Yup. She is afraid Madge will go all weepy the way she did the time she told her she couldn't have more kids, not long after they first met. They were having a drink together and the subject of kids came up. She mentioned the operation which meant she couldn't have any more after Alan.

At least you have the one, Madge says, her face crumpling. She had to get out a hankie.

They haven't found anything wrong. Not exactly. Advised us to wait. Wait. So we waited. She laughed, Aye, we waited for years before we tried the IVF and everything. But nothing. I mean, you have to give up eventually. Get on with your life.

Madge made her swear not to tell anyone. She never did, not even Gavin, although it was not as if it was anything to be ashamed about, for God's sake, not being able to have weans. Madge could be funny sometimes. Like two nights ago she was drinking like there was no tomorrow and now she is teetotal. She doesn't totally believe it's all down to the cystitis. She's probably testing herself to see if she can do it. Well, she has no need. Come Saturday night she'll be home in Glasgow and her and Gavin'll be saying bye-bye to the drink for a long time. They both agreed on it in bed last night. Before they had sex they snuggled up and went over their history together. That was what Gavin had called it – history. She has been married to the guy fifteen years. Fifteen bloody years. She knows him as a sensitive guy – oversensitive even – but she never thought of him as an intellectual till that moment. Intellectuals are supposed to go to university, be professors, all that. These days you couldn't call everybody with a degree an intellectual, there's far too many of them. Anyway they all go to university for the fine jobs and the money. Look at Stuart. Although Madge doesn't earn that much more than her, right enough.

Aye, history.

We have a common history, you and me, Sheila, he says. But it goes back deeper than our relationship even. It goes back to our class history. Our fathers and grandfathers and their fathers before them working down the pits, slaving to make the middle classes rich.

It was true both their grandfathers were miners. Only Gavin never knew his. His old man, as far as she could tell, was an old bastard. Got the sack when Gavin was only wee and spent his life on the dole, abusing his wife and weans. It wasn't just the fault of the class system Gavin had no life as a wean, it was his ain father's fault. By comparison her father worked like buggery to give his weans a decent life. There was a limit to how far you could stretch this shared history business. But she hadn't the heart to say that.

He's a lovely kid, your Alan, Madge says suddenly.

Aye, well, he'll no be a kid much longer, I suppose. You've been very good to him. Helping him with his French. I mean, I noticed. Gavin has as well. I mean, we appreciate it. Us not really speaking the language like you do.

Och, I've been doing it for my own benefit as much as his. There aren't enough opportunities, really, on a holiday like this to speak it. Need to go on a course or something. Holidays, being a tourist like, it's just no the same.

You did all right wi the guys at the bus stop, though.

Aye. Madge smiles, remembering. God, I was pleased wi myself, to tell you the truth. Then I started thinking, Jesus, Madge, you're sad, so you are, being that chuffed wi yourself just because you spoke to a guy at a bus stop.

You did very well, she insists. You'll get your A level next year no bother if you can speak that well.

These young guys – young black guys – had approached them at the bus stop. She was embarrassed feeling that way, but she had felt this tinge of fear when they came over. Not that they were swaggering particularly, no more than young people their age swagger but there was this association, she thinks, between black people and poverty. Or was there? Was that the racism in her own background made her think like that? The people who sat around the filthy streets with their begging bowls – most of whom did not ask you for money, right enough – they were mostly white, weren't they? She wasn't afraid of them. They just made her feel guilty.

They were asking for the bus to the airport. She caught that much.

Madge had it off to a tee. Told him to take *le quatre-vingt dix*. Points across the road. Explained about the other one, *le dix sept*, only it wasn't the express.

She worked it out afterwards because she knows the numbers, up to a point anyway, but she could never have said it off like that, spontaneously. The guy thanks her and crosses the road. She starts shouting then. *Mais pour le quatre-vingt dix il faut aller à la gare.*

Aye, you were pure brilliant, she says.

Och, you're exaggerating, Madge says but you can tell she is dead pleased, dead chuffed with herself. The holiday must be doing her good, right enough.

Gavin

They are walking down the road to the bus stop. It is just a short walk, thank Christ, so there will be no time for an argy-bargy (will there?) He knows the number to get. There is even a timetable on the bus shelter. He lets Alan stand in front of it and read it. He can't read it himself when the boy is standing that close to it but no matter. No way is he going to interfere.

He can't remember the last time him and Alan had a good time together, just the two of them. For years now it seems there has been this argy-bargy. He has felt like crying a lot of the time. He knows weans don't do what they're told the way they had to in his day. He knows they have rights, the way they never had in his day but the constant argy-bargy still makes him want to cry.

He wanted a girl to start with, it is true. Maybe because he thought Sheila would know what to do better than him. Even fourteen year ago men weren't supposed to know automatically what to do. He was there at the birth but even then he didn't really know what to do. Just hold her hand, the midwife said. He even had to be told to hold her hand. The truth was he felt like greeting. Crying like a wean. He did actually end up greeting.

It's OK, it's normal, the midwife says to him but it didn't feel like normal at all. He was greeting for himself as much as anything else. He was such an arsehole. There was nobody he could tell how he felt. Sheila was the last person who needed to know what an arsehole he felt. He was supposed to be strong, for her, for his new family, and here he was the big eejit, greeting like a wean.

He thought they would have a girl later, but after the operation Sheila couldn't have any more. Sheila never said she wanted a girl. She just says they were lucky to have the one and they should be thankful when he said it was a pity they couldn't have any more. They never talked about it after that. Only years later they had this big row and Sheila starts casting up, about how he never took Alan to the football, or even out for a kickabout or any of these things men were supposed to do with their sons (whatever they are). He was flabbergasted. His old man never took him anywhere in his life. His old man would come in of a Friday night stotious drunk and his mum was lucky if she got half his pay packet (when he had a pay packet). The weans were lucky if they didn't get a hammering for nothing. When Sheila says how he was stingy wi Alan's pocket money he was astounded. He thought he gave the boy plenty. He had never had pocket money in his life. Not till he was earning. Even when he was at home he had to hand his pay packet over and he never got much back, only what he needed for his bus fares and sweeties. Sweeties! It was ages before he even got the money to buy his own dinners. Ye can take a piece, his maw had says. A bloody piece at sixteen year auld.

Here's the bus, says Alan and they get on. Thank Christ the boy was looking out for it. For a minute he was away with the fairies. Lately he has been like that a lot. When he isn't wound up. Distracted. It's either the one or the other. At least the asthma hasn't been too bad since he came away. Not after the first few days, anyway.

Dad, Alan says on the bus, Are you sure you know where to get off now?

Och, we'll be all right. That was the kind of thing his mum used to say to him, even though things were never all right. A big fob off. Kids always know too. And Alan is no fool.

We'll just look out for it, anyway, Alan goes.

Aye, that's right, we'll just look out for it. He isnae even complaining. Thank fuck. His own kid makes him break out in a sweat these days. He is afraid to open his mouth practically. You cannae open your mouth without the fear of somebody jumping down your throat. That is the state of things nowadays. It isn't that he doesn't think children shouldn't have rights. He just thinks he should be able to open his mouth without the fear of his own son jumping down his throat.

Look! There's a *Go Sport*! Alan goes. Another one. God, it's ginormous!

Aye, so it is. He wants to say, Jesus, Alan, you're not wanting to go in bloody sports shops again, are you? He was away yesterday looking in this place in the town. All the fancy Reebok and Umbro and what have you. He used to go along with it when he had the money but now he is broke it kind of sickens him, all the consumerism of it. It makes him nauseous these days if he spends too long in a shop. Unless it's food. Although even then he just prefers the wee shops. Supermarkets are just disorienting because there is too much stuff on the shelves. Too much fake choice when really the only choice is whether you can afford something decent with the right vitamins and minerals and everything. Something fresh rather than processed.

You're too clever to get into all this crap, he wants to say to his son. All this consumerist shite.

But he says nothing in case his own son jumps down his throat. It is his own fault anyway. A couple of year ago – longer even maybe – when Alan started all this carry-on he was right into it himself. Not that he wore any of the stuff himself, you understand. He is not that ignorant. He has no desire to go walking about the street with great big letters spelling out meaningless drivel or, worse, advertising capitalists. He should have said all this to his wee son at the time, when he was of an age when he would never in a million years have dreamed of going down his father's throat. But instead he encouraged him in it. Sheila as well, they were both at fault. And now they have spawned a monster.

There it is, dad!

So it is, son, so it is. Ring the bell, quick!

For a minute he thought Alan was going to say, Ring the bell, or maybe the fucking bell, yourself, but, no, he goes and rings the bell, right enough, with not a word about him calling him *son*. He hasnae called him son in ages. He's afraid to – even Sheila thinks *son* is a bit over the top these days. Patronising, was what she said the other day. Ye cannae fucking win.

Off the bus they know from the map where the *Parc Floral* is but can't find the entrance to it, exactly.

I think it's this way, Alan goes.

Meekly, he follows. Better than having a row. Sheila will never forgive him if he comes back and it's obvious there's been a row. Sometimes Sheila will stick up for him but sometimes she'll say it's his fault. It doesn't matter if Alan called him an effing b for nothing. He must have provoked him or something. It's difficult enough being a teenager with all the raging hormones and whatnot without your own da provoking you, disagreeing with you or saying it's your fault because we got off at the wrong stop, or your fault we couldn't find the entrance. You were too meek because you just never use your initiative, or you should be more meek and let the ones who know what they're doing (i.e. the kids) take the lead. Just because you're a parent doesn't mean you know what you're talking about. Just because you've been on this planet for forty bloody years doesn't mean fuck all.

They have come to the entrance of the museum, the *Musée Départmental des Arts Asiatiques* but they have agreed no museums the day. A lighter day. Still educational but. Biology. Or what is it they call the study of plants?

I think it must be the other way, son.

There he goes again, calling him son. Alan'll be going daft in a minute with this patronising father of his, treating him like a wean.

Well, *obviously*.

Aye, the *obviously* was predictable, anyway. Still, if he is getting away with an obviously things cannae be that bad. Christ, things may even turn out to be good.

It is not that far away really from the bus stop although as usual the cars are flying past. He is afraid the fumes will start up his asthma again but he is afraid to open his mouth. His son already thinks he is a weirdo because he is afraid of the lunatic speeding drivers because lunatic speeding drivers are normal in Nice and when you are fourteen you want to be normal as well, or at least your own father mustn't go criticising other normal people and thus showing himself up (and you as well) for how weird he is.

When they get to the park there are all these palm trees. Never mind that the *Promenade des Anglais* is full of palm trees and so is Nice, already he is beginning to relax. Even though there is a crowd of wee weans at the entrance and he knows nothing about weans, does he, he is not *au fait* with twenty first century ones at any rate, he feels, absurdly, he has arrived somewhere. Absurdly because he should know fine well the worst has yet to come. Only then he almost has a panic attack because for a fleeting moment he thinks maybe they have come to the wrong place after all. If there are all these four year olds queuing up with their wee backpacks and their minders with their boxes of sandwiches and buns and peaches – well-fed weans – maybe Alan will think he is too big for all this.

Only Alan is smiling as well. For once he decides to take the plunge and he barges ahead of the weans. They are just loitering anyway. They cannae be expected to wait all day for a bunch of weans. He says loudly to the woman behind the glass, *Un adulte et un enfant, s'il vous plaît.* He does not know if he should have said *une adulte* but it does not matter because the woman is smiling at him. He hands over the money feeling on top of the world that he has spoken to this woman in her native tongue and she has understood. She has even smiled at him.

When he hands over the *billets* to the man at the gate Alan is smiling too. This place looks brill, he goes. How much was it?

He tells him.

That's wrong, Alan says. It cannae be. Here, let me see. He grabs the tickets off him, even though he doesn't know if they are supposed to keep them or something, in case somebody asks you if you've paid. Hey, he goes, you've only paid half for me.

58

Well, you are a half, aren't you?

Nup, halves are for under twelves. It's always like that.

Like he was born and bred here or something.

Och, well, it doesn't matter. Saves us some money, eh?

Aye, well. But I didn't do it intentionally, Alan. I mean, I didn't mean to commit fraud or anything.

Still, it's a good feeling, saving some money, for a change.

Will we follow the wee path? his son goes, heading towards this lake where there are these beautiful black swans. Swan lake. Perfection. It is like heading off back into an idyllic childhood, the kind he never had.

Have you got the camera? Alan is saying.

Aye. He reaches into his pocket. Come on and let me take you with the swans.

No, I'll take you but.

He is smiling a genuine smile – not just one for the camera – as Alan pushes the button. Although it will be nice to look at it afterwards and remember all this. Nice to show Sheila too him and Alan had a good time thegither.

Madge

She has known for three whole days now. Three whole days without telling a soul. She bought the tester kit when her and Sheila separated for an hour at the shops. She couldn't wait to try it out in the toilet. She nearly had a fit when she saw the results, even though she was four days late and she is never a day late. She was convincing herself it was the bloody menopause right up till she saw the deep blue line so there could be no mistake. She even thought she would tell Sheila, she was that high. It almost slipped out. It would have been the perfect moment when they were discussing Alan, or even before that when the cystitis came up. She probably would have told her except she has to tell Stuart first. She has tried to tell Stuart several times only it is like he is avoiding her. He wouldn't even come to the bloody shops with her. Not that he goes to the shops with her at home – he never goes anywhere with her these days at home – but when they are on holiday you would expect some change of behaviour, for Christ's sake. She knows they have been married long enough not to be in one another's pockets all the time but holidays are for precisely that, aren't they? With the baby coming they should be spending more time together, because when babies arrive you get no time at all for yourself. She has two sisters, after all, both with three kids each and if she has heard that one once she must have heard it a thousand times.

Less than a week ago she was telling herself she didn't want kids, was past that stage. Funny how you can turn things right round in your head. One day you are determined you will be childless the rest of your days and the next you are wanting to go and buy bloody babygrows (do they still call them that – God, she doesn't even know), wanting to go and look at babies in their buggies. She could get one of those fancy American (or is it European?) -style strollers with their big, tough wheels. Make a statement about late motherhood or something. She will stay on at work, of course. Maternity rights have never been better. She can take six months no bother. Some women in the department she knows have negotiated more. Maybe she would decide not to go back, after all. You never know. A woman she knew a couple of years ago but has lost touch with did that. They met up for a drink once or twice afterwards but then she just faded out the picture. Said she didn't realise how she was going to feel after the baby was born. For all she knows maybe she has lost touch with everybody. She wouldn't want to do that, end up with nothing to talk about but babies.

And yet right now she could talk about babies all day long. If she got the chance she could. What is difficult to imagine is Stuart talking about them. This is partly why she has not got round to introducing the subject. There have been moments when she could have just come out with it, but it is not as simple as that.

If this had happened to her fifteen, ten, even five years ago her and Stuart would be shouting it from the rooftops, no question. Her sisters, friends, colleagues at work, neighbours even, just everybody she knows really, they would all know about it already. Only her sisters' kids are getting big now. They go out with their friends, they sit in the house with their playstations and their stereos and make a mess in the bathroom. They have seen it all before, her sisters. Motherhood is nothing new.

Who is she kidding? Her sisters will be delighted for her if she is truly delighted for herself (and Stuart). They will give her all the support she needs. Stuart is the one she has to face with news of this pregnancy (*this* pregnancy! As if it happens every other year!) If Stuart cannot cope maybe she cannot either. Jesus, he hardly talks to her these days. And the worst bloody awful thing is he thinks he is being bloody nice. He is not even being rude or horrible or snidy any more, the way he was before they came away. He has become the perfect, polite stranger. The kind you meet on a train who helps you with your bags and everything, but you know is going to leave the minute the train stops and you will both say goodbye and be happy never to meet again.

She is just being ridiculous. Stuart is not going to leave her. Jesus, he can hardly look after himself. She wouldn't admit it to anyone (least of all Sheila or her colleagues at work) but she does everything for him in the house. Washing and ironing and all that. She always has done more than he has, but in recent years she has just taken on it all. What with Stuart being away so much it has just sort of happened. Not that she was unaware of what was happening and not that she didn't protest, at least not at the beginning, although maybe not enough. When she says to Stuart about the housework he comes out with this stuff about getting somebody in. They could afford it, he says. Aye, well, maybe, but she just didn't fancy the idea. It just wasn't second nature to her, having some stranger in round her personal possessions. She shared flats years ago, as a student but only for a few years. She wouldn't want to go back to all that. Anyway, maybe she just can't see herself ordering folk about.

And that is one of the funny things about Stuart this holiday. Unbelievably, he has started doing his own laundry. Maybe it was when he saw Gavin doing the washing in the bloody bath (the bloody bath, for Christ sakes – said he wasn't confident about going to the laundrette round the corner even though the wee card at reception said they spoke English. Wasn't confident with the machines either, he says. It's different with your own at home. Sometimes you would think the man is a bit mental or something, the way he goes on). Only instead of going away to the ordinary *laverie*, the way she'd've done, what does Stuart do but head to the *pressing* even though she told him it's really expensive, like your mother sending the sheets to the laundry when you were wee before she got the washing machine, but only the sheets because it cost a fortune.

Still, they can afford it. She shouldn't be so stingy. She'll not be stingy when this baby comes, no way. It's going to have the very best of everything. Isn't that what late babies are for, spoiling?

She is definitely going to tell him tonight. She can't spend another day in this agony. She is going to force that man to talk about babies, about their relationship, their future together, if it's the last thing she does. Only not in bed, not the very last thing they do, apart from sex which they don't do very much anyway. She has calculated the day she must have conceived because they have done it so little in the past year or so. It has got worse in recent months. It has reduced to about once every three or four weeks. Not that having less sex is the end of the world. As you get older the drive diminishes and all that, doesn't it? Although as far as she can see (or hear, even though they are obviously trying to be quiet about it) Gavin and Sheila do it often enough, although maybe they are at it more now they are on holiday. Well, maybe the news about the prospective patter of tiny feet will have a beneficial effect in that department, if not others. She bloody well hopes so. It is not just the quantity that is the problem. She is randy as fuck since she became pregnant but it is like he never wants to. He even avoids coming to bed until she is asleep.

Not in bed then, although hopefully that is where they will end up, randy as fuck after she has broken the news. Not wham bang like the last six months. The obvious place for a *tête à tête* is some nice restaurant. She will let Stuart pick because he always goes for expensive places. Well, he's going to have to be dipping into his pockets for the wee one and it'll be bye-bye to meals out for a wee while, no doubt (not that they go out much together) so they might as well splash out for once. Champagne even. She will order champagne. Not for herself, naturally, because of her condition (condition, ha!). But Stuart will have no bother downing a whole bottle himself. Better champagne than him starting on the whisky. Maybe they will even share it with the waiter or something equally daft once she has broken the news. Sometimes you are allowed to do daft things. There has to be a time in your life when you can be daft and not have a care in the world what anyone else thinks about you.

Stuart & Madge

He wakes with a headache. A tension headache. It is only half past six but he can't get back to sleep. He remembers what he has to do before he even tosses a glance at the sleeping woman beside him. There are still a couple of nights to go, but what the hell, he can't keep putting it off forever. He will just have to tell her the night. There is nothing else for it. There will be tears and tantrums and sour grapes, nae doubt, but fuck it, sometimes you have to take the bull by the horns. In the morning he will phone Karen at her work and tell her he is leaving his wife and she knows. He could try her mobile early, even the night he could try, but that bastard might be mooching around. He cannot discuss his future with the love of his life while the slimy bastard of a husband is footering about in the background where he's not wanted but is too thick to appreciate the fact.

In the meantime he is going to spend the rest of the day avoiding her. He will spend the whole day in the water if need be, because you cannae discuss things if you are swimming. Even if you can talk in a swimming pool (and it is something that he has noticed middle-aged women tend to do, instead of just going to some teashop or something they just go and pretend they are getting some exercise), even if you can do that with any ease it is that much harder in the sea because the water moves about that much more so it is easier to swallow it. It tastes disgusting, although so does the water in a swimming pool, come to that.

When him and Karen get together, for good, they will have to come somewhere like this. Only not a pebbled beach – somewhere along the coast, somewhere sandy. Upmarket but still with some history, culture. Karen is an educated woman, after all. She is no fool.

It was tough telling her he was coming here. Had to make out it was all arranged behind his back, which wasn't far from the truth, anyway. He realised, in the telling of it, that it might sound like some romantic holiday, taking the wife away to the Côte d'Azur. Thank Christ they were going EasyJet and staying in a cheap dump because he could lay it on thick.

We'll go somewhere real luxurious in the autumn, will we? he says to her.

She smiled that easy smile of hers. She has that rare thing, Karen does, a way of communicating without too many words. She doesnae need words. Women that yap all the time like bloody dogs are common as muck but not his Karen.

He eases himself out of bed, careful not to wake her but it is too late. She must have sonar detectors inside her brain or something, that woman. Spying on him.

Stuart.

Yup.

We need to talk, Stuart.

Christ, aye, but not yet, not yet. Now is not the time, but he kens it cannae wait forever. Only he is only just awake. He needs to prepare himself. At the very least he needs a bloody cup of coffee before they start down this road that has no turning. A cup of coffee, Jesus. A bloody drink even, even though it is only eight o'clock in the morning. But there is no escape.

We need to have time to ourselves, Stuart. Let's go out to dinner tonight. Just the two of us.

Dinner. Aye, fine. Just us, eh? He feels mildly resentful she said it first. He was going to break the news over a meal but she said it first. Maybe he would have put it off till tomorrow, right enough. Nearer the end of the holiday. Because it will be the end, after all. There can be no doubt about that. It will be the last night they are a couple. No more family holidays pretending everything's hunky-dory, no sir.

Do you want to book us a place?

Och, there'll be no need to book, will there? There's tons of places, isn't there?

Yeah, I suppose so. It isn't Glasgow, after all. Maybe it would be a mistake booking, right enough. The guidebook has plenty of entries, including prices, even if they are probably out of date, but it is not the same as seeing the place yourself. There is supposed to be this place with fish in the floor (real live fish, in an aquarium) but they are not kids and she doesn't want him looking at the floor, anyway, she wants him looking at her. Then there are the Negresco's restaurants – one of which is supposed to be the most expensive in Nice but, even though part of her wants the attention, even the lavishness of it, she has to admit that would be over the top. She might be on top of the world because she is pregnant but he would be suspicious, apart from probably unwilling because of the expense. Lastly, she doesn't want to go there because she wants him to pick, the way she wants him to start behaving responsibly, the way a father should. Because tonight is the last night they are going to be a couple. After the night they will be a family. They will be thinking in terms of three, not two (or one, as Stuart often seems to these days).

Stuart is away in the bathroom. At least he's up early this morning. Every other day she has been the one to get up first. She wonders if it has anything to do with her pregnancy, all this waking up early. She remembers vaguely her sister saying something of the sort. The mild nausea is another negative aspect of the pregnancy, although if she gets up now and has a cup of tea and a dry biscuit it will probably dissipate. Certainly by the time they go to the restaurant she will be back fancying food proper. Already she thinks her appetite has increased.

They will probably go to *Vieux Nice*, she thinks. It is the most romantic part of the city. Although she has to keep reminding herself she is to let Stuart do the picking. It is part of reminding him he has to take responsibility now. A family man. The thought makes her want to giggle. Only she desperately needs a pee. If she laughs too much she might just wet herself. Christ, she thinks she hears the sound of the shower. He's not having a bloody bath, is he?

Stuart! she calls. I need the bathroom. Can you be quick?

There is no reply so she batters on the bathroom door. Stuart! I'm needing! Hurry up, will you!

She'd shout louder only she'll wake Alan and Sheila and Gavin.

I'll no be a minute. He sounds resentful which is a bit ridiculous really. She doesn't see why he can't let her in. Embarrassed maybe because of Sheila and Gavin and especially Alan. You have to be careful with kids right enough. They are so sensitive, aren't they?

This is getting ridiculous. She should have told him ages ago. Then he'd understand how she's desperate for a pee. Because pregnant women get that way, don't they? Although she's often desperate first thing in the morning anyway. But then Stuart isn't around that much first thing in the morning at home.

She really can't wait and she hasn't seen a toilet at reception. There is nowhere else she can go. Even if she put her clothes on and dashed to the train station as luck would have it the toilets would be closed for cleaning or something. If she could find them. She'd probably piss herself on the way. A woman of forty pissing herself in the street. Worse than the beggars who look relatively decent really, considering they charge two francs for the bogs. She could be arrested. She heads into the wee kitchenette-type place and lifts a bowl — it's on the inventory and it says they have to pay sixty francs or something ridiculous to replace it. But it's worth bloody sixty to her right this minute, in fact it's fucking priceless. Back she goes into their bedroom and opens the window wide and then draws the curtain closed again. Then she shuts the door and crouches down with her back to it and pisses into the bowl. As the pee sparkles into the bowl she breathes a sigh of relief. She is practically laughing with glee that she thought of this instead of pissing herself as she chucks the piss out the window. The smell of her own urine hits her briefly. And now here is Stuart.

Holding the bowl low, hoping he can't see (or smell) it, she brushes past him and rushes to the bathroom where she is violently sick. She steps out of her stained nightie and gets in the shower. She starts to soap herself clean. She leaves the shower running, for once not worrying about the water going everywhere. By the looks of things Stuart has made a right mess himself. Expecting her to clean it up no doubt. They should've got a place with a cleaner, right enough. It was her fault for asking Sheila. She must've pitied her, but folk don't want your pity, when it comes down to it. Och, it wasn't just about pity – Sheila would be mortified at the very idea. She asked Sheila because she was looking for some sort of closeness there. At one point she was even hinting about just the two of them going on holiday. The sort of thing she should've done years ago but now probably never will. She can quite see how women with weans get tied. The commitment. The totality of it. She feels it already, the permanent presence. But this could be her only chance. There is a miracle growing inside her that will never happen again. What is a holiday on your own with a pal compared with that? Your pals cannae do for you what your man has just done after eighteen year of marriage. Suddenly a marriage that was getting downright stale, if she is honest, has new possibilities. And you never know, whether it's a boy or girl Stuart could end up going completely daft, completely overboard. Because the man can be passionate. There are many who would never guess it but when he was a younger man Stuart could be bloody passionate. Oh, he could be bloody passionate all right about the rights of workers and about socialism and there were plenty who had the benefit of Stuart's passion apart from her and she's no just meaning the politics either. Aye, she's not daft, she kens fine there were plenty of girlfriends before her. Some even told her what a catch he was etcetera. But he was passionate about her too, in the good auld days and she doesn't just mean the sex. Their love life has been in cold storage for a bloody long time now. At best the sex is mechanical and she orgasms the once, after about five or ten minutes. At worst he comes just after he has entered her and then says, sorry but he is too tired for more. Too tired my arse, she thinks. At worst he is a fucking liar. Only even if the love thing (which is bound up with the sex, after all – she is coming back round to the perhaps puritanical notion that you cannot really have the one without the other), if that cannot be rekindled perhaps a child will reawaken passion in Stuart McCracken. If a child will not do it then nothing will. And if that is the case then perhaps it will be time to call it a day, after all. Not that she has any wish to end up a single parent but there are worse things, aren't there? And she has a job and a roof over her head which she is determined to keep, come hell or high water. And Stuart will pay. Oh, yes, he will bloody pay. Aye, one way or another, Stuart will definitely be paying for his wean. There is no doubt at all about that.

* * *

This is the first time he has masturbated in ages. God, did he need a good wank. He hasn't had a bloody wank since he started going out with Karen – if you could call it going out because it has, of necessity, been secret. Which has meant not an awful lot of sex. Not enough anyway. He has carried on with the occasional perfunctory sex with Madge because sex is what you do with your wife. Besides, he knew Karen still fucked that bugger from time to time. Not that she'd say so in so many words. She was too sensitive for that. But once he just came right out with it.

Do you and him – do you and he, he asked. He couldn't bring himself to say the actual word, to acknowledge that she did what they did with her husband.

He's my husband, Stuart, she said. What do you think?

Which was pretty clear, after all. Although what was also clear was that she was unwilling. Unwilling because ashamed to talk about it, like he was ashamed to ask. She was putting on the good wife act the way he was playing the good husband. No, wait a minute. He *was* the good husband. It was something he was always proud of. It is just that he is now acknowledging to himself the way he never acknowledged before, that all good things come to an end. Although it's a pity to let a good thing go stale it's a damn sight worse to let it disintegrate altogether. This is simply stating a fact. Madge, like him, is a rational person. If he puts it to her like that she will not be able to disagree. If he goes about the business in a rational way there'll be no need for recriminations. No need for any emotional blackmail shite. Madge is too stable a person for all that crap anyway. As long as she gets her fair share (exactly half) Madge will see what has to be done. Although it will be two years for a no-fault divorce (he has been looking stuff up in the library) unless the two of them agree she can sue him for adultery. The only thing about the two years is that if Karen wants a baby (because he has never told her about him and Madge – there are some things he cannot tell even Karen – at least not yet), if Karen wants a baby then there could be a problem. But best to wait and see first (unless Madge wants to go for the adultery which is, however, more expensive).

Somebody is battering on the door, wanting in. You cannae even have a bloody wank in peace in this place. Oh, well, once he is back with Karen there will be no more need for wanks. They will be at it every night, him and Karen, if not twice a night. When he is away she can come with him. He should be able to arrange to take his partner. There will be no more of this stupid secrecy. Fun while it lasted but you can prolong secrecy too much. He has sensed recently Karen herself was growing a little weary of it. Wanting honesty. Well, honesty is what she's about to get, her and Madge both. Madge will probably thank him one day. There's no reason why Madge shouldn't get a new partner herself. It's not as if she's past it, not at all. It's just that they are no longer good for each other. Tonight they'll both acknowledge that.

The battering has stopped. When he opens the door he can see no-one. Only a split second later Madge nearly knocks him down in her rush to the toilet. So it was her, right enough. The woman will have to learn to slow down, to learn that rushing about does you no good. Although she was probably desperate for a piss, right enough.

Tonight they will take it slowly. They will have the best going. If he spends a fortune (and it will be the last fortune he spends on Madge – he will not suggest they go Dutch – he will say he is paying, although he will not call it a treat – that would be an error of judgment) then no-one will be expecting them to leave quickly. Although there is no need to prolong it if that is what they wish.

He will just let things take their course, see how it goes. Although he will not procrastinate. If he is going to take Madge somewhere like the Negresco then he is definitely not going to procrastinate. No fucking way. And Madge is not stupid. Madge will know fine well that they are not going to a place like that for nothing. She will suss out right away that it is something of a momentous occasion, and it is not their fucking

69

anniversary after all. Only he will not order champagne (unless she wants to). Like he will not call it a treat, he will not order champagne although he will dress up (they will not even get in unless he dresses up, according to Madge's guidebook). Although maybe they will not get in anyway because he has not brought a suit. On second thoughts he will not suggest the Negresco. A bit over the top, likely to make them both overreact, maybe. Somewhere more sedate, but still expensive. He will have a look through the guide again. Maybe even book. Because he has to be in control the night. They cannot, after all, go wandering the streets like bloody eejits when he has to be firmly in control of the situation.

Alan

The *Parc Floral* is one of the coolest places he's ever been to. The crazy thing is his dad really enjoyed it as well. All those plants and flowers from all over the world. And the terrapins. The two of them were mad about the terrapins. Hundreds of them, crawling about in this pond, in the open air.

It's great all this being outside, his dad said, even though much of it was in the greenhouse, but he knew what he meant.

It makes a change frae the museums, son? his da had says and he had to agree. The museums were fine but this place was something else. He might be a horticulturist when he is older. Only not in Scotland for you can't grow bamboo and bananas and kiwis in Scotland, can you? Unless they're in greenhouses and that would make them too expensive. Unless you were cultivating rare species like orchids. Because that is what horticulturists do, isn't it? That's what distinguishes it from gardening. Unless he lives somewhere else when he is grown up. You should be able to live anywhere within the European Union anyway, provided you can speak the language. That would be the only problem. That and getting the job you wanted. Which might not be harder than getting a job in Scotland, right enough. It's all down to who you know, his dad likes to say sometimes, but his mum says that is rubbish. But then his mum is doing what she wants, so it's all right for her.

He imagines his tutor asking them all what they want to do when they are grown up. Or writing an essay about it and having to read it out in class. A poof, they would call him. Only poofs and girls are into plants, especially flowering plants. If he said that to his mum she would just say, That's stereotyping Alan, and you shouldn't say poof. Except maybe he is one after all. He has been worrying about this for about two year now, if not longer, without admitting it to himself. There was one boy at primary school he always sort of thought of as special. Well, not always. Only in the last year really. He wasn't in the same class but he'd see him in the playground and they were both doing cross country for a while. It got so he couldn't wait for the cross country. Not that they really spoke to one another much, not really. Just stupid stuff about the running and where they were going, stuff like that. He got this funny feeling in his stomach when the boy spoke to him. Not as bad as being sick — it was a good feeling really but it was awfully like butterflies. It was getting a bit ridiculous really. The boy wouldn't have had a clue what was going on inside his stomach. How could he? He was relieved, really, when he found out he wasn't going to the same high school. Relieved they hadn't got to know one another too well too. The boy was called David but there were loads of Davids at the school. David didn't sound that different. He probably wasn't a poof anyway. He would probably have freaked if he'd had the slightest clue. He would have got beaten up if anyone had a clue, even at primary school, probably. Only at high school it is definitely worse. His old man thinks things were bad when he was a boy but at least he wasn't a poof. At least if he got beaten up for a million things being a poof wasn't one of them.

Except they do have a bullying policy these days. Some things are better than in his dad's day. Probably most things are better. You get sent to the head if you are caught fighting, bullying someone. And if you are the one being bullied there are procedures to follow. Like you tell your guidance teacher, or your tutor, or if they are not available, you tell the nearest teacher. Except there are some teachers you couldn't imagine telling you got battered because somebody thought you were (or because you are) a poof. Especially some of the old fogie types. The idea of going and telling them you are a poof is just ridiculous. They would think you were taking the mickey or something. They would probably hand you out a punishment exercise for taking the mickey. And even if you thought some of them might be OK it might still be too late. Like if you got battered to fuck and got carted away in the ambulance or worse. Although maybe you could tell someone you are scared of being bullied. You are supposed to be able to go and speak to your guidance teacher anyway. Mr McKay seems sort of OK. He definitely wouldn't hand you out a punishment exercise. He might not be embarrassed either. He can't imagine Mr McKay being embarrassed about anything, although he must be some of the time. It's normal to be embarrassed about some things some of the time. Even total extroverts get embarrassed some of the time. Not as much as his old man but. Imagine telling his old man he is a poof (if he is). He hasn't a clue how his old man would react, apart from being embarrassed. Like, would he mind? Would it make any difference to him? He knows his mum would try and come to terms with it because she sees herself as good at dealing with problems but why, after all, would it be a problem?

When all the palaver about section 28 was all over the news his mum said the Keep the Clause lot were just a crowd of prejudiced bastards but she couldn't say that at work, except to colleagues you knew well.

Why not? goes his old man.

A, said his mum, because the word bastard is unprofessional and B, because I can't afford to offend groups I work with. I have to accept that people think differently from me.

Prejudice is prejudice, his old man said but his mum just shrugged.

Maybe his old man, when it comes down to it, is less prejudiced than his mum. Not that his dad would say anything against her. There's nobody like his dad for loyalty to his mum. You can never say a word against her in his dad's presence.

This is the first time he's been round the place on his own. He could've asked his dad, but he wanted to spend some time on his own, to think. That is the trouble with holidays abroad (not that he has had that many of them), but it is like you get treated like a wean all over again. Just when you thought you were getting your independence you go your holidays and you are never by yourself. They can't trust you not to get lost, or read a map, or ask someone the way, or not get mugged. You've probably got a better chance of getting mugged at home than here.

He is walking along the *Promenade des Anglais*. Today is Thursday so there are really only two more days. You cannot really count Saturday because the plane leaves in the early afternoon and anyway they have to be out the apartment. Two days and all this will be over. The sun, that his dad especially loves so much and which even seems to make him happy – maybe it makes them all happy, right enough, the beach, even if it is pebbles, and that his mum likes because you don't get sand in your hair and everywhere else. She bought them all those plastic shoes eventually even though they may never wear them again, because where will they find the money next year when his dad's redundancy has run out? Except maybe he can go when he is grown up if, as his mum says, he makes something of himself. He doesn't know if he wants to make something of himself. Not if making something of yourself means turning into a guy like Stuart. And if it doesn't mean that what else does it mean, for fuck's sake? He thinks he'd rather be like his dad even though they haven't always seen eye to eye – even though his dad can be a real pain in the arse, worrying over nothing and being embarrassed at being ignorant when it isn't his fault. The worst ones anyway are the ones who think they know everything just because they went to university and have these fancy jobs telling other people what to do, when really all they are is wankers. He knows now Stuart is definitely a wanker, not just because of the remark he made about the Matisse collage, but because he saw him this very morning going into this place that sells sex. It says SEX in great big letters (the cheek) right on the front so it must be a brothel. I mean, what else could it be? The man is a dirty bastard. Poor old Madge, married to a dirty bastard like that. It must be worse than being married to a poof. At least if you were married to a poof and you found out you would know it was just because he couldn't help it. That it wasn't anything to do with you personally, that it's just the way he was made and he made a terrible mistake marrying you but you couldn't really take it personally, could you? Whereas if he goes with other women, Jesus, it's because he used to fancy you once and now he doesn't. And he'd rather pay than have sex with you. It must be just terrible, terrible. Poor old Madge. The least he can do is to be kind to Madge for the rest of the holiday. It is so obvious the poor woman doesn't have a clue. She seems dead happy which sort of makes it worse, really. Ignorance is bliss, his gran likes to say sometimes but that is a load of crap. He'd rather know, if he was going with somebody (especially if he was married except he won't be getting married if he is gay, will he?) He'd rather know if they were going to be unfaithful. Whether he was married (or gay) or not he'd rather know.

He crosses the road. He cannae spend all day looking at the sea. He is supposed to be away buying presents. He doesn't know where to go or what to get. At least he does know where to go – that narrow long street that runs parallel to the *Promenade des Anglais* where folk are getting themselves tattooed – mad bastards when they could get AIDS. He knows all about AIDS. Well, bits anyway. He knows dirty needles is one way and that includes tattoos. Apart from the folk sitting in the street doing tattoos there are all these stalls and shops flogging souvenirs. Except it's a bit obvious. Why should you just go to the souvenir places for tourists if you want to buy presents? Just because you are a tourist doesn't mean you have to have the same taste as all the other tourists. Although some of the stuff is not as bad as all the crap they sell in Scotland to tourists – tartan tammies and all that shite. Still, some of the stuff at the stalls is pretty cheap. Not all of it but. Like there's these African guys with their carvings he knows he couldn't afford without needing to ask the prices. He's not daft. He wonders if they made the stuff themselves or if they're just traders. Even if they told you they made the stuff themselves you wouldn't know whether to believe them. That is what his mum said anyway, even though she usually reckons herself a good judge of character.

He has walked as far as the *Galeries Lafayette*, right next to *Go Sport*. An African guy is sitting on the ground. He has always walked past these guys before, as have his mum and dad and Madge (Stuart hasn't really come with them shopping). He is tempted to have another look at *Go Sport*. The stuff in there is pretty good value for money, he thinks, and maybe he has enough left, but then he wouldn't have enough maybe to buy presents. And, besides, Madge was going on about local culture. Apart from the beggars which he finds embarrassing (even though there are beggars in Glasgow, although not as many as Edinburgh) maybe this guy is the nearest opportunity he's going to get to experience local culture, something real. His dad and Madge were in agreement about that one. Funnily enough his mum was sceptical and so was Stuart, but he would have predicted Stuart would be like that. A cynic.

Pas cher, pas cher, the guy goes. This is what he always says. This is his line. Only he has stopped. Without really realising it he has stopped. He starts to look at the stuff on the cloth on the ground. He is not even sure he wants anything. He has not really looked closely at the guy's stuff before. It is all girly stuff, you might say. Wee bags and bracelets and necklaces, stuff like that.

T'as envie? the guy goes, beaming at him, holding up this wee bracelet made of different coloured threads woven together with ceramic or clay beads at the end. He is not even attempting to speak English. He quite fancies a bracelet. A souvenir so he will always remember Nice. Not just the *Promenade des Anglais* but this guy here, who is too poor to have even a table to lay out his stuff. Too poor to go and eat meals out. Too poor even to have somewhere to sleep at night for he has seen these guys sitting here with their few bits of stuff late at night. If he buys something here it will keep for ages because it is definitely not the sort of thing you need to wear all the time.

He smiles and shrugs. *Je ne sais pas*. Although he does know. He just does not know which one he wants.

The guy smiles back. *Très joli, celui-ci. Trente francs, c'est tout.*

His own French is still terrible. He is dead slow in translating in his head but he gets it eventually.

Pour une fille? the guy goes, as Alan picks one up and hands over the money.

Non, c'est pour moi, he replies, adding, as an afterthought. *Je suis*

75

gai. He glances quickly at the guy to test his reaction but he is only smiling the way he did before. His intuition tells him he has got the word wrong – that *gai* does not mean gay at all. *Je suis homosexuel*, he adds. And now there is definitely a hint of surprise on the guy's face. He saunters off, feeling in some little way triumphant. He has come out, he realises, for the first time. To two people – himself and someone he hardly knows. Only that was the easy bit. Now he has to tell people he does know and that will be anything but easy.

Sheila

Something has happened this holiday. To all of them. She is not claiming to be psychic but she always was an intuitive person. Firstly, there is Gavin, her own husband who was downright bloody depressed when he came over here. No bloody wonder, losing his job. Not that he was that fond of it, but getting used to the one wage, trying to go easy on the redundancy, was bound to be a strain. For the three of them sure but especially for him. Being dependent. Men always hate that, don't they? Being dependent on a woman. All that and on top of it that cough of his.

Gavin's cough seems to have lessened a lot anyway. Gavin reckons it is the damp at home that does it. Maybe it's bronchitis he has although the doctor calls it asthma. He could live over here, he reckons. Or he says that one minute and then he is laughing when he discovers this statue to Jean Medecin, not so much because of the statue but because the bugger had an avenue named after him. One of the biggest streets right in the centre of Nice. You have to be very highly thought-of to have an avenue named after you. And what was he but the bloody mayor, it seems. Aye, could he fuck live over here. At least in Glasgow you know where you are and Christ knows the place is corrupt enough. Aye, there was corruption and nepotism aplenty in Glasgow no that long ago either. The state o the housing has to say it all. There is his old man spending his last days in a maisonette in Easterhouse that's riddled wi the damp. If Stuart thinks Gavin's got a bad cough he should hear his old man's.

Normally she doesn't pay that much attention when Gavin goes on like this but this holiday she has been realising, slowly, that Gavin is the most sincere person she has ever met. Or is ever likely to meet. There is never a dishonest word from him. Whereas people like Stuart, whom she meets day and daily – for local authorities are riddled with bureaucrats like him, people who create empires for the sake of their own promotion and care not a whit about the masses of people whom they are there to serve – aye, people like him are just out for their own ends. Words for him are for winning arguments. Never mind that the argument was based on wrong premises or is it principles? Although she knows that there is no such thing as a totally principled stance, the way Gavin likes to make out sometimes. I mean, you have to be pragmatic in this life, otherwise where would you and your weans be? A friend she worked with years ago, when the two of them were just part-time and she hadn't qualified, well, this friend Josie risked her career for the Peace Movement. She can understand why she did it, sure. She went with Josie on quite a few demos but drew the line at getting arrested. OK, so maybe it wouldn't've made that much difference, a few arrests at Faslane and Greenham, all for a good cause. Not like getting done for shoplifting or other criminal-type stuff. But still, you never knew. In social work and community education they always insist on a criminal records check. While there are some managers who think nothing of a breach of the peace conviction at Faslane there are others she is less sure about. Managers that remind her of Stuart, all go-go-go and it's not their fault if they knock someone down in the process. The idiots should have been looking where they were going.

She met Stuart just this morning, in the street. He was coming out of that sex shop. He went red, as you would expect anybody to, at being caught coming out of a place like that but he laughed when she remarked on it.

Spicing up the old love life then? Maybe I should take a walk in myself. Better than saying nothing, she thought. Good on him if him and Madge were into kinky stuff. She couldn't deny her and Gavin were a bit – well, muted, sometimes, in theirs. Not stale though, definitely not stale. Christ, she still came just about every time and Gavin is, if anything, getting better in middle age. No premature ejaculation for a start. Over the years the two of them have bought a few books, too, but never really used them much except maybe indirectly. The books probably encouraged the two of them to talk more, right enough, and things went from there. Only up to a point but. Everybody has their limits. Gavin, more than she, is vehemently opposed to any kind of sadomasochistic stuff.

I had enough of being beaten when I was a wean, he would say when they were looking at this book once that raised the subject.

That's different, she said.

How? he said.

It's the power balance, she said. When there's two equal adults. Equally responsible.

But then you get domestic violence, Gavin pointed out. Adults aren't always equally responsible. Or at least people can take advantage.

They left it there.

Bloody pricey, all that stuff, Stuart said. Although he never said he never bought anything. (Well, Christ, he wouldn't tell her, would he?)

Fancy a coffee? Or a drink?

Aye, why not?

So there's the two of them sauntering off down the street and into this restaurant/coffee place.

She ends up having a drink with him, even though it is only eleven thirty. Plus a *panini* because she has been up early, after all. And it is nearing the end of the holiday, for Christ's sake. The *panini* is lovely. Hot and crisp with *saumon fumé*. Probably Scottish salmon too.

All good things come to an end, she said, partly for something to say.

Aye, says Stuart, I don't think I'll be back here though.

Aye, the dog's dirt and all that. Still, part of it's lovely, though, isn't it?

Aye. But I like sandy beaches. I mean, there's plenty in Brittany, I know, but it's too cold there. I like Florida, as a matter of fact.

Aye, well, I suppose there's no language problem right enough.

Och, I can *parlez-vous* if I want. I got my Higher French years ago.

The surprise must have registered on her face for he waves with his hand. Don't go spilling the beans now, will you? I mean, obviously Madge knows but your Gavin and young Alan. Especially young Alan. I don't think he'd be too pleased somehow. Probably write me off as a lazy git.

She laughs but she is appalled herself in a way. It is the height of laziness right enough. And she can't really imagine keeping the knowledge to herself for ever. It is a bit cheeky of Stuart to even ask, expecting her to keep bloody secrets for him.

The thing is, I don't see the point, Stuart went on. Madge is making a big deal about this communication thing, but when it comes down to it the more you think you know the less you do. I mean, it was Madge made that stupid mistake about the wolves.

Well, it was all of us, but, surely?

Aye, but we all followed Madge, like bloody sheep, didn't we? Whereas if we'd just bloody asked folk – the waiter like – what it meant then we wouldn't have gone on believing all that crap. Getting taken in. Do you see what I mean?

But did you not translate *le loup* as wolf yourself?

Naw. I mean, I've forgot it all anyway. Not that it was ever that strong in the first place. I mean, what's a Higher French? Fuck all, really, I would say. Even the A level Madge is doing. Where's that going to get her? It's not going to get her a fucking job, is it?

Well, I don't think she expects it to get her a job. I mean, there's more to life than work, Stuart. Even you, a workaholic, should know that.

He has been grinning the whole time he has been with her but now he is frowning. Who said I was a workaholic? Madge?

No, no. Jesus, what has she said? The last thing she wants is to come between a woman and her husband. It was just a joke. I just know you're a career type. I mean, so is Madge. So am I, come to that. It's just that sometimes you need more.

Oh, aye. His face has relaxed. You're right there. There's more to life than work. I'll definitely drink to that. And he raises his glass.

Listen, he says, as they are finishing their drinks and sandwiches. Listen. You won't say anything to Madge, will you?

She doesn't understand. He has already said Madge knows he got his Higher French. What's the big deal?

The Sex shop, he says.

Oh. She attempts a laugh but can't quite manage it. He means he didn't buy anything after all. Of course she wouldn't mention anything to Madge anyway. God, they are not that bloody close. God Almighty.

Och, I might as well tell you, he mutters before she gets a chance to say anything. There's someone else. I'm going to tell her the night. It's been on my mind all week. Me and Madge are – well, let's just say we're no longer an item.

There's someone else? She is stupidly just repeating him. Because it is too bloody awful to contemplate, what he has just told her. That he has told her this awful thing before he has even had the decency (if there was ever any decency in any of it) to tell his own wife.

You don't need to know who it is. I just wanted you to understand I wasn't in there for me and Madge. That's all. She'll know soon enough. I can trust you, Sheila, can't I?

If you mean would I be so low as to tell her what you've just told me then no, I wouldn't be that low in a million bloody years. She is raising her voice and she knows people are looking at them but she can't help it. I just hope you have the decency, she splutters, to tell her as soon as possible. She gets up and stumbles out of the restaurant without a backward glance. It is only minutes later she realises she has left him to pay the bill.

Out in the street she does not know where to turn. She is afraid to go back to the apartment in case she meets Madge, afraid her face will give her away, afraid to meet the bastard again, afraid to meet him especially in the presence of Gavin and Alan. Only the holiday has been completely spoilt. Ruined. Poor, poor Madge. Jesus Christ, poor Madge. Compared with Stuart her husband is an angel. There is Gavin, going on, incessantly, sometimes, about the importance of history. He has hardly shut up about it since he was at those bloody museums. He takes everything so personally, Gavin does. It is the same when there is a TV programme on about some issue or other. The other month he was on about how they should consider giving up the car because it was damaging the environment. Not use it less but bloody give it up. Now it looks as though they will maybe have to give it up anyway because they cannae afford to keep it on the bloody road.

There is something very comforting about having a shared history and wanting it to continue. It was more than a little shocking Stuart speaking like thon about his wife of eighteen year before he even mentioned the carry-on, the adultery. And the way he put it, like it was fucking nothing, so fucking casual-like. There's someone else. Someone else. I fuck someone else as a matter of fact. In my spare time. I am not a workaholic. I just go fucking someone other than my wife in my spare time. Madge guessed wrong. OK so he is entitled to disagree with his wife about learning French or anything else, only the way he spoke about her. Fucking hell. Not the actual words, but she could sense the aggression in his voice. Leading up to the big revelation. Couldn't wait to let her friend know he fucks someone else. It is the worst thing she has ever heard, for the husband to go telling the wife's friend before he even tells her. And is he even trying to get her to tell Madge in a roundabout kind of way? Because he hasn't got the bloody guts to do it himself? The way he hasn't the guts to speak French. Jesus, it's no that bloody hard. Her and Gavin were even having a go the other day. Walking down the street looking in the shop windows and translating. Trying out their accents on one another because they daren't try them out on anyone else. Like a couple of kids. Well, it is like it will be their last chance to play at being French (some hope!) for some time. The holiday has meant more to her than she ever dreamt. Look at how Alan has come on. Not just the language, although he was great that night at the restaurant. Ordering in French. She was really proud of him keeping it up even though he obviously thought – rightly or wrongly – that shit Stuart was trying to do him down. After the day's revelations she has started reassessing every opinion she ever had about Stuart. A right dark horse. Jesus.

But Alan has been picking up more than the language, she senses. That is the great thing about going abroad, you get this sense of your place in the scheme of things. Even seeing the jobs other people do, a wee glimpse of what they eat, the houses or apartments they live in or don't live in, the wee women with the wee dogs, the beggars, the guy selling the Macadam journal that only Madge could read and even then not very well. All that, if not all the touristy stuff (although probably that as well). It helps you develop a sense of perspective. Not that it makes you grateful exactly for your own lot but it makes you realise where you're coming from. Maybe Gavin even has a point about the toilets. Today is the first time Alan has gone off on his own, not just on this holiday but on any other holiday. Today is the first day neither her nor Gavin felt obliged to stick to him like glue, petrified he would get lost in a strange place. But he is fourteen, after all. He is old enough to manage a couple of hours on his own even in a foreign country. And it helps him knowing a wee bit of the language. It helps a lot. Him and Gavin and Madge are away to the *Musée des Beaux Arts* later on.

We might go some place else after, Madge says. Unless you want them returned to you? Meaning Gavin and Alan.

It's crazy. Madge was in such a good mood this past while. Like she didn't have an inkling. Like she was high even. It is crazy. Or maybe it is a nervous excitement, trying to cover up what was wrong between her and Stuart, keeping her end up. Well, no way is she going to tell her because no way is it her place to tell her and especially no way is she going to do that bastard any favours. No sir. But just because she isn't going to spill the beans doesn't mean she is going to do absolutely nothing. Letting sleeping dogs lie is precisely what she isn't going to do. Because you owe your friends. Empathy and consolation is what friends are for. She will have to let Madge know, in a roundabout sort of way, that she will offer a shoulder to cry on, be there any time she is needed. In an ideal world (ideal apart from the selfish fuckers like Stuart who inhabit it) Madge would end up guessing the truth without having to be told. The proffered shoulder will be accepted, gratefully, and the selfish git spurned like he deserves. Except spurned sounds less than inadequate. The fucker should be hung, drawn and quartered when it comes down to it. But the shit will get off Scot free. Especially because they have no kids the shit will get off Scot free. If Madge divorces him – and if she knows Madge there is no *if* about it – it will suit him down to the ground because he will be free to do what he likes. There is no fucking justice.

Gavin

Aye, this is a right turn-up for the books, him and Alan and Madge (Madge!) away to the *Musée des Beaux Arts*. *Beaux Arts* – it has a lovely ring to it. He is beginning to appreciate why Madge is so keen on the French. There is no such thing as an exact translation. The literal English translation just sounds stupid. He imagines telling somebody – one of the boys he used to work with – he went to the *Musée des Beaux Arts*. They would gie him looks but he thinks he would be able to explain all right, about not being able to translate it.

The place is really wee. No café or nothing but in a way that suits them. They got here quite early so they can ponder and take their time. Makes a change after rushing for the bus. The first bus was so crammed full they decided not to get on. Then they ended up getting a different bus and it never took them all the way there. They had to walk a good bit and, though Madge was chatty, he was worried all the time that Alan was going to complain. Or he was worried Madge wouldn't understand that what teenagers do is complain, and Madge would say something and Alan wouldn't say anything at the time, but he'd suffer for it afterwards. He always ends up getting the blame.

Only Alan never said a word. Just walked on ahead and even sounded dead pleased when they found the place at last because, although there was a sign, the building didn't really look like a museum – it was too wee, so they walked up the hill past it and then had to come down again. This is the kind of thing that gets Alan in a tantrum sometimes – the stupid mistakes you make on holiday just because you don't know your way around. Kids just expect to find their way from A to B these days. Only when he was a kid he was in some constant daze. Never knew where he was with adults. You could take nothing for granted – not even your dinner.

Dufy donated a lot of his stuff, it seems. He tries to work out whether he thinks the guy is any good, whether it is a genuine representation or whether it is just style without substance. He probably wouldn't dream of even asking himself the question if it wasn't that he's heard all this stuff about corruption. Except he donated them, didn't he, rather than the city buying them? You can be too paranoid about a thing. Although maybe the fact that he donated them has as much reflection on their worth as on Dufy's generosity. But he is being unfair. He lacks the education to make an informed judgment. At the shop on their way out he fingers the books but of course they are all in French. Too dear anyway.

Madge comes over. They have Dufy in the *Beaubourg* in Paris. The Museum of Modern Art. One of them anyway. D'you like his stuff, then?

Aye, well, he goes. Because he's not sure. I don't really know, he confesses. I'd need to find out more about him.

Madge smiles. He wonders if she thinks he is stupid, if people who haven't been to all these fancy places like her and Stuart have are just stupid. Maybe he is stupid. Should he not be able to say if he likes a thing or not? Only you need to be able to compare, don't you, to judge? Only how can you compare like with like in art when there is no such thing?

I've been to the *Burrell* in Glasgow, he says, stalling. At least he has been somewhere. He has been to the *Gallery of Modern Art* too. Quite a few times. Maybe that is a more appropriate comparison. Thinking of the period, like. The timescale.

I think so, he adds, after a bit. Madge is still looking at him. I think I can see Nice in his work. Know what I mean?

Oh, aye, Madge says, all enthusiastic. Me, too. The character of the place. Definitely.

He beams at her but already she is looking away, fingering the books. He goes back to them as well.

Maybe he could find something on Dufy in Glasgow when he goes home. Maybe even in the library he could find something. It doesn't have to cost him a thing. At least he has the time now to do stuff like that. He doesn't have to spend it all in the house. Although he likes being in the house right enough. He likes being by himself. The peace and quiet of it, as well as nobody telling you what to do. He thinks about the mural he started in the kitchen. Maybe he could do a different one somewhere else in the house. Focus on something less domestic. Something he can remember this holiday by. Maybe he could have a go at copying the *Promenade des Anglais*, à la Dufy. Only he can put his own interpretation on it too. Already he is beginning to imagine the work – not the finished article, just in progress but it is amazing that you can draw in your head before you have even taken out a pencil or a brush.

He picks up a wee print – the wee ones are not too dear. Do you fancy anything? he asks Alan.

Naw, I like the sculptures the best, Alan goes.

He nods. There is some fantastic stuff, right enough. Classical-type stuff as well. There's artists here he could look up in the library or something when he goes home. It is great to be able to travel the world and see what other cultures make of their existence, how they interpret it. The same as us and yet not the same. And this is all history too.

Madge is looking rather tired as they make their way out.

There's still plenty of the afternoon left, Madge says on the way to the town centre. They have decided they might as well walk as footer about waiting on a bus all day.

I felt ill on that bus going there, to tell you the truth, Madge says.

Aye, well, the heat, right enough, he says. She looks pale but he doesn't say so. Some women hate you discussing their appearance like that. I wouldn't mind going to the beach, to tell you the truth.

Great idea, Madge says. I know I could do with a swim. Only we'll have to go back to the flat to get the swimming things.

Aye, he says. Maybe I could get some stuff for dinner – pizzas and salad or something – in the supermarket. I'll prepare it. I'll make something for all of us.

Thanks, Madge says. Only Stuart and I have arranged to go out to dinner the night. I'll head on back, if you don't mind. Have a lie-down for half an hour. Maybe we could have a bite to eat at the flat right enough. We never really had any lunch, did we?

Back at the flat Madge has fallen asleep and there is no sign of either Sheila or Stuart. Well, they might still be back. If not, they could leave a note, saying they are at Blue Beach or something. Blue is the one they've been going to most of the time. Madge looked up Nice on the Internet before she came and discovered which beaches were the cleanest. The woman is amazing in some ways. Taking the trouble to do all that.

Alan helps him prepare a light meal. There is enough salad for everybody plus cold meats and other stuff they can keep in the fridge. But they only put out the three plates.

Will you go and waken Madge, son, or will I?

Wait a minute, dad, Alan says. See how she didn't look too good earlier on? I think I know what it is. I didn't like to say but.

What, son? He's not really paying much attention. He is starving. He can hear his stomach roaring. How would a boy of Alan's age know what was wrong with a woman like Madge? It is probably that time of the month or something. Only he has to watch what he says to Alan.

It's that bastard Stuart, Alan says with sudden venom. I saw him this morning coming out of that brothel. Dirty bastard. I bet she knows.

What?

The brothel down the road. You must've seen it.

He stares at his son. Of course he has seen the women with over-made-up faces and their low-cut blouses and their short skirts and glitzy shoes and flashy wee handbags hanging about but how would he, let alone Alan, be able to identify a brothel? Has Alan seen something he hasn't? Like a half-naked woman sitting behind a red light or something? Christ, is he getting that old he doesnae notice they things? No that he knows what a brothel looks like, right enough.

It says Sex Shop in great big letters, Alan says patiently. It's just along the street. On the other side.

Oh, he says slowly. Aye, I've seen it. He is trying not to laugh. Alan will definitely get mad if he laughs. That's not a brothel but, Alan.

What is it then?

It's – it's a place where people go and buy – well, like, sex aids. Videos and stuff like that.

And dirty magazines?

Aye, I suppose so. I don't know exactly what they sell. I mean, I've never been in a place like that myself.

Alan is blushing now. Embarrassed at the discussion as well as at his mistake. Anybody – especially a kid Alan's age – can make a mistake like that. It just shows you how innocent he is, in a way. He has spoken to him about the facts of life but only briefly. It was a while ago. The boy didn't seem all that interested. Sheila found a book they could give him but it was a bit babyish. She said not to worry. The main thing was not to show any embarrassment about sexual matters and to make it quite clear you were available to answer questions. You cannae sit and give them a lecture wi all the details and expect them to take it all in at the one go.

I didn't think you'd go to a place like that, anyway, Alan says, matter-of-fact.

Aye, well, it's not that I'm saying there's anything wrong with them. I mean, I don't really know if there is or not since I've never been into one. But I'm not that sort of person, like.

Me neither, Alan says. I don't fancy women anyway.

Oh, right. In his day it was girls. Fourteen year old lassies are still girls, surely? God, what does Alan mean? That he's too young to fancy them yet or that he doesn't fancy them full stop and he never will? Which means, which means something that, for all him and Sheila talked, and talked to Alan, he has never before considered.

That's all right, he says at last, hoping he hasn't hesitated too long. Everybody has to make their own choice.

You're not bothered, then, about me being gay?

Nup. Why should I be? I mean..., he gives an embarrassed laugh, ...in this day and age it shouldnae be a problem, should it? Although, he adds, worried, if there was any trouble at school, like bullying or anything, you'd let me and your mum know, wouldn't you?

Aye. Only I haven't said anything to mum yet.

No. Do you want me to tell her?

Naw, you're all right. I'll tell her myself. Only, he hesitates, maybe if I don't get round to it, you could. I'll let you know. OK? I'll go and tell Madge the food's ready.

Aye, that'd be great.

Only he doesn't go. Instead he hesitates. While he stands there and smiles at him, like some big eejit. Grinning like a fucking Cheshire cat. The first time his son has confided in him in bloody ages, the first time he's got round to telling him something really big, something that could have an effect on his life forever afterwards.

It's no big deal, dad, is it?

No big deal, son. Naw, not at all.

The boy is walking away. Walking away as cool as a fucking cucumber after making a stupendous announcement like that.

Alan, he goes, son.

Alan turns round. He isn't smiling at all. He looks scared. It must've fucking killed him to tell his da that. Because he has never known how to encourage the boy. Because he was never brought up to it himself he hasnae a clue.

Son, he goes, his voice going all shaky because he is afraid at any minute he will burst into tears or something and Alan will take him the wrong way and that will be it, the chance blown forever. Alan, I think it's great.

Great? Alan looks puzzled.

Aye, I think it's great you told me. That I was the first. He feels stupid saying it because it makes him sound as though he is just thinking of himself, but that is not it, not at all. What he meant to say was that it is great his own son has the confidence, that he is not making himself sick to his stomach bottling things up the way he did when he was his age, the way he still does even. That and it's great he has the confidence in his own da too, the way he never had in his. Confiding in was not what das were for in his day.

87

Alan nods. I'll away and get Madge then.

The three of them sit down to eat.

This is brilliant, Madge goes. God, I wish Stuart would do stuff like this.

Och, it's nothing. Neither it is. It's not as if he did any cooking, not really. Apart from putting the pasta on the ring and because it's fresh it only takes a few wee minutes. And the sauce is dead easy as well. You just have to chop up the tomatoes dead small and add fresh parsley and coriander and stuff. It's dead easy after you've done it a few times.

Stuart'll be busy all the time with his work, he says, apologetically, although a meal like this takes no time at all. This is dead easy, he goes, pointing at the salady stuff. Curly lettuce with fresh peppers and red onions and black olives. It is all about presentation. Although it's easy to say that when you have the time to think about such things. He is no longer embarrassed, he realises, about being out of work. He potters a lot in the house. Lately he has been doing a lot of cooking. Learning all these new skills. He has been enjoying the domestic bit. Maybe that is one reason why Alan suddenly felt he could tell him about being gay, because his own da is not the macho wanker some das are.

I'll have to cook us all a proper meal, he says, before we leave. Tomorrow night I'll rustle up something grand. A grand finale. A wee celebration.

He beams at the two of them. Alan smiles back.

As it happens, Madge says, between mouthfuls of the salad and pasta (she has fairly found her appetite, that one, and he always thought her bordering on anorexia practically). As it happens, I have something to celebrate. Something very special. She leans forward, half-whispering and again he gets the impression she is a wee bit drunk, if he didn't know better for he spent the morning in her company, didn't he, and she never touched a drop? And even if she hid a bottle in her room she wouldn't be able to hide the smell, would she?

Only, she goes on, not smiling anymore, looking scared rather, you have to promise not to tell a soul. At least not until I've told Stuart, because I haven't got round to telling him yet, only I can't keep it a secret any longer and I'll burst if I don't tell someone. And now she is nearly in tears and he would put his arm round her if it wasn't for the fact that he is terrified of putting his arm round anyone who isn't his wife and he wouldn't want to be taken the wrong way.

Aye, well, he goes, only shouldn't you wait until Stuart is home?

I can't, she goes, I can't. I'm even scared to tell him because I don't know how he's going to react. And now she is nearly crying, Jesus, and he has to get up after all and put an arm on her shoulder because he can't bear to see a woman cry. As he does so a sob erupts from her throat. This is worse than he anticipated. He carries on holding her shoulder, already feeling a great eejit, completely unable to offer any words of comfort.

It's all right, Madge, Alan goes. We won't tell a soul. And the boy reaches forward and touches her hand. Something he would have been afraid to do last week, in case his father took him the wrong way.

If this had happened ten, fifteen years ago, Madge goes, God, even five years ago, Stuart would've been over the moon, I swear it. We always wanted kids. We were both devastated when we thought we'd never have any. And we were really good pals to start with, me and Stuart, although you wouldn't think it now, to look at us. I mean, it's like he's always avoiding me. I've known for days, days. I nearly said to Sheila the other day only then I thought, Christ, I can't just go round telling folk when I haven't said a word to Stuart, it's ridiculous. Only there never seems to be the right moment, the time when I feel I have his full attention. Only I'm definitely telling him the night, when we go out for this dinner.

You're pregnant, he says slowly. Jesus, Madge, that's brilliant.

Congratulations, Madge, Alan grins.

Stuart'll be fine about it, he says. Once he gets over the shock.

Aye, I hope so. Only whether he's fine or no, I'm keeping it. Even if it's handicapped I'm keeping it. I feel like it's a miracle or something, you know, after all this time. I even thought to start with it might be the menopause. I mean, that's how shocked I was. I wouldn't blame him for being shocked, not at all. I mean, I would think it was normal, you know. After all this time.

Aye, it'll be a big change for you, for the two of yous. A baby, God, that's great, Madge.

I've a surprise as well, Alan says. For a split second he isn't sure what Alan means, then he knows before he says it. He tries desperately to give his son an encouraging smile but worries it will come out all wrong, that his features will be all twisted instead with the stupid anxiety he feels.

I'm gay, Alan says.

Congratulations, says Madge. I had a idea, right enough. I had an idea. You don't mind me saying that, Alan, do you?

He stares at Madge. How could she possibly have known a thing like that? Except women are awfully intuitive sometimes. Maybe Sheila will have had an idea herself. After all, the boy's own mother must have a better idea than a stranger, for Madge and Alan hardly know one another. Right now all he feels is this great sense of relief that the announcement is over with and as he glances at his son he knows he feels the same, except how many times will he have to go through with this? The whole of his life because there will be no letting up. Except it should get easier, shouldn't it? Even now he experiences this wee twinge of jealousy that Alan seemed to find it that wee bit easier to say the words to Madge. Only he said them to him first, didn't he? He will always remember that. He will always remember today not just as the day Alan made his stupendous announcement but as the day relations with his son became more – intimate. Only already the stupendous aspect is diminishing just that wee bit for it should not be such a big deal these days, should it? He'd better watch what he says or Alan will be calling him an arsehole. For the first time this holiday he decides it is not himself, but Stuart, that is the arsehole. An arsehole for not being there for his wife who is about to go through one of the most major experiences of her life. Except he will be happy about the baby, won't he? Any man would. Any man who had been waiting years like they had. Any man who loved his wife would be over the moon at her having a wean at forty odd. These days they have all the medical attention and everything, don't they? No especial need to worry on that score. Over the bloody moon. Except the operative word is love, isn't it? He doesn't know either of them well enough to make a judgment on that score but Madge greeting the day said it all. Or maybe that is rubbish. Pregnant women get all emotional, don't they? He minds Sheila when she was expecting Alan. Highs and lows all the time. For the briefest of moments he is jealous of Stuart. Him and Sheila would have loved another one, after all. But you have to be thankful for what you have. Him and Sheila have plenty, Gods knows. Plenty to be grateful for. Which makes him wonder where the hell Sheila has got to. He was never one for keeping tabs on his wife but surely she should've been back by this time? He is beginning to be worried for her safety. Only he can't tell Madge that, her that has enough on her plate. And he cannae say anything to Alan either. The boy will still be wondering how to say it. Maybe he just told Madge because it is easier telling a perfect stranger, or an acquaintance rather. He was always closer to his mother but maybe that just makes things more difficult because when you are close to people they have these expectations of you, they make more demands, don't they? He wishes he could turn to Alan and say that Sheila will be all right but he doesn't know that for sure, not for definite, he doesn't. Sheila would be all right if it was anybody else's son but when it comes to your own it is different. It occurs to him now that maybe he doesn't really know Sheila all that well after all. Just because they have been married all these years doesn't mean there aren't parts of her Sheila wants to keep private. Maybe he doesn't really know Sheila any better than Madge knows Stuart. And that is a terrible thought.

Sheila

To an outsider she's strolling along the *Promenade des Anglais* without a care in the world. This is what people come here for, isn't it? The perfect holiday. It looks like paradise. Fucking paradise my arse. This must be the worst fucking holiday she has ever had. All the petty little squabbles her and Gavin and Alan ever had are as nothing compared wi this carry-on. Carry-on. Jesus, there she goes again, underestimating every fucking thing that happens to her these days. If Madge had just told her Stuart was having an affair it would have been bloody awful, but for Stuart to go telling her himself. Takes the fucking biscuit. All because the bastard is too cowardly to go and admit the truth to his wife. Men are such fucking awful cowards, right enough. If she thought Gavin ever did that to her she would fucking kill him, so she would. Not that he ever would. Not just because he wouldn't dare (although he wouldn't) but because at heart he's a decent man, Gavin. He thinks about other people. He doesn't have an ego inflated to the size of those balloon-things you see out there in the bay, those hang-glider-type things towed by a motor boat, that Alan and Gavin contemplated going on before they realised it cost an arm and a bloody leg.

Jesus. How is she going to keep all this from Alan? Should she even try? He is growing up, after all. He needs to know relationships are problematic (if he doesn't know that already from his own home) but some things you have to protect kids from. He is still a kid at fourteen. He has never had a girlfriend, for example. Although he is beginning to have a wee bit of a moustache and for the past three years or so now neither her nor Gavin has gone around naked in front of him, and for the past couple of years Alan hasn't gone around naked in front of them either. She had to speak to him about that. About putting on a dressing gown or at least a T-shirt when he's going for a shower. Not that she is prudish but she is trying to protect him, after all. He is a naive wee boy who wasn't even that interested when she gave him books on growing up. The only stuff she could find was rather babyish – ridiculous really when it is adolescents who need to know the most and adolescents who are hardest to talk to.

Anyway she will have to explain to Alan. She will have to try and be non-judgmental about all this although that is very difficult when Madge is her friend.

She has stopped in front of the newspaper stall. They sell the British papers here. Not the Scottish ones of course, but lately she has been reading *The Guardian*. We all need to broaden our outlook, she thinks.

She is sitting on the beach trying to work out the problem of who to tell what to, and in what order, when one of the young men selling drinks approaches. She has never bought anything from any of them before, treating them all like hustlers in a way, when all they are doing is a job. The stuff is cheaper than it is at one of the beachside cafés as well. She beckons to the young, black male and he comes over.

O-ah-seez, she says, pronouncing it the way he does, and smiles at him. He smiles back at her the way, she imagines, he smiles at all his customers. He is gone before she has time to consider whether she should tip him. No, of course not. You would not dream of tipping somebody who worked in a shop. Although this young man does not work in a shop although maybe he would prefer to. Or maybe not. Maybe the job is not as bad as it looks. Out here in the good weather. Humping a heavy coolbox up and down the stony beach. Who is she kidding? If they even had it in a rucksack it would not be such a dead weight although the drinks and icecreams would not be so accessible.

She was talking to Madge the other day about these young guys.

When we were in Brittany, Madge says and for a moment she stiffened for she hates other folk bragging about their fancy holidays abroad only then she relaxed for she knows fine Madge is not like that, not at all.

There was this woman – about my age – sold the ice-cream. Just ice-cream, I think it was, up and down the beach at Benodet. Only what with it being sand, instead of pebbles, she had this wee trolley. A wee trolley and a sunhat and a big bottle of mineral water. It made the job tolerable, I think. Although she did the same singsong bit, *Vende de glaces, allez, venez, vende de glaces, demande la glace*, something like that, she said. Her voice went up and down like a song. All the time practically. When it would have been better, I think, to have had music or even a bell or something. I mean, it must be terrible for the voice. All day long.

Aye, just for lazy tourists, who cannae be bothered their arses walking to the shop.

Except it's a living, I suppose. I mean, maybe she couldn't get anything else, Madge said.

Aye, only it's a crap way of living. Like these guys who come round your door selling crappy cleaning stuff at dear prices.

Aye, I know. With their wee badges explaining about how they used to be unemployed and how this gives them a chance to be independent.

Aye. The hell it does. I never buy anything off them. Gavin does sometimes, right enough. Guilt, I suppose.

Aye, I suppose that's why I buy the stuff too. That and to get rid of them quicker.

She said nothing to that. It was only afterwards she realised it couldn't really be true for it only took a *no thankyou* to get rid of them whereas if you bought something there was all this footering in the bag and whatnot. A right carry-on.

Madge has more experience than her of holidays abroad. She will still have the money to carry on going abroad, Stuart or no Stuart (and it will definitely be no Stuart for he wasn't bloody kidding, was he?) Having no kids means you are better off. All your money is just for yourself. Only it's different – or she assumes it must be, for she's never really tried it – looking for someone to go with you, instead of assuming you're going with your family. Not that the three of them really compare with some families. Some families she knows go away and the kids do the one thing and the adults the other. Sometimes she has envied them. It is always harder when you have just the one hanging on, for that is exactly what they do. That's why Alan is lacking in maturity, because he's an only and he's never had to compete with siblings, or just get on with them. People have sometimes turned to her and said she's lucky, or her and Gavin are lucky, having just the one for when there's more than one they fight, so they do. Aye, maybe, but they don't fight all the time. They are there for one another too, the way her and her sisters were when she was wee. She used to kid herself that him being an only meant he grew up quicker, with two adults to relate to instead of brothers and sisters. But instead it is the exact opposite. The exact opposite and it has taken years to find that out.

Aye, it takes years to find some things out, yet some things can destroy your life in a minute. No way is she going to be the instigator of any of that. She might prepare Madge for the horrors to come but she could easily make matters worse – whatever she does – opening her big mouth, or pretending she knows nothing when she knows far too much. If she could go and speak to Gavin about it and be sure she could speak to him on his own... but there is not much chance of that. Anyway, she could make matters worse just by doing that. How is Madge going to feel if she finds out Gavin as well as her best friend knows all about her man's sordid affair?

Sordid. Maybe she is overreacting calling it sordid. For all she knows it is a genuine love match. There is such a thing, isn't there, at his age even? Why shouldn't there be? Maybe, for all she knows, Stuart has found his soul mate. Maybe part of her is a wee bit jealous. She is as fond of her man as anybody would be, neurotic and all as he is, over-anxious, obsessive even (Jesus, that doesn't sound very complimentary at all – poor old Gavin) but when you've been married to somebody all these years and plus, when you get to their age, well, you can't expect miracles. Like, she gave up the notion of the knight in shining armour a long time ago, before she met Gavin probably. She tries to imagine Stuart's fancy woman (for want of a better word – how the hell else is she supposed to think of the woman who is, after all, betraying her best friend, fucking up her best friend's life – correction – it takes two to do that and if any one person is most responsible then it must be Stuart, not this unknown creature). She tries to imagine her but she can't because Stuart didn't say anything about her.

The sun is too hot. She has no hat and only a wee drop of suncream left. Thank Christ she remembered the sunglasses. Although she could always go and buy a pair. For that matter she could go and get herself a swimsuit somewhere. Something not too expensive. The place is full of shops. Her and Madge were looking at bikinis the other day. Only she knows she will be as depressed as hell if she leaves the beach and shopping is what she does at home, not what she came here for. Anyway it is too fucking hot to do anything apart from lie in the shade and she doesn't fancy any of the urine-smelling grassy areas, beside which the shady areas will all be taken up. She eyes the water's edge. Masses of people are having the time of their lives and here is she being a miserable old goat. What she wouldn't give for a swim right this minute. She glances down at her clothes. She is only wearing shorts and a wee top. They are both a mixture of cotton and polyester so should dry quick enough. The only thing is her bag. It is only a bumbag and there isn't much in it so it wouldn't exactly weigh her down swimming but the banknotes will get all wet. Only they will dry out, won't they? It doesn't even matter that much not having a towel. What with it being a pebbled beach there is no need to worry about sand in your clothes, in your hair. She prefers pebbles, after all, she thinks. Only she cannot really swim with these sandals on. And she'll look stupid wearing a top when there are all these topless women. And why should she even get her bra wet, after all? She experiences a sudden sense of freedom, of achievement even, as she flings off top and bra together and, kicking her sandals off at the water's edge, slinging them to join the rest of her clothing, she throws herself into the cool, calming waters, pretending for once she has not a care in the world. Or maybe she is just dreaming without being asleep. Dreaming she is sweet sixteen again and that the notion of a knight in shining armour has not quite evaporated. Dreaming, as she revels in the waves slapping against her bare breasts, that she is quite as desirable as Stuart's young woman. As she shuts her eyes and floats on her back and bares her tits to a perfect sky she is at last able to forget her cares and woes. Then the buzzing of the police rescue helicopter overhead jostles her from her reverie. In her haste – Christ knows why – to hide her nakedness under the cover of the waves, she swallows some water and its saltiness almost makes her sick. She stumbles from the water clumsily, scratching her tender feet on the rough pebbles. She must have water, some drink, something, but the *O-ah-seez* man is nowhere to be seen. As she lifts her bra to put it on she spies Madge and Gavin and, oh, Christ, Alan, coming down the steps yonder. Eating ice-creams, the three of them. Ignorance is bliss. Thank Christ they don't appear to have seen her. Thank Christ there's still time for her to shove on, first her sunglasses, then top and sandals and head, bra hanging undone beneath her top, wet shorts sticking to her like she has pissed herself, away across the undulating terrain at the water's edge, past the rows of folk on their private couple of metres square of pebbles with their own sunbed for a day or an hour or whatever, past all the folk who probably think, like Stuart, that everything has its price and that you can buy happiness the way you can an ice-cream or an *O-ah-seez*.

Alan

He feels light and free. Well, to an extent he does because his dad was OK – no, more than OK – brill. His old dad was bloody brill, when you consider how ignorant some people's parents – or just people generally – are about being gay. Ignorant fucking bastards, a lot of Scottish people, so they are. He is not so sure about France. He wishes he knew more about other countries, about how people in other countries live. Maybe they're not that different from the Scots after all. Although you see folk kissing outside more maybe it is just because people are outside more, because of the good weather and that. He has not noticed gay couples kissing, for example. He has not noticed gay couples full stop because how the fuck are you supposed to notice them if they do not even go around holding hands, for example? Are there poof bashers over here as well? He bets there are. He knows some places are worse than others, like Zimbabwe, for example, so he'd better stay out of places like that (ha! ha! as if!) but what about the rest of Europe? Or the States? He has heard about San Francisco, of course, but there must be other places.

Aye, he would love to travel the world when he is older. Only he would want to do it because he wants to see somewhere, not because it is the place for gays to go. I mean, gays should be able to go anywhere they like, same as everybody else, shouldn't they? You should be able to go around with pink triangles on your T-shirt or whatever you fancy and no-one should be allowed to stop you. It should be an offence to try and stop you.

But in the meantime he has to grow up and there will be plenty of other things to worry about. Being gay is just one thing. There is the passing of exams and getting into uni and then a job, not forgetting finding somewhere to stay unless he goes to Strathclyde or Glasgow when he could stay at home, to save money. Except maybe his mum and dad wouldn't want him to stay at home if he is gay. It is all very well his dad saying it's great but what if he meets someone? What if they fancy each other and want to go to bed together? What would his dad have to say about that? He can't even ask him because he is too young. Even if he wasn't gay he'd still be too young. He doesn't want to go to bed with anyone. Maybe he won't want to for years and years (although not too many years, hopefully). Or maybe they will be just great about it. Or at least his dad will. Only he doesn't know about his mum.

Although it is great about his dad, the trouble with his dad (or his mum) is that his mum doesn't always listen to his dad. Sometimes he thinks she listens even less since his dad lost his job. As if he's stupid or something just because he doesn't have a job. If his mum doesn't listen to his dad maybe she won't want to hear about her son being gay. Just because her man thinks it's OK doesn't mean she has to think the same way. Women are different to men. He isn't stupid but maybe he doesn't really notice women the same way as non-gay boys notice them. Maybe there are things they pick up on he hasn't noticed. He loves his mother but deep down he can't sure about her. She used to go around the house with no clothes on – well, first thing in the morning and last thing at night she did anyway. Only not anymore.

Are you ready, Alan? His da is standing beside Madge with his bag all packed. A wee while ago they all decided to go to the beach. Just for an hour or so.

Aye, he says. I've got my trunks and my wallet. I don't need anything else, do I?

His dad and Madge smile together. He wishes he hadn't said that. He is growing up, he should know what he needs himself, like he knows what to get ready for school. Even his mum doesn't ask him all the time now, have you got this or have you got that?

They go out together. To see them in the street you would think they were one happy family. It just shows you. Except his mum and dad are quite happy together, aren't they? He thinks things have been better over the holidays. He has been happier anyway. Mostly. No worries about school or anything. Being gay is a doddle in the holidays.

They've left a note for his mum and Stuart. They are going to Blue Beach again. *Plage Bleue*. They have been to Blue Beach loads of times but he doesn't think he'd ever get tired of it. He has only been abroad twice before. A few years ago now. They went to Majorca both times. The first time was the cheapest, his mum said. They overdid the cheapness bit, his mum admitted when it came to near the end of the stay. His mum and dad were going to the wee shop and buying potatoes and stuff and boiling them on the wee two ring stove when you could get pretty cheap pizzas in this place just round the corner. Only, they only noticed the day they were leaving. They had so much pizza to eat before they came home they had no appetite on the plane for the free food. What a waste, his mum goes. At least she never stuffed it all in her bag, the way he thought she would. He'd've died of embarrassment. He nearly died of embarrassment just thinking that she might try it. His mum could never stand waste and he knows why, even though it is still embarrassing, stuffing things in your bag.

Whenever he used to ask why they had less money than some folk the answer used to be that his mum wasn't working. Like when she was at uni. Then it was the mortgage. Now it is because his dad has no job. There is always some reason. It is not that he feels hard done-by. There are people at school he knows hardly get a decent dinner because their old man drinks it all or loses it in the bookies. When they were in First Year there was this boy came out and said that. That he had no money for the geography field trip because his da had lost his wages in the bookies. The teacher just went all red. Some people's das are real bastards. And some kids' das beat them up as well. Or their mas do. Or they drink. Or both. His own are all right really, even if his ma doesn't understand about being gay she isn't that bad. He will just have to cope if she isn't understanding. As long as she doesn't go on about it all the time he reckons he can cope.

His da and Madge are talking about art again. He only half-listens. Half of him is interested in all this Dufy/Matisse stuff but the other half of him is enjoying getting into his own head. It is one of the privileges of childhood, or adolescence, paradoxically, that you do not have to join in a conversation. You can just be politely uninterested and nobody will think you are being rude if you are not an adult. Part of him doesn't want to grow up. Only now they are talking about Picasso and he is mildly annoyed that they have not tried to draw him in. Do they think he is too thick, just because he is only fourteen?

I went to the Picasso museum in Paris, Madge says. There must be hundreds of his paintings there. I bought a book. In English. I can let you see it, if you want.

Aye, that'd be good, his da mumbles. First he heard of his da being into Picasso although why shouldn't he be, right enough?

He did thousands of paintings and drawings altogether, Madge goes on. Can you imagine? Although he never even signed loads of them. Which just goes to show you, I suppose, he didn't mean anyone to see them.

I suppose with him being so famous – and dead, of course, his da says, people want to get their hands on anything they can. Even if he didn't mean them to.

Aye, I suppose there's nothing wrong with that, Madge says.

He doesn't say anything. He's not sure if he agrees with Madge. His dad isn't saying anything either. If you want to keep some things just for yourself he doesn't think it's right for just anybody to come along after your death and start digging everything up. People are entitled to their private selves. Like coming out. You shouldn't be forced to come out to everybody, all the time. Or even anybody really if you don't want to.

It's like they're trying to recreate him as an artist. He realises he has spoken his thoughts aloud.

Aye, well, his dad says. I suppose the artist is more than his intentions, eh? I mean, other people are entitled to their interpretations and everything.

He doesn't reply. Maybe the subject is too difficult for him. Maybe he is daft making comparisons with being gay but they are talking about identity here, aren't they?

They have arrived at the beach. His da and Madge are scanning the place for his mum (and Stuart too, he supposes). His eyes wander to the horizon where a topless woman, about his mum's age, is coming out of the water, hopping about on tender bare feet. A woman with pale skin like his mum's, roughly the same height. But it can't be, can it, surely to God that isnae his mum there with her tits flopping about everywhere, in those wet shorts? And now she is shoving on her top double quick. At first he wasn't certain because the first thing she did when she came out the water was to bend down and put on these sunglasses. But it is definitely his mum. He cannae differentiate between women's tits, but no-one else has a flowery top like that. Huge wild flowers like Van Gogh's Irises. He doesn't usually think of his mum as a wild dresser except for this one thing. He wants to shout but he doesn't want to embarrass her in front of Madge (or even his dad). Only what is she doing but hurrying away along the water's edge, trying to avoid the three of them (or is it his dad, or Madge or just him?) What the fuck is he supposed to do? And if she is embarrassed how come, because is it not more embarrassing to be topless in front of hundreds of strangers than in front of your husband, your best friend and your son who you used to wander about naked in front of not all that long ago really? Except maybe he does understand, just a little bit, because, after all, he told that guy in the street, didn't he, that trader, a guy he didn't know from Adam. And it was easier telling Madge than telling his da. Sometimes you feel safer with strangers than with your own kind.

Madge

She knows she should've kept her big mouth shut about the baby. Jesus, a baby is how she is already thinking of it — a fully formed chubby bundle you can touch and hold. As a rational person she knows it is really just a blob less than a couple of centimetres long and she has had blobs, as big as this probably, put inside her before. She cannot now remember whether she thought of those too as babies, although they warned her about the possibility of miscarriage, about not building up your hopes. Her hopes have been dashed that many times it is ridiculous to expect everything to go hunky-dory even if it weren't for the uncertainty with Stuart, but sometimes you need to be a wee bit ridiculous. It might be ridiculous too, telling your best friend's husband and son you are pregnant before you tell your own husband, but if you cannot be a wee bit ridiculous on your holidays when can you be?

This looks like a good spot, Gavin is saying, pointing to a tiny bit of space on the crowded beach. She nods and they all sit down. She never was one for crowded beaches but they don't all come for nothing, do they? She has her swimsuit on under her dress so the minute she slips the dress off she is all ready.

Which one of you is going to look after the stuff, then? she asks, realising it is easier than asking one of them to join her.

I'll stay, Gavin volunteers. You two go and enjoy yourselves.

You mean you're not going to enjoy yourself too? she grins.

Aye, well, you know what I mean.

She smiles and nods because she does too, although it's interesting that he expects her to read his mind in the short time they have known one another. She and Alan head off towards the water. He is quite an unusual man, Gavin. It makes her wonder how him and Sheila got together, for she can't imagine him chatting up a woman. He is too self-conscious. He doesn't flaunt himself. She can see, even now, donkeys' years after Sheila met him, what must have attracted her. Modesty sounds inappropriate — at once too childish and naive or feminine, even, but it is the best she can come up with. Only you do not usually associate sexiness with modesty but there is something ever so slightly sexy about this man's modesty. Not that she wants him for herself. Even if she wasn't into stealing other women's husbands (least of all her best friend's) she still wants to make a go of things with Stuart. It is

101

definitely not too late. No way is it too late for the two of them, now they are having this baby. Because having babies is definitely a two-way thing and she doesn't just mean the procreation bit.

Don't go too far out! she calls to Alan, partly because she remembers his mum calling that to him, partly maybe because she is going to have a kid herself and something subconscious in her is reminding her that this is what you have to do when you have kids, or are responsible for somebody else's, keep an eye out, all that. Except Alan's frown tells her she is being too fussy.

Och, you're all right, she shouts back, contradicting herself. You're a good swimmer, aren't you? And away he goes.

He is not, after all, exactly a kid. *Jeune homme* is how the waiter referred to him in the restaurant, she remembers. That awkward inbetween stage, when you aren't the one thing or the other. Except that maybe in deciding he is gay Alan has crossed the boundary between childhood and adulthood. In her day kids were either the one thing or the other. Only these days there is all this awareness about protection from sexual interference. In her job it has become issue number one, practically. God, you can hardly put a hand on somebody's shoulder without worrying if you're going too far. Not that she doesn't agree with all the changes. Too bloody right. Too many pompous pricks in the profession getting away with murder for fucking decades. One guy she encountered when she was in residential was up in court last year. She met him when she was a young, unqualified care worker, years before she did the postgrad course. When it was all over the news and everything she was afraid to speak about it – still is, come to that. Afraid to admit to anybody she knew him, that she had worked alongside the bugger, in case she got – in case she gets – tarred too. In a way it is ridiculous – how was she to know he was to go on to bugger wee boys in his care? (Or was he already buggering wee boys in his care when she knew him? Christ.) She never liked him, always found him a right smarmy git, bloody know-all and she never liked the patronising way he treated the kids. She remembers him giving this kid a right bawling out. But it wasn't as if he was the only one. Jesus, when she thinks about it. The notion of kids having rights in they days was only in its infancy. Like hitting kids. I mean, everybody practically did it in they days. One woman she was quite friendly with – Joan McGreevy – they'd been to uni together. She remembers going to her house after she'd got married to this teacher bloke. She didn't dislike the guy. He didn't come over as intimidating or anything. Compared

102

with Stuart he was the quiet type. Then he goes away up the stair to mark homework or something and suddenly they are discussing kids, discipline, all that. They were both hoping to have them in they days. Then Joan just comes out with it about her man (she can't even remember what his name was now) belting some of the boys at the school. Justifying it. She can't remember the conversation exactly, just that it made her realise how little she knew the woman, that the woman thought it was OK to beat boys, that she was as complicit in the matter as her husband. She hardly saw her after that. They never went to one another's houses again anyway.

Only she didn't feel responsible for what Joan McGreevy's husband did – although if she'd agreed with her she would've been complicit as well. The thing was she noticed Peter Traynor putting his hands on wee boys. Having wee tussles, like they were playing. Stuff like that. Nothing untoward, most of it, except for the time he put another wee boy over his knee once. He never skelped him or anything. Well, he gave him the one skelp, a wee pat on the bum. Made out he was just kidding. Although he took down his trousers the kid laughed about it too – she remembers that. It was an embarrassed laugh, of course. Traynor was always looking for some excuse to touch the kids. She worked alongside him for over a year. Why couldn't she have seen what he was up to? Or was she just turning a blind eye?

Aye, it will be a constant worry, looking after a kid. Maybe she should give up the job. There are enough worries with the job, God knows, without taking on all this responsibility as well. It's hard to imagine Stuart becoming a family man, after all this time. Even though they talked about it for years. Having kids. Talked about it that much they left themselves nothing else to talk about. After the non-event came the talk about jobs. She never shuts up about her work. It has become her life. A kind of torture, although it brings in money. And what if she gives up her job and becomes dependent on Stuart for everything? What then? Well, with her experience she could always get something else. She should take more risks, so she should.

Alan is swimming back. Swimming like billy-o. Like something was after him.

Jesus, he shouts. Jesus. Madge. Fucking hell. Christ.

What is it? She has never seen him in such a state.

Out there, he goes. Something nibbled at me. I think it was a shark. I'm sure it was a shark. I'm not going back in there. Jesus Christ.

He clambers up the slope towards the water's edge, towards his father who has been keeping a watchful eye, evidently.

What is it, son?

He recounts the tale about the shark. She is tempted to laugh it all off. Whoever heard of sharks in the Mediterranean? Well, not attacking anybody anyway. What a dramatist the boy is. A wee attention-seeker.

Could it not have been something else? Gavin goes. Like a dolphin?

God, I never thought about that. I suppose it could.

She remembers seeing a T-shirt in one of the souvenir shops the other day. They have all these T-shirts with NICE on them only this one had a dolphin as well. Maybe there are dolphins, right enough, right here in the Med.

If it was a shark it was a friendly one anyway, she says, smiling. And dolphins are always friendly.

Although dolphins usually show themselves, don't they, but she is not going to say that. Maybe he is genuinely frightened. Growing up is a frightening enough experience without being frightened to death in the water. She is scared of the water herself. She doesn't usually think of it as being scared but why else would she stay close to the shore, where other people are?

I'm not going back in there, Alan repeats, like he has a phobia.

You could always stay closer to the shore just in case. Not go out any further than most people. Just in case.

It might just have been a fish, his father offers.

No way. No way was it just a fish. No way was it a fucking fish. Do you think I'm stupid or something?

He is really raging now. A raging bull with raging hormones. Christ. Gavin is going all red in the face. He looks a bit like a raging bull himself. For a second or two she is petrified there will be an almighty row. Moments ago these two people were her friends. A couple of hours ago she was close to crying on their shoulders. She has to try and calm the waters. Either that or walk away.

OK, but it was something friendly anyway. Let's be thankful for that. You weren't actually hurt, were you? You were only nibbled.

He nods, slightly calmer. But no way was it a fish. No bloody way.

He reminds her of some of her more unpleasant clients. One minute you think you can manage them all right, the next they are off their trolleys about the slightest wee thing. At least here she can excuse Alan because of the hormone business. Only not entirely. She remembers only now Sheila moaning about the troubles of adolescence, meaning Alan. She doesn't know the half of it. In fifteen odd years time, if all goes well, she will have a teenager like this. Full of raging hormones. Only she won't be able to walk out on him or her, like she has done when some horrible client has exhibited aggressive or abusive behaviour. At work she can walk away or call the police or whatever. There are other avenues. But you cannot walk away from your own child. It is worse than marriage, having children. Indissoluble.

Gavin is away for ice-creams and five minutes later everything is hunky-dory again, or would appear to be if she didn't know better. She feels angry at herself for exposing her and Stuart's problems. They don't have any more than anyone else. How come Sheila never let on about Alan's temper tantrums, for example? She should keep her mouth shut. In future she will. Once you are a family you cannot just go exposing your problems like some social work client. Not that she doesn't understand how people get to the stage where their lives become some sort of public exhibition. But if you are not careful you will wind up being an involuntary exhibit. Like Picasso's *Weeping Woman*, Picasso's contorted women. But she is no weeping woman. She is strong. Not that she blames folk for attention-seeking, the willing exhibits. Some people's circumstances are such − their social deprivation is such − that they have to share the agony beyond their close friends. But it is one thing to share things with Sheila and quite another to share them with her bloody husband and son − neither of whom she knows from Adam, scarcely. It is quite inexcusable to have told Gavin and Alan she is pregnant when Stuart doesn't even know. Even to have told Sheila would have been inexcusable.

Only it will not be long now. She glances at her watch. Half past five. A couple of hours at most.

You two go and enjoy yourselves in the water for a bit, she says when they are licking up the last of the ice-cream. But don't be too long. Remember I have to get ready to go out.

Aye. We'll go in for a wee dip, will we? Just keep near the water's edge. It's deep enough anyway. Come on. Gavin can be quite persuasive, it seems, when he has a mind to.

The two of them are away. Peace at last. If only. There will be no peace till she speaks to Stuart. Once she and Stuart have discussed the baby everything will be fine. Everything will settle into its own place. Peace will come and there will be no more worries.

Gavin & Sheila

It is completely fucking ridiculous, so it is. If it wasn't for the fact that the woman is obviously in a pretty precarious mental state he would say so too. What an effing b the man is, disappearing like thon till yon time. Aye, ten o'clock and no back yet. Madge was all dressed up to the nines at seven o'clock. In a good mood even till seven thirty. Getting kinda uptight between then and eight thirty and then verging on tearful and at last crying her eyes out. When Sheila landed in at the back o nine he was ready to hit the roof himself.

Jesus, Sheila, this is a hell of a time to come in at without saying anything. Could ye no have said ye had plans or something? Phoned reception or something? He was trying to whisper because he didn't want to upset Madge. He has to admit he wasn't hell of a bothered about upsetting his wife. It took him a minute or two to notice how upset Sheila was already.

I'm sorry, she half-whispers back. Jesus, I've had a hell of a day. Are Stuart and Madge away out?

Naw, he says. The bastard never turned up, did he? She's in the kitchen, crying.

I met him this morning, in the town, she says. He was in a hell of a mood, she adds, because she feels some additional information is expected of her.

Aye, moody auld bastard. Just watch what you say to her, that's all.

Maybe that was why she never says a word to him, in the end, apart from Stuart being in a mood, and what was new about that? The minute she saw his face, before she saw Madge's, she sensed the tension in the place. No way was she going to make it worse by opening her big mouth. If the look on Gavin's face wasn't enough to persuade her, the minute she saw Madge she knew, no way. She remembered seeing Madge crying before, years ago, when she told her about not being able to have kids. Sobbing her heart out. You wouldn't expect your man coming in late (well, he is bound to come in sometime, isn't he?) would have quite the same impact, but maybe there is more to this than meets the eye. Staring at her friend now, her face swollen in her misery, Sheila wonders if Madge has, after all, an inkling about the affair. Being married to him all these years, she must know him well enough, what he's capable of. What seems clear, though, is that Gavin doesn't have an inkling himself, that Madge hasn't really said anything to him if she does have an idea. And anyway maybe she doesn't. Do we really know another person through and through to the extent we could guess they are going to come away with you on your holidays only to make the big announcement that they are going to leave you for another woman – and, aye, I'm afraid she is (in all probability) younger and sexier and prettier than you? Is it the kind of thing any woman, indeed any person, would reasonably expect from their partner?

What she does know is no way is she going to be the bearer of bad news. Madge has suffered enough and no doubt she will suffer more but she is not going to hear it from her best friend. Heaping agony on agony is not what best friends are for.

I'll make a cup of tea, she says. In a minute. I just need to go to the toilet first. They will be wanting to quizz her. Only Gavin comes out and stops her on her way into the toilet.

Don't bother mentioning you saw Stuart at the shops, he says.

OK, she says. He is letting her off the hook. Not that it is her fault the bastard never came home. She hasn't seen him since mid-day or earlier, for Christ's sake. Only funny how Gavin just assumed they'd met at the shops. It annoys her just a wee bit that he has to assume that is always how she spends her free time. As if she shops till she drops or some crap like that. Well, she can't deny she does when she is feeling low. As often as not though she buys something when she is feeling low and then takes it back to the shops a few days later when she is feeling better. If she doesn't like it or decides she can't afford it, that is. She is no bloody shopaholic. She has more control in her life than that, for Christ's sake. Even though her life isn't exactly going how she planned. Not that she ever got as far as planning, not quite, but when you are young you visualise yourself as being happy all the time, when you get older, away from parent's constraints and all that. You do, don't you? You don't imagine being constrained by stupid wee things when you are in your mid to late thirties. Wee things like your husband assuming you wouldn't go for a coffee or a drink with someone else's husband. Especially when the husband is someone who is a complete and utter bastard.

When she gets out of the toilet, eventually, for she has diarrhoea, has had it all day, even though she hasn't eaten a thing since that bloody panini she had with Stuart, Gavin has already made the tea and the three of them are sitting at the kitchen table. She has the distinct impression they have been talking about her behind her back.

I have something to tell you, mum, Alan goes.

Oh, she says, relieved. If it is Alan who has something to tell maybe they can forget all about this Stuart business for five minutes anyway. What is it, Alan? Then, seeing the look on his face but not quite able to interpret it – not fear exactly, but a certain apprehension there, without a doubt, Is it something private, Alan? Do you want to come in the bedroom and tell me? She feels a sudden pride that she has a son who tells her things, who shares parts of his life with her that are secret and private to everybody else, his father even.

Naw, you're all right. My dad and Madge know anyway.

The wee bugger looks angry, for some reason. Or embarrassed or something.

What have you been up to? she half-laughs. He is still a child, after all. What is he afraid to tell her that he could just tell his dad and, of all people, Madge?

I'm gay.

What? An automatic reaction for she heard him well enough although it takes a moment or two to sink in.

You're kidding. A really, really stupid thing to say and one that she regrets immediately for his face is aflame.

Aye, too right I'm fucking kidding! he roars at her like a maniac. Like gays are one big fucking joke! Fucking queers and poofs are just a joke! It's all right for other people, right? All right for anybody but your own son to be fucking queer! And he stomps off, away to his bed presumably.

She is about to go after him, another automatic reaction even though she feels like he has hit her across the face but it is his dad who is going after him. Madge is saying to stay here and he'll be all right, as if it was her had the outburst and she can apologise later.

The door behind her is ajar. She can hear muffled sounds from Alan's room. Gavin muttering about how his mum is just a bit taken aback and she didn't mean to say daft things, that he'll speak to her later. She is mad enough to go and slam the door loudly.

There was no need for that, Madge says quietly.

She stares at the woman she thought was her friend. The woman whose feelings she has spent the day trying to spare, but who has failed to consider her feelings.

You think it's OK for him to speak to his mother like that? To yell abuse at me? She is ready to cry. She has had enough, worrying about other people all the time, people who do not care about her. She has given up her life, she sometimes thinks, for her kid. And for what? For them to speak to you like you are dirt.

No, of course not. Madge is hesitant, shy almost. But all teenagers do it, don't they? It's normal, really. The hormones and everything.

She wants to say, How the fuck would you know, you've never had any yourself. And never will. But she knows she's being unreasonable.

It was a big step for him, saying that. He thinks you're rejecting him but I know you're not.

It's just a bit of a shock, she says, picking up the tea that has gone cold. I didn't expect it, that's all. I thought he was still my wee boy. That he had all this time to grow up and now it's like he's grown up already.

Oh, no, he's still got all his growing up to do, Madge goes on, as if she has brought up half a dozen teenagers herself. It's just he's made a decision about his sexuality. He must have been thinking about it for ages. He's probably been unsure for ages, before he got round to telling any of us.

I can't get over him telling you first.

Madge smiles. So that is what is eating her. She can't blame her. No doubt she'd feel the same if it was hers. He didn't tell me first, she explains. He told Gavin and then he told me. I think he was wanting to test the water before he told the person closest to him.

Meaning me, she thinks. Aye, well, I suppose. God, but, I don't know what to say to him.

You could start by telling him it's OK to be gay.

Aye, well. Aye, you're right. I'll go and speak to him in a minute. I'll let him and Gavin have a blether first. Man to man and all that. I'm not making excuses or anything but maybe I feel a wee bit left out. I mean, I've known a few gay men in my time – at work and that – but not really well. Maybe she doubts she can get to know a gay man really well. Maybe she has been operating under these unconscious assumptions of prejudice all these years.

Anyway, how are you?

Madge shrugs. Aye, well, I suppose it's pretty obvious, isn't it? Stuart's let me down – yet again. Must've got drunk or something. She looks at her watch. I mean, there's plenty of time for him to come home and everything. It's just he must've forgot. She shrugs.

Sheila doesn't know what to say. There is something else, something Madge is keeping from her. Only why should she expect to know everything about Madge and Stuart? Madge never struck her as a particularly dark horse before. But for her not to even say a bad word about the bastard is a wee bit unusual. Maybe she is jealous. Jealous of her and Gavin's relationship. The thought is almost comforting. No, it is exactly that. Comforting. Partly it is the thought that Madge is actually jealous of her – strong, persuasive, forceful Madge that has no need to be jealous of anybody except when it comes to the husband front which is not exactly nothing, of course. Partly it is the fact that she and Gavin have something that is worth being jealous of. Something she has taken for granted for years and years. Christ, she even resented the fact that the poor soul lost his job. As if it was his fault.

Gavin has come back into the room.

I'm sorry, she says quickly. I'll go and speak to him, will I? Normally she would never do that, ask Gavin's opinion on how she behaves towards her own son. Since he was born she always felt she knew exactly how to respond to him, that the two of them had a special relationship really. Obviously there have been problems in the last year or two. Problems she put down to hormones and all that. She felt she was coping then, coping with a wee boy still but. Today is the first day really it has dawned on her he is no longer a wee boy at all.

Alan, she mumbles to the figure huddled under the bedclothes. I'm sorry.

There is no response. Jesus, she has left it too late. She is just like one of those stupid parents she is always criticising, who cannot cope with their growing kids, who lose their temper too quickly, or are always thinking about themselves. Not that she does it openly but the feelings are there just the same.

Alan, she goes again, and now she is crying. I never meant to hurt your feelings. Alan, please.

He lifts the bedclothes from his face and reaches out to her. He looks alarmed. It's all right, mum, he says, cuddling her the way she cuddles him when he's been hurt or is unhappy. I'm sorry too.

I'm glad you're gay, son, she says, through the tears. It is a bit of a fib but it is what he needs to hear.

When he agreed to come away here he thought of it as a time of celibacy really, insofar as he thought about it at all. He probably envisaged the time passing slowly, just waiting in a kind of limbo with Madge and Sheila and co. as a kind of obligatory entourage while he was forced to do without his love for three hundred and fifty odd hours (counting the travelling and the times immediately before and after the holiday when he would not see Karen). The last thing he envisaged himself doing was wandering into some seedy brothel and paying through the nose to get wanked off but, after all, he hasn't hardly had a chance even for a wank this holiday, what with all this carry-on sharing a bathroom and hardly a minute to yourself. And the whore is OK, really. Nothing brilliant but OK. He is able to fantasise Karen wanking him off so that is OK too. Better than with Madge doing it. He finds it hard to fantasise when he is having sex with Madge these days – the little sex that they have – because he always feels her beady eyes can bore through him. It was the thought of those beady eyes that made him decide he could not, after all, face the meal out, the confession. What, after all, does he have to confess? A relationship with another woman is a thoroughly modern thing. Jesus, everybody, apart from prudes and those nobody fancies anyway, does it. Unless they're too scared. Like Madge. Madge is scared of her own fucking shadow.

It is already ten o'clock and the business is finished. Says his goodbyes and is away out. He prefers the way they ask for the money upfront. He isn't wanting to hang about anyway although he will have to decide where he is going. He should've just stayed in the pub, got drunk. He only had a couple of drinks before he landed in here. It didn't exactly need Dutch courage, this anonymous act. If he'd had too much he couldn't have got it up and that would've been embarrassing. Christ. Only he can still go out properly, maybe chat up some Americans or something, or some French bird that speaks English. Although maybe not too much English wouldn't be a bad thing. Ignorance is bliss. Anyway, the night is yet young. No way is he going back yet. If he goes back at all, that is. Madge will be cursing and roaring because he never turned up. He remembers the last time he forgot they were supposed to be going out thegether. That woman expects him to have a memory like an elephant just because she has one herself.

He has been wandering the streets for a good twenty minutes or so but he is heading for where the action is. You wouldn't expect posh nightclubs to be too near the red light district anyway, would you? This holiday has ended up costing him plenty. Just as well he loaded the plastic before he went. He had to fib to Madge about it otherwise she would've been asking all sorts of awkward questions, not so much about why he wanted to load the cards but where the fuck had the money gone? And although it could be said that it doesn't matter now if she finds out about the prostitute, never mind clubbing it, there's no way he's goinae risk her telling Karen because he wouldn't put it past her, no sir. Too many of his mates' marriages have gone up the spout. The first thing the women want to know when the game is up is what is happening to the money. You could understand how the ones with weans have an excuse but sometimes the ones wi no weans are nearly as bad. The weans are probably just an excuse anyway. All they are out for is themselves.

Well, so are this crowd, without a doubt, he thinks as the doorman hands him a tie. At least he is wearing a shirt, although suddenly he feels all sweaty. He could do with a bloody shower, so he could. Maybe he could still have one if he booked himself into a hotel only maybe it is too late for that. Plus he has no luggage. He could always make up some cock and bull story about losing it or something but he is not a good liar, not really. It does not come naturally to him. It is just that sometimes circumstances force you into things. If circumstances had been different, if him and Madge had had kids, then maybe his life would've been completely different, he thinks, as he gazes at his face in the washroom mirror. He could have been happy with domesticity, he thinks, as he washes his face and then his armpits, scrubbing at the hairs with his soapy nails. His shirt is all wet now – he should've took it off but he didn't like to. Just undid a few buttons. Aye, there's plenty he knows happy wi domesticity. Work during the day, and the wife and weans evenings and weekends. Trips to the grandparents, theme parks, stuff like that. It's a different ball game for folk wi weans. Whereas folk without are often just – wankers. He definitely wants Karen to have his wean. By IVF if necessary although maybe it will not be necessary. It is not the blood succession he is bothered about. He has met folk who were adopted and were perfectly happy never to meet their natural parents. Why should they need to when their adoptive ones gave them everything they could ever ask for? He wasn't sure about kids before but he is sure now. Well, he was when he was younger but the longing went out of him, didn't it? Him and Madge both – they just got on with their lives, or in Madge's case, she didn't, or let it stop her advancing whereas nothing has ever stopped him. Life is what you make it has always been his philosophy. Although everyone has their doubts now and again. Only now he has never been as sure about anything in his life. It's not that he thinks him and Karen couldn't make a go of things wi no weans (well, they'd have none to start with, of course). It's partly the identity thing. That and the living forever thing, through your kids. You can earn all the money you'll ever need and have all the fucking status you want in a career and still there can be something lacking. Still what you have and what has been passed onto you for generations – your national heritage even – it all ends with you if you don't have kids. In less than a dozen years you are forgotten. There will be no monument to what he has achieved in his lifetime because achievements like his are not recorded in stone. It is the fate of the working classes and their immediate representatives to go unrecorded, unthanked. He is an Unimportant Person. He is no politician. His name will not be entered in the history books. At best there will be recorded (in some tiny print in some specialist publication) that there were x number of cases in such and such a year or a decade, x employment tribunal successes, x union increased in size from x hundred thousand to x hundred thousand. Only for the numbers to drop again (after his death). Unknown, unrecognised, unnoticed. Here lived another boring old fart. Without a wean he is fucking lost to all eternity.

He is almost weepy at the thought of it. Only when you have kids you have to keep level-headed (hasn't he always?) Let's face it, kids confer on you all this respectability, don't they? Even Madge, he suddenly feels sure, would understand. She will be jealous, of course, for Madge has wanted weans as much as him. But she'll get over it. Eventually. Get another life. Or a life. A decent job for starters. And it's not as if she'll have nothing. Half a house isn't nothing. Enough to buy herself a wee flat for the mortgage is nearly paid up.

Before he went to the whorehouse he tried to phone Karen. Only, even though it was her mobile he phoned, that prick of a husband answered and he just put the phone down. That was why he went to the whorehouse really. Because he was that depressed he couldn't speak to her. He realises now he is sitting on his ownio – he'd be bored out his brain if it wasn't that he has his own thoughts to occupy him. He'd be outraged at the price of the drink if it wasn't that he is beyond outrage. He needs a woman like Karen to keep him in check, to have his babies and to come home to at the end of a long and tiring day. He has had enough of affairs, enough of the wild life. He wants domesticity for real. What him and Madge have had all these years wasn't real domesticity at all, they were just faking it. It is worse than women faking orgasms when you think about it.

He cannae be bothered talking to anybody because he doesn't need a fake existence like this. He needs what is solid and real but he has left it all back in Scotland. The sense of homesickness is profound. He glances at his watch. It is only midnight. It will only be eleven o'clock in Scotland. That is no way too late to be phoning. His Karen has too much energy to be in bed at this time of night. He heads for the toilets and finds a cubicle where he can phone in peace.

It is Him again that answers the phone. He must be a right controlling, sexist bastard to go answering his wife's mobile phone every time. To want to know who is phoning the woman he thinks of as his property.

Can I speak to Karen, please?

I think she's gone to bed. Who is this?

Lying git. It is a bit bloody much when you cannae get to speak to the love of your life on the phone without some prick of an unwanted husband interfering and trying to control her life. He would just love to say, Look here, sonny, it's her lover. Who the fuck do you think it is? He would like to think he is just one step away from saying it too but he isn't that pissed.

Tell her it's Stuart. Stuart McCracken. It's about work. It's something important I've just remembered. I'm sorry to disturb you at this time of night. I realise it's late. The lie comes incredibly easy. The thing is he's got used to this association between Karen and lying. It isn't right. He doesn't want this deception to carry on. Prick and all as he is, the man has a right to know. As does Madge. The thought comes to him that Madge may know already, depending on what Sheila thought fit to tell her.

Right. Just wait a minute, would you?

Jesus. The bugger is away to tell her so it just shows you it worked. Mind you, the git must've been lying as well about her being in her bed. Otherwise he wouldn't've agreed. He would've said to leave a message or something and then what could he have said?

He has to wait a good few expensive minutes (but no more expensive than the whorehouse and this place) before she turns up. She sounds quite crabbit although she is whispering.

For God's sake, Stuart. What are you doing phoning me when I'm at home?

He is shocked really. There was no real understanding that he wouldn't phone, after all. And it isn't his fault hubbie keeps picking up the damn thing. But now is not the time for recriminations, he reminds himself. He is a wee bit shocked at finding in himself such negative feelings towards Karen – the woman he usually goes around thinking about as perfect half, or all, the time.

I just wanted to speak to you. Can you talk all right? Absurdly, he is whispering too. Well, it is a private conversation after all and the place could be full of Americans. Look, I'm sorry it's no the right time. It's not just that he needs to keep her sweet. He doesn't want her to get mad with him.

I was in bed. She sounds weary, right enough. He should've waited till the morning but he really does need to talk to her. And he cannae keep Madge hanging on forever.

I didn't expect him to get you out your bed. Are you no well or something? Really he wants to call her love but something in her voice stops him. Hubbie is probably listening round the corner. Just as well he never phoned the house right enough or he'd be on the extension, nae doot.

Look, Stuart. Things have changed. We can't go on as we were.

He waits for more, too terrified to ask though.

I'm... I'm pregnant.

Jesus. That's... that's brilliant. He wants to bloody weep. Jesus. Does... does your husband know?

What do you mean, does he know? Of course he bloody knows. It's his baby, for Christ's sake. Jesus, Stuart, she whispers. Jesus, you couldn't possibly have thought otherwise. I mean, Jesus Christ, Stuart.

Of course they've been using condoms and it's not as if one has ever burst or anything but still and all there are little miracles sometimes, aren't there? Why wouldn't he presume the baby was his? This time he does start to weep.

David's really happy. Says it changes everything. And he's got promotion so it'll be easier to afford a baby. Look, Stuart, you and me, it wasn't really working out anyway. I mean, we were just a fling, Stuart. Be honest, Stuart.

He is sobbing more freely now so she must be able to hear him but he cannae help it. He hardly knows whether he is crying for the baby they'll never have or his lost love, the love he probably never had either, that was little more than a fantasy.

As he creeps back into the dimly-lit bar he knows for certain now that Sheila will have told Madge, that it will be too late to make amends. That he has thrown away a marriage of eighteen year for what was always a middle-aged fantasy. It must have got worse coming away here. Nobody to talk to in his own language hardly except in his own head. That Alan boy hated the sight of him. He could see that fine. Couldnae take a bloody joke about the wolf. It was Madge that started it but him that got the blame. It doesn't seem funny any more, right enough. Bunch of fucking arses, the whole lot of them. God, he is so fucking jealous of that guy David he can hardly hold it in. Except he could have, would have forced himself, if it wasn't for the fact that he told Sheila who will by now have told Madge. Sheila hates him now as well. Gavin too will hate him. They will all hate him. He feels the most misunderstood person on the planet. He doesn't even understand himself. What a fucking arse he has been. OK so him and Madge weren't exactly an item but he could've patched things up if it weren't for him and his big mouth and Sheila and hers. To think that a stupid wee holiday has ended up fucking up his whole life. Because of a stupid wee holiday he didn't even want to come on he has to rearrange his entire life. His work as well as his personal life. He will lose the house. He will have to try and avoid Karen at work all the fucking time, while watching her belly swell from a distance. Only what if she is lying and the wean is his after all? He could go the whole hog, away to a solicitor and have DNA tests and everything done, couldn't he? Wreck Karen's life as well. He hasn't got a fucking hope in hell. Not when him and Madge have been barren all these years. He would look an even greater arse than he does now.

He beckons to the guy behind the bar and orders a bottle of whisky. None of your rubbish, he says, realising he is drunker than he thought. Good Scotch. The guy points to a whole load of bottles. Right enough. He's reasonably knowledgeable on the whisky front, even for a Scotsman but he is not exactly what you'd call a connoisseur. Price wise it'll be six and half a dozen. Though what the fuck does he care about prices, never mind anything in the fucked world?

Bowmore'll do very nicely, he smiles at the guy. Very nice. He offers the woman beside him a drink. A drink for the lady, he says. She nods and says something in French to the barman who pours it for her and she smiles at him and then walks off to some table to meet some other guy.

He never saw himself as the other guy before. It has been quite an eye-opener, this holiday. If it had been ten year ago now he would have been planning the future, or at least his next step. This time there is no next step. The dice are down and there is nowhere to go. Even at work he is a bloody failure. People think he is old-fashioned. He has heard as much. Till now he put it to one side, other folk's opinions, thinking they were less important than his own. But he has miscalculated, the way he miscalculated the day when he was speaking to Sheila. What the fuck ever got into him he'll never know. He might as well drink himself to death for all the attention anybody ever pays to him. Even the whore the night wasnae paying any attention. You could tell her mind was somewhere else. Trying to make out she didnae speak English. Just because she couldnae be bothered talking, or listening. He wasn't really after a fuck – well, he was but he wanted somebody to listen to his woes too. If he'd only known what woes were. All he thought he had to worry about was Madge's reaction. Jesus, Karen must've fucking plotted this. Women are always fucking plotting something. She didn't just go and get pregnant just like that. Her and this David guy must've been talking about it. For all he knows David knows all about him. For all he knows Karen used him as blackmail. If you don't give me a wean etcetera, I'll go and sleep with whoever I like. I know a man who can etcetera, etcetera. Women are such fucking secretive, manipulative creatures. They just pretend to love you but they don't know what love is. Nor, apparently, does he. He is not worth loving and maybe he is not capable of love either. It is just one big fucking mystery. He should have carried on fucking whores. They are less hassle. OK, so if you are found out it would be embarrassing. Especially with all the politically correct wankers in his line of work. But at the end of the day it would not be the end of the world the way it is now. He is a bit of a fucking nobody when it comes down to it. It is not the same as a cabinet minister, or even an MP, being reported by a whore. He is just a fucking nobody. So much of a nobody the folk at work will dare to feel nothing but contempt. Till now at least he has had the respect of his colleagues. He does not think he can go on working alongside people who will feel nothing but contempt when the beans are spilt all over the fucking place. He does not even have enough anger left to sustain a defence against the onslaught that will come. He doubts he can save himself from them all, or even from himself.

Gavin & Sheila

He has hardly slept all night. He knows Sheila hasn't either, thanks to him probably for he spent ages tossing and turning. If he was at home he'd've got up but here there is nowhere to go in the middle of the night apart from away out and he wasn't going to do that, not after Stuart. One clearing off was bad enough without him starting.

Him and Sheila went to bed about midnight. Madge said she was going to wait up for Stuart. He considered staying up with her but he didn't want Sheila getting the wrong idea. And especially after her getting upset over Alan. God, he was a bit bowled over himself but at least he had the sense not to show it. Sometimes you have to keep things to yourself. He lay awake, waiting for Stuart to come in. Sure he dozed off a few times so he could've missed him but he doubts it. He heard Madge getting up and going to the toilet, not once but two or three times. Pregnancy does that to women. It is a long time ago now but he minds fine Sheila being the same. They have been together a long time, him and Sheila. A lot of water under the bridge. Not as long as Madge and Stuart but. He doesn't know how the bastard could do that to his wife, staying out the whole bloody night. Unless he's had an accident or something. I mean, Christ, he really could have had an accident. People have accidents all the time, don't they?

Madge says the same thing when they meet in the kitchen. Sheila thankfully has gone back to sleep. She is always like a bear with a sore head if she doesn't get enough sleep.

I haven't slept a wink, Madge says. I'm worried something's happened to him, Gavin. I mean, he's never done this before. I know we haven't always been the happiest couple in the world and there's many's the time he's not come back till late but the whole night, never. I mean, if he had to be somewhere he'd always phone me first.

He realises he doesn't know Stuart at all hardly. He has no experience of people who live in that kind of world, where they have to be somewhere else late in the evening, let alone all night. Away from their families. Where their work is that important to them or someone else or they have so many fingers in so many pies they can just dart off here, there and everywhere. He is ignorant about a lot of things, right enough. He hasn't exactly done much in his life, just strived to be happy. To keep Sheila and Alan happy. Still is striving for it is an uphill struggle, sure. Aye, some folk would doubtless find his *raison d'être* a wee bit weird. Madge might be out of her mind with worry but Stuart must have given her a lot of excitement in her time. Still does for all he kens. For all he kens the bugger will land in after the night on the tiles, presents galore (he can afford them, after all) and everything will be hunky-dory. Especially with the news about the wean-to-be everything will be hunky-dory. It takes all kinds. So if everything is going to be hunky-dory then he should watch what he says.

Except what if it isn't? Which is quite possible after all, wean-to-be or no wean-to-be. He might not want it, after all. Madge must've had her reasons for keeping her mouth shut. She knew for days, she said, days before she said anything to him and Alan. And that is only if the bugger turns up, unscathed. The unhunky-dory state of affairs could be even worse. Unthinkably worse. This is not just some assessment by the pessimist he freely confesses to being. It is a fair and reasonable explanation based on objective fact. The fact being that Stuart has been out all night. All bloody day and all bloody night too. He would have no hesitation in phoning the police if it was his Sheila that had disappeared. OK so Stuart is not his Sheila, in no way whatsoever resembles his Sheila and is a bit of a wild yin by all accounts, his ain included. But he is still somebody's (namely Madge's) man and, moreover, he has (so she says) not stayed out all night before without saying he was going to in advance. He could easily have been mown down by a lunatic driver. Especially if he got pissed which is more than likely. I rest my case.

Do you want to phone the police, just in case?

She shakes her head. Not phone, no. But, look, if he hasn't appeared by the afternoon or something then maybe you could come with me – to the police station. I mean, it'd be easier to talk to them face-to-face than on the phone. My French isn't that good.

Sheila is behind him. I couldn't sleep, she goes. Look, isn't this all a bit premature? I mean, we should at least wait until this afternoon or something. I mean, it's not as if he'd freeze to death or anything, having a night out on the tiles.

He doesn't have to mention his own fantasy about the hit-and-run driver. It would make him look weird, thinking a thing like that. He glances at Madge who gives this wee shrug, looks slightly offended but.

Sheila catches the glance and the expression on Madge's face, simultaneous with the shrug. As if she shouldn't make remarks like that about her husband. Christ, if only she knew. If only she knew the

119

half of it. And now it finally dawns on her, what should have dawned on her last night but with all this carry-on with Alan and whatnot she wasn't thinking straight. It finally dawns on her that she will have to tell Madge after all. She could tell Gavin first but she might not have the opportunity and anyway probably it is not fair to pass the buck. Gavin might even be mad, say, Why the fuck didn't you say before? That lassie's been worried sick all night with nothing to be worried sick about because it's obvious the bastard is away home to his sweetheart rather than face the music. She might have guessed from day one what a coward the bastard is. She might at least have guessed from yesterday morning instead of waiting till now for the truth to dawn on her.

Except maybe she should mention it to Gavin first. Or even Alan. Take the boy into her confidence. He's going to have to know sooner or later and it's not as if he is a wee boy anymore. And maybe she should listen to Alan's opinion on the subject too, instead of getting carried away. She does have this tendency to get carried away sometimes. And besides it is a real burden, but a burden shared is a burden halved, isn't it? She is not wanting to burden her own son who has enough to contend with, though. No, it would not be fair on Alan who has enough on his plate. And, besides, for all she knows Stuart will be walking in the door any minute. Let the bastard tell her himself, that's all. Lastly, aye, lastly, there is the possibility – slim but still a chance – that Stuart will have changed his mind about leaving Madge. That his conscience will be pricking him. Surely the man still has some conscience left? Surely to Christ?

Aye, maybe we could wait till the afternoon, Madge is saying.

Right, she goes. She is thinking, Thank Christ for that. I'll make a pot of tea, she says out loud. It gives her something to do. Only they cannae wait like this, Christ, can they, till the afternoon for Stuart to show his face (fat chance).

Maybe we should go out and look for him? she says, without looking at Madge.

I wouldn't want to miss him but, Madge says.

Aye, right enough.

We could take turns, Gavin says.

Aye, that's an idea, she says. We could take turns. That would give her time to think, to decide.

We could walk along the *Promenade des Anglais*, she goes. It seems the obvious place to look for someone. Although not if they're not wanting to be found. The most obvious place is the airport, when you think about it but she doesn't say that. How can she?

***

He is in a quandary. On the one hand it is not his place to tell Madge who to tell about her pregnancy, but on the other hand isn't it unfair for him and Alan to have that kind of knowledge when Sheila doesn't? He ponders this. Does the lack of knowledge do Sheila any harm? It makes the situation awkward, certainly — especially his situation, because Alan will likely have his mind on other things — but he has dealt with awkward situations before (or not dealt with them as the case may be), has had awkward situations to deal with all his born days and maybe it is character-building, after all. Although maybe he will have a word with Madge if he gets the chance because it is not just for him but for the whole lot of them that the situation is awkward. Maybe it is Alan he should be speaking to, saying, Look, just watch what you say. Now, Madge told you a secret, or just, If Stuart comes walking in the door now just keep your mouth shut, OK? Except he has to watch what he says to Alan in case Alan goes down his throat. As if I would, the boy will say, do you think I'm stupid or something, you stupid bastard you? Except so what if he says that? Well, quite a lot, as it happens because it is not just himself, his own ego, not just a question of his own personal humiliation. He is thinking of Madge too. If Alan goes over the top the whole fucking lid could be blown off this thing. The whole fucking lid.

Sheila will be hurt when she finds out they knew before she did — if she finds out that is — because maybe there's no reason for her to, though the thought of pretending they didnae know sounds ridiculous. Even if he could do it himself — put on some act — he could hardly expect Alan to, could he? Encourage the boy to be dishonest when he has always brought him up to be honest and to tell the truth. He's beginning to wish Madge had told them nothing. Only the woman couldn't help it. She was just desperate to tell somebody — anybody could see that. And he was glad to be there for her. And so was the boy. His son has that much care – consideration – for other folk — for a woman in distress. The way he touched her hand. Made him proud, so it did.

Stuart

Four in the morning and he is still undecided. He should be as drunk as a lord but he feels sober. If he felt drunk maybe he could face heading back and face the fucking music – but he doesn't. Being drunk isn't the same as feeling it. His breath might be stinking and he might not be able to able to speak without a certain amount of slurring but he is not that drunk to mind the hassle, to notice that any hassle would be focusing on the fact that he is drunk (quite apart from any hassle that might be connected with what he has told Sheila and he is not that drunk he cannae pretend he doesnae gie a fuck about that). He doesn't need hassle. He doesn't need the judgmental looks he knows he's going to get from that Gavin, never mind Sheila and even the boy, Christ. Judgmental fucking pricks. If it'd just been him and Madge maybe he could've stood it but it isn't just him and Madge.

He gets talking to this American couple in their thirties. From Wisconsin.

Great place, he says, stupidly, not because he is drunk but because he doesn't know where the fuck Wisconsin is, doesn't know the slightest thing about it. Except he has a notion it is in the mid-west somewhere (cattle, maybe – rings a bell – O grade Geography possibly but he is only guessing). He means America is a great place. Well, great for your holidays anyway. Maybe he is just drunk right enough. I mean, what the fuck are holidays for, anyway? Who needs holidays, for fuck's sake?

They get into some kind of conversation. Inane to begin with but the couple are focusing on him, because he is British maybe. Although it's not as if he's the only bugger here who speaks their lingo.

We've been to England, the woman says. The Tate. The National Gallery.

Oh, have you?

The clubs, the pubs, the woman says, grinning away, maybe suggestively. He is no interested. She is an ugly-looking bitch but there is no-one else to talk to. He hasn't spoke to another soul all day. Apart frae Sheila and that fucking bitch Karen. He has nothing against a blether, even with ugly bitches, although he has to look at her face, right enough. But he can manage that. Sometimes ugly women can have quite a lot to say for themselves. They have to, right enough, he supposes, have to be more interesting. How else would they ever get a fuck? Except if she is just going to sit there reeling off lists she can just fucking forget it. He might just come out and let her know he's no interested. Just to see her face. Except there is the guy to contend with. The guy is about the same size as him except you never know wi these Americans. Might have a gun or anything.

We've hired a yacht here, the man says.

Have you? he says, genuinely astonished. God, that must be great, being able to go out in the bay, do your own thing. They should've done that, him and Madge. They have the money. Instead of coming away with those poor fuckers, him and Madge could've had a rip-roaring time away on a yacht. He has been an arsehole, he sees that now. Him and Karen were never an item, never. She was leading him up the fucking garden path, so she was, the fucking bitch. Maybe, even after all this time, Sheila will have kept her trap shut. She doesn't seem the gossipy kind, when he thinks about it. Only it would be stupid to land in assuming the trap has been kept shut when it could have been opened yonks ago. That's the trouble with speaking to people you don't know about intimate matters – matters of the heart. Now if he didnae even know Karen, as it has turned out, how the fuck would he be able to predict what somebody like Sheila (whatever the fuck Sheila is like) would do?

Do you want to see it? the woman asks.

He nods. Why the fuck no? Two weeks at the seaside and the first time somebody has suggested a boat trip. Aye, brilliant, he adds, not wanting to sound unenthusiastic. It is decent of them to ask, really. Although probably they are just wanting to show off. Typical fucking yanks. Wanks.

He must have been that drunk he doesnae mind how they got to the boat, yacht, whatever it is called. Only he is not that daft to realise the two of them are out their heids, once the engine is on and they are roaring away out into the bay. Fortunately it is some other bugger who looks less obviously mental that is at the wheel. Thank fuck for that. He wouldn't want to put himself at risk, after deciding he is going to go back with Madge after all. Water under the bridge, like. He's been there before.

They are snorting cocaine. He shakes his head. He had a wee drag of a joint in the club, but that is as far as he would go. He is beginning to wish he'd never come. Fucking cocaine, for fuck's sake.

So, you had a row with your wife? the man goes.

He shakes his head. Not exactly. God, is that what he told them? He can't even remember.

The woman has taken off her top, is sitting in this really low-cut bra and this evening skirt. Come and sit beside me, she goes. It's crazy but he feels he has been set up. Although what would these two rich bastards want with him? Unless it is sex, of course. He would recognise this as a sexual advance right away if it wasnae for the fact that the woman is with her husband, for fuck's sake. He has never been into kinky stuff like that. Truth to tell he has never been into much at all. There was stuff in the sex shop he wouldn't've known what to do with. Although the guy was trying to be helpful, right enough. Telling him what you do with this and this and how some women like to dress up this way or that. That was why he went and got this daft waitress's outfit. For Karen. He can see now why he went and got it – it was an act of desperation, so it was. Deep down he must've realised Karen would never be his in a million years. This was his way of making her his – trying to get her involved in a wee act of subordination, subordinating herself to his power. The panties had practically the whole of the backside ripped out of them. It made him think of spanking her then, although he had never spanked a woman in his puff. As if he kent what he was thinking the guy goes and hands him this wee whip then but he shook his head. There were other things he could use, he thought, with the arrogance that comes with the absurd confidence he had less than a day ago. He wears a belt round his trousers, for example. He could just take that off. Apart frae anything else it is one thing to go about wi women's underwear in your briefcase but a whip is something else. So he shook his head, even though afterwards he imagined himself using it, imagined Karen's face when he brought out something like that.

The truth was it was just a fantasy. He didnae have a fucking clue whether Karen was into sadomasochism or no. That is how well he kens the woman, that is how often, how well, they have fucked. Whereas Madge likes her bum getting a good rub now, Madge does. In twenty odd year of sex wi her Madge has never asked to be spanked and he has never offered but Madge does not always like to ask for what she wants. He knows that much about her. The waitress outfit could be a bit of a peace offering but. See what she thinks. Thank fuck her and Karen are the same size. He has always liked skinny women. That Sheila is a bit too well-padded for his liking. And this American woman here. Fucking disgusting. Not that he's surprised. Americans eat too much.

The guy at the wheel has turned the motor off now. He has joined them for a snort.

No my scene, he says, playing up the Scots. They speak a foreign language, right enough, these druggies. He should never have come. He is fucking marooned out here while these three druggies sit and snort their shite. Some folk would sicken you.

How about going back then? he goes, after a bit. He is not sure if he nodded off for a bit.

The guy that was at the wheel just glares at him, as if to say, Who the fuck are you kidding?

The woman smiles at her man. I thought we might take a trip to Africa. It's not so far. Right, Al?

Why not? the guy goes.

Very funny, he says, not smiling. He can see them for what they are now. A bunch of fucking sickos. Getting a kick out of freaking folk out. Getting him out here under false pretences.

No kidding, buster, the guy Al goes, the sicko bastard. If he wasn't away out here on a boat he would smash the bastard's face in.

The other guy is looking at Al as if to say, will I away back to the wheel? Any minute now they will be speeding away somewhere. If not Africa then up the fucking coast. Somewhere he doesn't want to go anyway. It is the fucking morning already. The last day of the fucking holidays, for fuck's sake, and him and Madge haven't even had that meal out. Not that these bastards give a fuck about that. He is suddenly sure, without really knowing why, that Sheila has kept her mouth shut after all. After all, it cannae be an easy thing to do, when you think about it, telling your best friend (because they are best friends, aren't they?) that her man is away with some bird and is about to fuck off for good. Doubtless Sheila will have taken the easy road and kept the trap shut. He would, in her place.

Except, he reminds himself, the trap may not be kept shut indefinitely. Madge, in the light of suspicious circumstances (what could be more suspicious than him staying away all night?), will be having her doubts and looking for the proverbial shoulder to cry on. Which naturally will be Sheila's. At which point Sheila may well open the trap. Except at this hour in the morning the two of them will naturally be in their beds. The problem will only arise at the time they will be waking up, having breakfast, talking to one another. He'd better fucking hurry up then.

It is now or never. He discards first of all the Versace shoes he is stupidly wearing and mentally says goodbye to them forever. The trousers that he flings off are not worth a toss anyway. He has his credit cards and his money in a wee wallet strapped round his waist. Great things, these wee holiday gadgets. The shirt he bought in Gap especially for this holiday he might have left on for it is light enough but he doesn't want any encumbrances whatsoever. No sir. He is away for an early morning swim. He is away back to his freedom and home comforts even if there will be a scolding first (a spanking even – well, hardly but he could always ask. If they are going to have a fresh start, get off to a new angle in their relationship he could always put it to her. You never know). He glances at the wee backpack with the waitress outfit inside. Pity to leave it behind but still. He could always get one mail order.

He is clambering over the side when the bitch tries to stop him.

Don't. There are jellyfish.

Ha fucking ha, he says and then he is in the water, swimming strongly towards the shore, leaving the sounds of an argument behind him. Then the boat comes towards him but he waves them away. No way is he falling for that one again, Versace shoes or no Versace shoes. They can go fuck themselves. It is not that far, really. He was always a strong swimmer. He's had a bellyfull, right enough, but he pisses in the water and it's like half of it has left him, already. He is soberer than when he went into the water. And, look, there are no waves. There is no current. The sun is rising like a great ball of fire. The fucking police, the fucking gendarmes will pick him up if he needs them to. It isnae that fucking cold. He has swum in colder waters than this, for fuck's sake. He heads on towards the shore. It's farther than he thought. It doesn't look any fucking nearer than it did when he clambered off the boat which must have been a good five minutes ago. He wonders now if maybe there's a current after all. The boat is near him again but again he is waving them away. Still, they'll probably keep nearby. Presumably they wouldn't want any possibility of an association with death by drowning, after all. They would need to watch themselves because of the drugs. They arenae fucking stupid. No that he has any intention of drowning. No sir, none whatsoever. No fucking way.

Madge

She knows they are only wanting to help but some things you have to do your own way. Although there is no harm in letting the two of them wander the streets looking for her man if that is what they want. The three of them, as it happens, for Sheila ended up making Alan come too, knowing fine if he didn't she'd be stuck with him and it was hardly fair to her when here is she up to high dough except she isn't, not any more. She is not calm exactly but she is suddenly beginning to take things in her stride. She has a lot of things to be thankful for, even if Stuart isn't one of them.

Maybe you'd like him for company? Gavin, said, as an afterthought, as they were going out the door. Alan and Sheila were already in the corridor, out of earshot.

She shook her head and smiled. It was only a few minutes earlier she had heard Gavin on at him.

Come on now, son. You ken fine the woman has enough to contend wi without leaving you here.

She could just about visualise Alan glaring at him at the thought of being told, practically, that he is something to contend with. Just when he has been trying to be so grown-up, too. Only Gavin was right. They are all something to contend with, except by the time they come back, with or without Stuart, she will doubtless be wanting company anyway.

Whether Stuart is back with them or before them she is going to tell Sheila anyway. Although she wouldn't be surprised if Sheila has guessed, or if Gavin has even said something. Spilled the beans, accidentally or otherwise. Or Alan maybe, kids being what they are. He must be curious, after all. She has had enough of all this secretive crap and Stuart has had his chance. Not that Sheila and Gavin and even young Alan wouldn't know how to keep their mouths shut if Stuart did turn up. Pretend they never knew.

She is calm now but if, and when, Stuart turns up (what does she mean, if – of course he'll turn up, what else can he do – his fucking passport is here, for Christ's sake) she'll get into a rage without intending it. It will just happen, the way it has happened time and time again. Unless she learns to let go. Unless Stuart has had some bloody awful accident which was not his fault, which is pretty unlikely when it comes down to it. When they were younger and he cleared off for hours and never came back till yon time she used to imagine all sorts of things had happened to him but no longer. She was being more than economical with the truth when she made out Stuart had never been away all night before without warning her. Not that she remembers specific details, least of all dates or times but not knowing where he is is not a new experience. But it is no longer agony the way it was in the beginning. She has not really worried about what might or might not have happened to Stuart for years. For years he has just made her unhappy or angry or tense or nervous, but only for herself. It is not because of anxiety about Stuart's welfare that she has sat up till the small hours and cried her heart out. For years it is herself she has been thinking about, her own welfare. Only last night she shed no tears at all. Now she has her baby's welfare also to consider. She is not going to let a selfish prick come between her and this child who means everything to her before it is even fully formed as a human being. She is not going to allow herself to lose an hour's sleep over its wanker of a biological father who cannot even give her sexual satisfaction because he is too fucking thoughtless or just plain lazy to notice whether she has come or not and what woman could come in a minute flat without so much as a caress sometimes never mind a fucking kiss? It must be years since they have kissed properly. A proper wet kiss where you delve into one another's mouths and just lose yourself and then the penetration happens as a sort of afterthought almost but the real ecstasy is in the kissing. She hasn't known ecstasy like that for fucking years. Sometimes she thinks she has never known it. For a wanker like Stuart sex begins and ends with the penis. A wanker who in all probability is unfit to be a father anyway, so she will probably just tell him to go and fuck himself. Just because she's pregnant doesn't mean she's going to let the bastard walk all over her. Precisely because she is pregnant she is not going to let any fucker have one over on her, ever again. That applies to snotty-nosed clients as well as as fat-arsed managers. She is going to fight everybody around for this kid. If your own kid isn't worth fighting for what is? She has never felt so fierce in her life.

Except if she has to fight so much for her and this kid's survival she will also need allies. Allies like Sheila and Gavin and even young Alan. She can just imagine young Alan coming over and babysitting. Why not? She would pay him, of course, although he would be probably be willing to do it for nothing. An excuse to get out the house.

Don't be too long, she said to Gavin, as an afterthought, calling after him down the corridor. Sheila gave her a funny look then but Gavin says, Righto, like it was the most normal thing in the world. She is glad now she said it, not just because she doesn't want to be left here on her ownio half the day when, bugger it, it is her holiday too, but because if Stuart does come back she is afraid of her own anger. Anger can be an emancipating thing but it can also be a form of imprisonment. She is not going to allow herself to be imprisoned in her anger. She is still on her holidays, for Christ's sake. Her last childless holiday for a long time, doubtless. She is buggered if she is going to let that man bugger it up any more than he has already. The minute they come back she is going to suggest a snack lunch out and then maybe they could take a look at *Vieux Nice* or something. And when the opportunity arises – as no doubt it will – she will tell her dear friend Sheila she is going to be a mum. It will be be time to celebrate this pregnancy at last.

Gavin, Sheila & Alan

It's all very well saying we're going to look for him, Sheila goes, but how the hell are you supposed to start looking for somebody like Stuart? I mean, do we go trailing round the pubs and clubs at this hour of the day because some of them wouldn't let Alan in for a start?

Gavin sighs. I ken, I ken. Only it's just a token thing, really. I mean, I know it's an impossible task, trying to find somebody in a place this size.

Well, not impossible, Sheila says. I mean, I bumped into him myself yesterday morning, didn't I? I mean, I suppose it's not that hard to find somebody in Nice, really. Not if they stick to the tourist spots. Easier than Glasgow, I would say. Or Edinburgh even.

Unless they don't want to be found, Alan says.

Aye, well, right enough, Gavin says and she looks at the two of them. Jesus, do they know something already? Whether they do or not has there not been enough of this secrecy? What difference does it make if she tells them or not? A whole bloody lot of difference, that's what. At least she'll maybe tell Gavin. She will tell Gavin eventually. Only why bother unless it is a run-up to telling Madge? And what would Madge want to know information like that for?

I never knew you met Stuart yesterday, Alan goes. They are walking down the street, heading in the general direction of the shops and the beaches but still aimless apart from heading towards civilization.

We went into a café, she says, automatically. She can feel the two of them staring at her.

Why? asks Alan.

What d'you mean, why? He asked me if I wanted to go for a coffee, that's all. What's wrong with that?

Nothing, says Gavin quickly, giving Alan a look.

Nothing, says Alan.

But did he give you any indication, like? About where he was going or that?

No, why should he? She feels the pry of their eyes again. Why would you go for a coffee with that swine?

We didn't talk about anything special, she says. I was just trying to be friendly, that's all.

I know, Gavin says, but he doesn't look as though he believes her. It is ridiculous but she is not going to mention the panini. Plus it wasn't even a fucking coffee, it was a glass of wine. If she needs to justify having a panini and a glass of wine with Stuart to her own husband, if her own husband can read that much into a bloody sandwich and a glass of wine then no way is she going to mention it. A bloody panini, for Christ's sake.

Maybe he's gone into the sex shop again, Alan says and she stares at him. How the fuck does Alan know about Stuart going into a sex shop?

What do you mean? she asks, trying to keep her voice even.

Just that I saw him coming out. He is flushing now, wishing he hadn't said anything.

Sheila is not blind, she can see her own son's embarrassment. She doesn't want to make things any worse. The thing is, though, when exactly did he see Stuart coming out the sex shop? Christ, did he see her as well? She passed it, after all. Did he think she was in there as well? If she admits she saw Stuart coming out Alan might even think she was in there along with him.

I think that's a bit extreme, his dad says. I'm not going into no sex shop looking for him. No way.

Neither am I, says Sheila firmly. I mean, there are limits.

Aye, Alan grins. I'm not allowed anyway, am I?

You certainly are not, says his mother firmly.

He is a bit miffed at that. It's one thing for the law not to allow you but parental censorship is something else. What do you want to do then? he mutters. He is trying to avoid antagonism. After all, his mum and dad have been OK this holiday, really, compared with some people.

They have stopped outside the railway station. They are quite near some shops now as well as the sex shop. They are next to a pedestrian crossing – or whatever it is they call them over here. They cannot stand here all day.

To tell you the truth, I'd like to go to the shops, Sheila says. I wanted to buy some chocolate for people at work. We've got quite a bit of cash left, haven't we? I mean, I don't see why we should feel guilty about doing a bit of shopping. You never know, she gives a short laugh, I might even bump into the bugger like I did yesterday.

I don't fancy the shops, Alan says.

All right, his da says. We'll go for a walk along the *Promenade des Anglais*, will we? Get an ice-cream or something?

Aye, all right, says Alan.

Only we'll meet back here, will we, say in an hour and a half? I mean, I told Madge we wouldn't be long.

D'you fancy just going for a quick dip? Alan asks when his mum is gone.

We've no togs but, his da says.

We could just go in in our underpants. There's not a lot of folk about.

Naw, his dad says, looking appalled, we cannae do that son. Even you. I mean, you're getting a bit big for that. I tell you what, but, I'll get you a new pair out of *Go Sport*. A new pair of trunks.

All right, says Alan. But would you not get yourself a pair as well? I mean, yours are worse than mine.

Aye, all right then. Just if I can get a cheap pair but.

You're always buying cheap things, dad, Alan goes and watches his da blush.

Aye, well, have to watch the money son. Know what I mean?

Aye, but better quality things last longer. Pays you in the long run.

His da laughs. Aye, but how often do you see me in a pair of swimming trunks? Mine'll last for ages.

You could go swimming at home. Swimming's good for you, Alan says.

Aye, I suppose I could. It's not that dear, is it?

We could go together. Imagine we were back in Nice again. In the *Baie des Anges*.

Aye, that'd be right. In the cauld and the rain. Although maybe we could go to the Pollok pool, right enough.

Aye, wi the fake palm trees, Alan says and they laugh.

He doesn't tell his son because it probably sounds stupid now but he minds when the Pollok pool opened, when Alan was just a wee baby and he took him along when he was only a matter of months. The waves were a bit much for a wee baby though it looked like paradise, he thought. The artificial beach and the gleaming white tables and chairs. Bringing the Mediterranean to Glasgow. Only he had never been to the Mediterranean in they days. Didn't know the real thing from the imitation.

I was thinking, right enough, about another mural. *The Baie des Anges, Vieux Nice*, all that. Only I don't know if I'll remember it well enough.

132

We could get some postcards to take back.

Aye, come on then.

Alan is still in the water but he is sitting looking round him. Not that there's much chance, no really. Even if the bugger does turn up all of a sudden he wouldn't want him to think he was looking for him. It could cause a rift – deepen the rift – between Stuart and Madge. And with the expected wean that is the last thing Madge needs. When all's said and done he's still the baby's father, after all. Judge not that ye be not judged.

Sheila is waiting for them at the station. They are ten minutes late but she looks OK.

I've only just got here myself. Only I've just been thinking I never got anything for lunch. I suppose we could see what Madge wants to do first?

Aye. Unless *he's* arrived, Alan says.

Aye, that's a point, his dad says. If he has we'll just go away out and leave them to it.

Aye, we can always do the packing later, his mum says.

Madge & Sheila

Congratulations, says Sheila. God, that's brilliant, Madge. I'm really happy for you.

I told them yesterday, Madge says, nodding at Gavin and Alan. Only I swore them to secrecy. It just sort of came out, you know. I couldn't wait and then I felt stupid.

Does Stuart know? The minute it is out her mouth she knows she has said the wrong thing. Of course he doesn't bloody know. That is how she swore Gavin and Alan to secrecy.

Madge shrugs. He'll know soon enough. If he hadn't gone clearing off in the first place I wouldn't have said anything to anybody first.

Gavin is relieved. Of course Sheila will assume Madge just told him and Alan late yesterday evening, before she came back. Although he hates deception he doesn't want Sheila getting the wrong idea. Not that Sheila would, and not just because she told the boy as well. Sheila knows he isn't into intimacy with other women. Except there has been a sort of intimacy there with Madge, hasn't there, but not in any inappropriate way whatsoever. And it is difficult to explain wholly appropriate intimacy with your wife's best friend.

Are you two wanting to go in again? he asks and they shake their heads.

We'll just sit here and have a wee blether, Madge goes and he laughs and heads away to join his son in the water.

I've decided I'm not going to worry about him any more, Madge says, her mouth full with the ice-cream the young man brought them in his coolbox. A final extravagant gesture, Sheila thought, as Gavin called him over and asked the three of them what they wanted. It was like he was being the big man now Stuart had cleared off.

Aye, boys will be boys, Sheila says and the two of them laugh. He'll be back in his own good time.

I might even kick him out, Madge goes on. After all, I'll get Child Support now, won't I?

Sheila tries a smile, not sure if she is joking.

Seriously, though, it's no way for a prospective father to behave now, is it? Madge looks at her.

This is the perfect opportunity for her to say something but she would never, not now, not in a million years say anything to hurt her dear friend who has waited so many long years for this absolutely brilliant news and who, despite all the trouble with that bloody man, looks radiant.

Aye, but he doesn't know he's a prospective father, now, does he?

Mmm, says Madge. Even so, it's bloody annoying.

Well, we'll just enjoy ourselves, anyway, says Sheila.

I wouldn't mind a look round the shops before I go. Do you want to come?

If you can wait till they come out the water, all right.

If you don't mind, Madge says, I think we should avoid mentioning Stuart's name from now on. He's caused enough bother without him spoiling the rest of the holiday.

Quite right. I agree with you there.

Except it is all very well agreeing not to mention his name but they must have got it into their heads he was going to come back sometime. That Madge would not have to worry about packing his bloody case for him. Except they have to have the room vacated for ten so what else can she do?

I'm going to leave his passport at reception, along with his case, Madge goes. I'm damned if I'm going to carry his case to the bloody airport.

They have agreed to get the bus to the airport. It's a lot cheaper than a taxi and Madge is insisting she is feeling OK although probably that's not quite true. Only it is difficult to say too much to her, to break down that wall she has put up again. Impossible. Last night they went to the pictures. Gladiator (*version originale*) was on. There was no problem getting Alan in because the censorship laws here are more relaxed. Alan was dead chuffed about it. Not that he hasn't been to 15s before but he has been refused entry many's the time too. They talked about it on the way home, about the extent of the violence and to what extent it was gratuitous. Gavin and Alan were walking on ahead, chatting quietly. Sheila was at last feeling the day had been near perfect (if it wasn't for the bloody Stuart business) only when she suggested going and getting a pizza or phoning up for a takeaway one Madge got all huffy all of a sudden.

But what about Stuart?

That was when she realised Madge was expecting him back after all, whereas she wasn't. She didn't want to think about it but what she must have been thinking but shoving to the back of her mind was that Stuart was away home to see that bloody girlfriend of his. Where the fuck else would he be? She was definitely going to mention the business to Gavin when they were in bed because he was still fretting the bugger had been run over or something, which was ridiculous in a way because Madge would have heard from the police if something like that had happened.

Only Gavin fell asleep practically as soon as his head touched the pillow and in the morning he was up before she was, in chatting to Madge, so there was no chance, none, of mentioning the subject.

So Stuart has become Him, right up to the moment of departure and beyond. At seven in the morning, packing the last wee bits, tidying the place before the staff come to do their bloody inspection, Gavin sits down on the bed. He looks drained as well as absolutely flabbergasted.

Jesus, we should have gone to the police. Jesus Christ. All his stuff's sitting in there. Jesus, Sheila, but, he could be dead, for fuck's sake.

Ssh, she whispers angrily. Shut up. Look, I think he's away back to Glasgow. I don't know for sure and I can't tell Madge but it was something he said. Another woman, she mouths silently at last.

Oh. The relief on his face is palpable. Why didn't you say before?

Why d'you think? she hisses.

Oh, aye. Aye, right. I see what you mean. Aye, well, that's all right then. Fine. Bloody hell.

It is only when Madge starts mentioning the passport they start to have their doubts.

Sometimes they don't bother with passports, do they? I'm sure they never bothered that time at Palma. Do you remember, Gavin?

Not really. Naw, I don't think so.

It is too late anyway to start contacting the police. Although it looks terrible, at the last moment, clearing away back without him. Obviously if he isn't back in Glasgow they'll have to phone the police then but there's no point worrying Madge unnecessarily.

On the plane Madge has her first drink since she found out she was pregnant.

It's only the one, she says apologetically to them. I really feel I need a drink after what I've been through.

I don't blame you, said Sheila.

Aye, there's nothing wrong wi the odd one, as long as you don't overdo it, says Gavin.

What neither of them is prepared to say is that what Madge has been through may be nothing compared with what she has yet to go through, whether Stuart is back or no.

Madge & Sheila

When Sheila invited her back for a coffee she wasn't going to say no.

Will you come over with me to ours after? she asked Sheila, not explaining why, partly because there was no explanation really, just an odd feeling.

Aye, sure, Sheila said, not querying either.

If he's not at the house then I'm just going to phone the police the minute I get in the door.

Right. This was a bit of a turnaround. Or maybe it wasn't. What else could you do in circumstances like that?

And of course he isn't there. All the way back on the plane to Luton and then the one to Glasgow she knew it. It's growing dark but there are no lights on.

Hi, had a good holiday? It's the next-door neighbour. Very friendly if not exactly nosey.

So-so, thanks. She would like to rush in the door but is impeded by the huge pile of mail behind it as well as by her luggage. She feels unbelievably stupid for leaving Stuart's stuff — especially his passport — behind in Nice. What an arse she has been.

He could be visiting somebody or something, Sheila says. The excuse sounds pathetic. What fucking drivel she talks sometimes.

You mean another woman?

No, no, I didn't mean that.

Madge ignores her. She picks up the phone and dials Directory Enquiries. The number of the local station will be in the book but she cannae be bothered.

Sheila fusses about making coffee even though they've just had one. It gives her something to do without making it look like she's eavesdropping. Madge always has real coffee in and that takes longer as well. Just as well for Madge seems to be on the phone a long time.

At last she comes into the kitchen.

Coffee's made.

Christ, it's a drink I need, Madge goes, then, seeing Sheila's face, I'm only kidding. Aye, I will have a coffee, thanks. Look, Sheila, they want me to come down the station. Preferably tonight. The guy said it's complicated because he went missing in France.

Sheila nods. Jesus. Will she have to reveal all eventually, if no the night? Jesus.

The thing is, Sheila, it's embarrassing. Me leaving his stuff – his passport and stuff – behind. Christ, I feel so stupid.

But we thought he was still there. Christ, he probably is still there, Madge.

Aye, but, like, the guy made me feel I was an eejit or something because I never went to the police over there. But, I mean, my French isn't that good. I mean, I know it isn't that bad but it's the stress of it and everything as well. The thought of trying to explain everything to these French guys. I mean, Christ. And, you know, Sheila, I just wanted to get home. I mean, I've got to go and see the doctor and everything.

Well, just say that to them when you go down. You have nothing to fear, Madge.

But what if something's happened to him? I mean, he could have had an accident or something. I mean, Christ, Sheila, he could be lying dead somewhere. Jesus, Sheila.

She makes the decision then, although it does not feel as deliberate as all that.

I don't think so, Madge.

Why not?

I just have this feeling. I met him, you see, the day before yesterday, in the town, when you and Gavin and Alan were away at the museum.

Go on.

We went for a coffee.

Did you now?

Oh fuck.. Oh fuck because she can sense more than puzzlement on Madge's face. There is definitely a tinge of hostility there – you couldn't call it anything else. Which is bloody ridiculous. She doesn't know which is worse – her own husband being freaked out (not that he would admit to it – not in a million years – not Gavin) over a bloody cup of coffee (never mind a panini and a glass of wine) with somebody else's husband or her best friend being freaked out at her sitting blethering to her man. And it's funny how you can change your mind in an instant over somebody's reaction to you having a coffee with her man. Because she has said enough, hasn't she? She ought to be patching things up between the two of them. And she doesn't know whether it really makes any difference to the likelihood of his whereabouts. The fact that the bugger is having, has been having, an affair doesn't really affect his chances of meeting with an accident, does it? He could still have got drunk and run over, or run over by a drunk, or both. Except surely to Christ the police would have been round? That is the big difference, isn't it? Missing for nigh on forty eight hours so if he'd had an accident surely to Christ the police would have been round?

Look, Madge, he just sort of hinted he might be – well, you know, he had plans or something.

Jesus, Sheila, I don't believe this. You're keeping something back, aren't you? Christ Almighty, Sheila, don't do this to me. You know the fucking state I've been in these past few days. Don't fucking do this to me, Sheila.

So she tells her. She should probably have kept her mouth shut but maybe not, maybe not. As she mutters, He said something about there being someone else, she realises she doesn't know that much about the affair at all. How long, for example. Least of all, who the fuck she is.

Did he say her name?

She shakes her head. It is a question she wanted to ask Madge, but didn't dare, if she has the slightest clue who the woman might be.

He just said there's someone else. That's all he said, Madge.

Someone else. Fuck. Is that all? The bastard. So I'm supposed to try and work out who the fuck she is? Jesus Christ.

She starts to say, No, you're not, meaning she wasn't supposed to tell her and then realises anything she says can only make it worse. How the fuck is she supposed to know what Stuart meant or didn't mean? Just because she sat and had a glass of wine with the bastard doesn't mean she knows sweet FA about the guy. Except for the remark about someone else which said everything.

But Madge's mind has moved on. I hope you're right, she is saying. I hope he is in Glasgow with her. I don't give a fuck about him any more but I sure as hell don't want any trouble with the police. If something happened to him in Nice they're going to find it very bloody funny I never reported him missing over there. Just went and handed in his fucking passport and his luggage. I could end up getting the blame.

I never thought of that, Sheila thinks, but she only says, Oh, no, Madge, you did what you could.

She is about to offer to accompany Madge to the police station but the phone rings.

C'est moi, Madge McCracken, Madge says. *Oui, non, je suis desolée.* I'm very sorry. Look, can I phone you back later because I have to go to the police station? My husband is missing. I don't know. Look, I'm very upset. *Vous pouvez garder les bagages, non?* Can't you put the stuff somewhere in the meantime? Look, if you tell me how much it is I'll send you the money. *Je vous enverrai suffisament d'argent.* Right. *D'accord.* She puts the phone down. Fuck, she turns to Sheila. It's the hotel place in Nice. They're harrassing me over Stuart's stuff. I knew I shouldn't've left it there. It'll cost me a fortune now to have it sent over.

I'll come with you to the police.

Aye, right, thanks. Only what if they start asking you questions? I mean, I don't suppose they will but will you tell them, like, about meeting him and what he said to you?

I don't like lying to the police, Madge.

Aye, I suppose you're right.

Drink up your coffee then and we'll go.

Are you not going to phone Gavin first?

Aye, I suppose I'd better.

The police were OK. She did tell them, in the end, only because she was there and the policeman asked Madge when she last saw him and Madge looked at her and then she came out with it. Inevitably, he asked what they talked about and she told him then, explaining (she hoped it didn't sound too contrived) that she only told Madge this an hour ago.

We'll get onto the police in Nice then, the policeman says. Although it sounds as though he may have just cleared off with this – erm, this woman, Mrs McCracken.

That was when Madge comes out with it about the passport. Instantly the policeman's face changes.

Aye, but he couldn't've got home without a passport.

I thought maybe he could. Maybe there was a chance, Madge says haltingly.

I doubt it, Mrs McCracken. Look, I'll have to go and speak to someone about this. I'll get someone to bring the two of you a nice cup of tea. Just you ladies make yourselves comfortable now.

Do you think that means we might be waiting a while? Madge asks when the policeman has gone.

Sheila shakes her head. No idea.

I've been in police stations quite a few times – seeing clients. Only this is the first time I've ever been to one on my own account. It's a completely different experience.

Mmm. I've been to a few to see clients as well. At least we're not in the cells, Madge. (Important to keep up the humour, stop Madge getting depressed, whatever.)

The policeman takes ages, right enough. By the time he is back they have long drunk the tea and finished the biscuits. They are sitting there with little to say to one another. How can you have a private conversation in a police station?

No news, as far as I can gather. I phoned the police in Nice myself. Wee bit of a problem with the French, you understand, but fortunately someone there had pretty good English. We're going to fax a report so they'll let us know if anything turns up.

Righto, says Madge.

So we'll be in touch.

It is two weeks later when Madge phones. She sounds hoarse, unwell. They have kept in touch by phone but, if anything, they are less close than before the holiday. It is as though the holiday has drained them of mutual goodwill. Although Gavin has been round to Madge's a couple of times.

She needs someone to talk to, he said. It must be terrible for her.

Yeah, she says. Only she doesn't know what to say to Madge. What the fuck can have happened to the bugger, for Christ's sake? According to Gavin (according to Madge who phoned his work to explain she hadn't seen him – Can you imagine her embarrassment? Gavin said. I mean, Jesus, having to tell them she doesn't know where he is. Jesus), on the one hand the bugger hasn't been near his work and nor has he phoned in sick or anything, which doesn't bode well at all. On the other hand if he is shacking up with some new dollybird (Madge's words, of course, not Gavin's), well then, you never know. And people go missing all the time, don't they?

Can you come round? Madge asks.

What, now? she asks, even though she is at her work and is seeing a client in five minutes, an emergency – like she can tell Madge's is, just by the tone somehow, even before she tells her he is dead. Someone else will have to deal with the emergency at work. Someone else will have to deal with this client who won't have the money for a power card, who has so little control over her life that she relies on the Social Work Department, the DSS for the bare necessities of her meagre existence. This client, whose situation resembles at least a dozen others in a number of respects (dozens more if you delete one or two of the common denominators) will have no food in the fridge (if her fridge, that is on its last legs, is working at all) or no means of cooking any food she does have. Her children will have had nothing to eat since yesterday and her boyfriend will, as like as not, have been beating her up again. She will have spent her last couple of pounds on ten cigarettes and be cadging in the office for more. This client, whom Sheila has helped out of her own pocket on more than one occasion, against all the rules, will be in desperate straits. But, for once, her friend is in still greater need. She phones her supervisor to explain. Her supervisor is understanding. She knows all about Madge's situation. Naturally Madge has been off sick since she came back from holiday. Stress, Sheila supposes, although it could be pregnancy-related too.

Madge has evidently been crying. Naturally.

You won't believe this, she begins. A fucking jellyfish. Talk about the oddest of coincidences. A fucking jellyfish that shouldn't even have been in the Mediterranean. A Portuguese man o' war, they said. Although apparently they sometimes get these other jellyfish, colonies of them. Medusa or something.

You'll have to go over there.

Aye.

Do you have anyone to go with you?

I was wondering if I could ask your Gavin. Obviously I'll pay the fare and accommodation and everything.

Aye, well, we haven't really got the money, Madge.

I know. It's not exactly going to be a holiday anyway.

Sheila & Madge

There's this place called the *Géode*, Madge tells her. You'll really have to go and see it. It's like this huge semicircular screen. You get, like, 180 degree vision. The films aren't up to much, I don't think, but it doesn't really matter because it's the visual experience you go for. It doesn't really matter if you don't understand the French.

Just as well then, cause I won't, Sheila goes. Although Gavin's getting on very well at this class he's going to.

They are in Paris. It's only October but Madge is calling it her last holiday as a single person. Wanting to make the most of it before the baby is born and she won't be allowed to fly after the seventh month anyway. Although that's still ages away.

It's cold for the beginning of October, Madge says when they are walking through the *Parc de la Villette* towards the *Géode*. It is as though peace has settled on them both, after the bustle and traffic noises of the city. After the massive injection of culture when all your senses are working overtime they can at last relax amid the grassy spaces, the undemanding modern architecture that is just flung about the park, almost carelessly, not requiring instant translation by the visitor.

Yeah, I thought Paris would be warmer. When we – me and Stuart – were here in October before, we were laughing at all these folk all wrapped up in the lovely weather, thinking they didn't know what the Scottish weather is like at this time of year. Although Paris can be cold in the winter, right enough.

She is starting to say his name again. Not that she was in love with him at the time of his death. She is not one to kid herself on about something like that. Only it was painful to start with. Painful not so much because of the circumstances which were, if anything, simply absurd. No, rather it was because of the woman hiding in the background. At the funeral she found herself not paying attention to people who came over to offer their condolences. Some of them she cared nothing for – they were simply adopting the conventional pose – but some were genuine enough. They must have thought her distracted when really she was quite the opposite, looking out greedily for prey. For the Someone Else Stuart had blabbed about. If it hadn't been for him meeting Sheila that time in the café and blabbing like that she would never have been looking out for anyone. But how could she know who to look for, except someone, perhaps, who was more upset than she should have been? In the end she gave up torturing herself, although what was maddening was the thought of being watched – of someone looking at her, pitying her, or even hating her, for all she knew. Pitying herself more like.

It was curiosity more than revenge that made her go through Stuart's things before she sent them to the charity shop. She had to go through his pockets anyway in case there was money or valuables. She wasn't looking for anything sentimental. Anything she thought might conceivably be of sentimental value she had given, or sent, to his mother. Not that Stuart thought highly of her (or that she did) but she had asked for stuff.

You'll not be wanting to live in that big house yourself, she says to her and that was when she told her.

At your age? she goes. After all this time? You're kidding me.

Do you think I would joke about a thing like that at a time like this? she hissed at the old witch.

She doesn't want anything to do with any of Stuart's family, although doubtless his mother will come crawling back when the baby's born. Meantime she gets treated as an unfaithful, if not murderous, wife. That is what's so maddening. When he was the one, not her.

She found nothing. Not until she opened the case she had hastily packed herself in the apartment in Nice. She picked it up, along with the passport, when she went along to identify Stuart's things. It would take some months before the French equivalent of an inquest could be held, before the matter would draw to a close.

The inquest that took place just a couple of weeks ago raised more questions than it answered. Some of Stuart's clothing was missing but why would he go for a swim in the small hours half-dressed? Had it not been for the man o' war it would have pointed to suicide, she was sure of it. You do not go swimming in your socks and vest. But the man o' war meant a verdict of suicide was impossible. He was drunk but that, she supposed, was not sufficient to point to attempted suicide (which is still not the same thing as suicide). Quite the reverse, possibly. He always was a gallus bugger.

She walked along the *Promenade des Anglais*, no longer marvelling at its palm trees, at the long stretches of beach that still glistened in the sun, quieter now, only wishing it was all over. It is over, except for the woman. Even after a verdict of accidental death it will not quite be all

145

over until the woman has been found. Although the lawyer she contacted after the identification business and before the funeral, after it was clear the insurance people were going to be shirty, said if it was an accidental verdict everything would be OK.

You'll have nothing to worry about, Mrs McCracken, he said. You'll be well provided for.

Which was true. Apart from the ordinary life insurance there was a few hundred thou to come from the travel insurance. At first she thought she would pay the mortgage off and probably go part-time after the baby is born. The insurance company will have to pay all the expenses she has already incurred. Rid of the burden of a selfish, domineering man in her life, a baby on the way and a sense that she has gained in status at work, perhaps because she has coped with this crisis so well, everything should be perfect. And it would be were it not for the invisible woman.

She could have let bygones be bygones but she isn't that sort of person. When she found the address book there were quite a few names unknown to her. Work contacts. How would she know? Some of them referred to only by their first names. None of them stood out. It was only when she flicked through the diary that she realised the name Karen kept cropping up. Just that, though, just a name. She flicked through the diary and, sure enough, there was an address as well as a telephone number. Only she would do a little detective work first. Except now she had her woman she could afford to wait. Until the financial affairs have been sorted out, at least. Maybe she could even hire a detective if the insurance company pays up. Why not?

She tells Sheila about finding the name in the diary.

But you can't be sure it's her, can you?

I'm as sure as I can be.

Do you not think you should drop it, Madge? Write it off as water under the bridge?

Madge shakes her head, bites her lip.

But what can you possibly hope to get out of it? She is afraid to utter the word revenge, perhaps in case that is the real explanation. What else?

Madge sighs. It's just curiosity, Sheila. I want to hear it from her lips. And I don't want her to pity me. And, Christ, Sheila, if she was having this wild love affair with him, as he claimed, she's the one whose heart should be breaking. You'd think she'd want to talk to somebody.

What? You'd go and pretend to be someone else?

No, of course not. She probably knows what I look like already. I mean, I'm assuming she went to his funeral, for Christ's sake.

Right. Unless she's married or something.

I never thought of that.

So that's it, then. You just want to talk to her? But, Madge, it'll just upset you.

There is another reason.

Sheila looks at her.

I just want her to know I'm pregnant, that's all.

I see. Sheila cannot resist a smile. I might have known you were up to something, Madge McCracken.

They head into the *Géode*. There is a film called *The Wolf* showing shortly.

We'll have to see this, Madge says and she does not argue for Madge is paying for this trip too.

Oh, you can get headphones with an English version, Sheila says, pleased.

Oh, right. Only I don't think I'll bother. Think I'll try the French myself. I can't see it being that difficult anyway.

Surely there's no harm in taking them anyway, just in case. The original soundtrack is English. It's a Canadian film, she says, reading the leaflet she picked up. You might as well.

Madge shakes her head. I'll not bother.

But much of the film is difficult to follow. She could kick herself for ignoring her friend's advice. Although, overall, she can catch the gist, about the wolf being a protected species, about what a beautiful creature it is.

I wish we'd seen that before we went to Nice, Sheila says, grinning, when they come out.

Aye, Madge says, but you cannot wish away the past. And would she want to?

I never expected to be in France once, never mind twice, this year, Sheila says over lunch which is a self-service affair in the *Cité des Sciences et de l'Industrie*, thank goodness, for she wouldn't want Madge going and spending a fortune on her. Although the food is lovely and they share a carafe of wine (Madge has apparently forgotten her intention to have an alcohol-free pregnancy – not that she blames her – especially in the circumstances – not at all).

147

I never expected to be here three times, Madge says, grimly.

No, no, of course not.

But, you know, I don't regret anything. Now I've got the insurance money I feel this sense of – freedom. I mean, obviously I'll have to bring the baby up without a father but, you know, there's no point in kidding myself that Stuart was going to be the decent father. He wasn't exactly the decent husband so why should he have been a good father?

Yeah, but I suppose you never know.

No, in his case I do. I definitely do know, Sheila. I've given him a decent burial and now I'm going to forget about him. Lay his ghost to rest for good. At least, once I've had a word with this Karen I am.

Sheila sighs. She has a feeling this Karen is going to keep on turning up in the conversation, like a bad penny.

Right, tomorrow the Louvre and the d'Orsay, if we have any energy left. Just bits, of course.

Sheila shrugs. She is beginning to think Gavin would have enjoyed the trip more than her. All she wants to do is sit around cafés and drink in the atmosphere. For a forty-something pregnant widow Madge is abounding with energy. She suddenly feels very old. Or maybe she is just missing Gavin. And Alan. She keeps wondering what they are doing without her. Even though Stuart was such a unfaithful bastard he was still Madge's husband. You would think there would be some regret there, still, some sense of loss. Suddenly she knows quite clearly that if anything happened to either Gavin or Alan she would be absolutely devastated. For all the squabbles they have had (over things so stupid she cannot now remember what they were) they are pretty close, the three of them. All the money in the world cannot make up for that and that is why, when Madge tells her exactly how many hundred thousands she expects to receive from the insurance company, she does not feel even a shred of jealousy.

148

He has started the mural at last. In the months after they came back from the trip that was supposed to be a holiday, but turned out to be a disaster, he could not do any work on it. He could not do any work on it because he could scarcely think straight, never mind wield a paint-brush to any artistic effect. He would never ever have contemplated going away with Madge and Stuart if he thought Stuart was having an affair and, moreover, planning to leave his wife. If he was religious he might think a divine retribution had been visited upon him or something like that but he is not religious, or at least his own idea of religion or spirituality does not conform to the popular conception, least of all the idea of a vengeful God, so the news has only left him stunned.

Sheila was onto him about decorating the hall. He cannae blame her. He is supposed to be a decorator, after all and although he still gets the odd bout of coughing it is not half as bad as it was when he first got laid off his work. At this rate the DSS doctor'll be pronouncing him fit. Not that he could complain about that.

But he is glad he never went along with the ordinary paint and paper idea. Even stencilling.

You could always try stencilling if you fancy being a bit more creative, Sheila said. He avoided answering her. Did she not trust him? Did she think the folk that did stencils could do better than his freehand? Not that he would condemn anything out of hand but he'd had a look in a DIY store and the look was enough. The price of they things as well. He could buy loads of paint for that money.

He knew Sheila wasn't really that bothered for the mural, although at the start, when he tried to explain it to her, she made out she was quite interested. Probably she was more keen on him taking an interest, the way she takes an interest, gets wholly involved really, in her job. He can see why a person would get completely involved in social work. Facing head-on all these crises, getting in there, doing your bit. Believing you can make a difference.

He has started going to Art as well as French classes. He is going to take Higher Art as well as Beginners French. The truth is he doesn't really want to go back to work now because there is so much to do. He does the classes during the day at a local college and they are free because he is not working. Only he has to do his studying in the evening, and the rest of the daytime when he is not doing housework he is concentrating on this mural. He has let the house get into a bit of a tip these past few days and he missed both his classes because of this mural. Last night him and Alan had fish suppers because the kitchen was such a tip. He wouldn't have the place in a tip if Sheila was at home. Sheila likes things in their place. He can't blame her. It is her house as well. He can't expect her to be enthused in the same way he is, not to the extent of letting the house get into a total and utter tip.

Sheila has been onto him about the hall for quite a while. Only he never mentioned the mural idea to her. Although he mentioned it to Alan that day in Nice when they were supposed to be looking for Stuart it was only the vaguest idea at the time. More like the initial inspiration that comes before you have really thought about what the work entails. He had to go a lot further than he thought for the research bit. It was a good idea of Alan's, that, getting those postcards, only it wasn't enough. After the holiday he went trailing round all the art galleries – the ones in Edinburgh as well as Glasgow. He wanted to get the sense of perspective right. He needed to acquire some of the perspicacity of the old masters. You couldn't just launch a work of art from a few wee postcards.

Christ, a work of art. Is that what he really thinks? He'd better watch himself, getting grandiose ideas. Although anybody can try. He can only do his best with what he has. He has no intention of Sheila finding the house a tip when she comes back at the end of the week. If he doesn't have it finished then (which is unlikely the way it's going) then he will at least have a wee bit ready – a wee bit that looks complete in itself – and he will just have to do the rest during the day when Sheila is at work and tidy up every evening. At the moment he is working about twelve hours a day on the business (Christ, the DSS doctor definitely wouldn't approve – that goes without saying) but he will just have to cut down, slow down.

He began with the beach. No, that is not quite true. He began with the vaguest idea about the light and the dry air in Nice. He hadn't really thought about the dry air (which is good for his chest) until he came home and realised how humid it was in Scotland. It sounds absurd, trying to paint the dry air, but not, he convinces himself, when he thinks of his work as a representation. The dry air as well as the sense of abundance is symbolised by the palm trees. Then there is the sense of history in the place. That is represented by the buildings in

Vieux Nice. There is one that Dufy did that he will use (but not copy) to assist him there.

He is not putting too much in. Not at this stage certainly but probably not anyway. Too much would clutter his thinking when he needs to separate out what is important from what is run-of-the-mill. What makes not just Nice but his own personal experience of Nice different from any other place that tourists visit and different also from someone else's experience of Nice. Although he wants it to be recognisable, accessible, he knows that anybody and everybody would think of palms, which is great, up to a point, but he possibly wants the shock of newness as well as the surprise recognition can bring. And the pleasure, of course – not forgetting the pleasure.

Are you no going to put in the dog turds then? Alan asked and he had to laugh but he knew what Alan meant. It is going to be no touristy picture, this. There will be more than the dry air and the lightness and the pleasure. There will be the pain too and the dog turds will be the least of that. But how to represent death in a picture that is supposed to be full of light? This is definitely not something that could be done in a matter of a week. No way.

He has varnished over the Still Life, the *Nature Morte* in the kitchen. Normally he would never dream of putting varnish on a wall because he knows it is murder to get off. Only it was Sheila's idea. After they came back from holiday.

Diamond hard, that's what it needs, she said. That'll stop it getting scratched and then it'll be wipe-clean.

He looked at her. We'd never it get off – the diamond hard stuff, Sheila.

Aye well, she said. That's the general idea. That way it'll last for years and years.

He has never really thought about making money out of the murals, making ones to please other people. It was Madge came out with it, the day she came back from Nice, after the inquest.

I'm goinae be a rich woman, she says, sitting down on the settee. Christ knows I never in my life thought I was going to be rich.

She went on to tell them about this travel insurance. How that, combined with this life insurance would mean not only that she'd be able to pay off the mortgage but she'd have a few hundred thou on top.

Aye, well, it'll be security. For you and the baby, he says, smiling. It'll be a comfort to you to know it's always there.

I was thinking about doing something with it. Going into business.

Oh, he says. But you've got a good job, Madge.

Och, I know it's not bad but I get weary of it. I'm not cut out to do social work, not like your Sheila. The job makes Sheila come alive but it just deadens something in me. It's not what I wanted for myself when I was young. Young and free. Doing my own thing. Something a bit wilder. Not constrained by the system. You know what I mean. Of course I'm free now, but maybe it's not too late.

Did you have anything specific in mind? he asks, curious.

Not till the night, she says. Not till I came up here and saw this. Jesus, it's fucking brilliant.

He couldn't help blushing. Sheila and Alan too had been enthusiastic but not that enthusiastic. At least for the first few moments after she spoke he was over the moon. But only for the first few moments. After that all he could think was she was flattering him, presumably because she felt sorry for him, being out of work. She was glad he was taking an interest in something, that was what it was. Besides which his head had moved on from the still life in the kitchen, even if his hands had hardly done a stroke on the latest idea.

We could go into business thegither, Gavin, Madge says then while he just laughs out loud. Aye, that'll be right.

Seriously. Bespoke Murals or something. I can see it now. Of course you probably wouldn't want to put quite as much time and effort into ones you were doing for the money – to make them commercially viable, like.

Madge, he says, a bit annoyed now that the joke has gone far enough, I'm on the Sick. I haven't a bean, Madge. I do this for – for my own amusement, Madge. Of course it is far more than that but how can he put it without sounding like he is full of himself?

Just think about it, she says. We could put a business plan together. Maybe get some advice. We'd need a lawyer anyway. Seriously, Gavin, you have talent. All I'm suggesting is you make a little money from it. Eventually a living.

Sheila was sceptical about the money. I don't know what's got into her. She's a good social worker. Setting up your own business is terribly risky.

Aye, he said. He couldn't disagree with a word but he felt regretful she didn't apparently want to discuss his art because already he was thinking of it like that. It was not just about a business proposition but about how good he was. Although probably you couldn't really separate the two.

Alan's response was touching. Aye, but, dad, real artists don't make money for years and years. Don't you go selling yourself short. Don't you go doing it just for the money. Just you do what you want to do.

Which is what he is doing right now, right this very minute. Which is all very well but he doesn't want to be financially dependent for the rest of his days – either on the DSS (he should be so lucky, considering their record for sending sick folk back to work) or on Sheila. Look at Stuart, the selfish bastard, only looking out for himself and look what happened to him, fuck's sake. Anyway art is not about isolating yourself, about living in a vacuum, is it? Art is about determining your relationship to the world out there, connecting that to the world in your head and forming, moulding an accurate representation of how you see those connections.

Of course any kind of business enterprise is inherently risky, Madge went on, while he marvelled at her cheek, considering Sheila wasn't there and he never did anything substantial involving money or risk (substantial risk, financial risk, anyway) without involving Sheila. What was she on about anyway? He didn't have a bloody bean. Not a bean.

You're having me on, right? he said, just to clear the whole thing up. He cannot stand uncertainties, untruths, however people try to hide falsehoods behind euphemisms, or jokes.

Nup, Madge says. And you don't need a bean. I'm the one with the funds, remember. Or I will be pretty soon. We'll talk about it again when I have the money.

There was nothing more to say. Although when Madge went away he reminded himself – something he wouldn't dare to admit to her – that really it is not just a question of beans. There is the pure pleasure of painting for yourself. It is not something he has really enjoyed since he was a child, or at least an adolescent. Even then there would be someone to stop you, to shout at you what were you doing and you had to do this or that. Plus you never had the right colours, never had the money for paints, brushes, all that. But now it is perfect (apart from needing money, from being dependent on Sheila, the DSS). There is nothing in this world comparable to standing here wielding your brush, deciding to put a spot here or there, changing the landscape at your will. While he paints he listens to Edith Piaf whom he never even heard of before but whom Madge introduced him to and whose CDs are selling, unbelievably cheaply in cut price shops all over Nice, and all over France, Madge says. The music, like the painting, transports him to a world he never knew, a world of the imagination, as well another era. Right now he is listening to *C'était une Histoire d'Amour*. He has never heard such a beautiful sound. When Sheila comes home he would like to take her in his arms and just waltz around the room. Only right now he is happy to do a little waltz with his paintbrushes. He is not quite ready for Sheila. There is quite a bit to get ready before he and Sheila can do any waltzing together. Quite a bit indeed.

Alan

It seems ages since he was in Nice. Ages since he was swimming in the sea, having come out as gay, ages since he saw his mum topless on the beach (although she never saw him, right enough, didn't know he was there and they have never spoken about it). Now he is confined in Glasgow it is like he is back in the closet. His dad never talks to him about sexuality or anything. Not that he did before but after his announcement in Nice, well, he thought it would have amounted to something, made a difference to the future. Only his dad is that wrapped up in this painting business it's like he never thinks about anything else. He can't blame him. He has never seen his dad so happy, so profoundly happy. He hopes it has nothing to do with his mum being away for he loves his mum dearly and he would never in a million years want them to split up. Although he doesn't think they will now. They have been getting on better since Nice, really. Although everybody needs a break and his mum admitted she was going to Paris as a favour to Madge. He was tempted to say, You're all right. You don't have to go. Just write us a note so I can get the week off school. Ha, that'd be right. It is one thing going away your holidays with your mum's pal (and her man – although a bit strange coming back without the man, right enough) but another going away yourself with a pregnant woman in her forties. The tongues that would be wagging! He is not daft.

He has heard that tongues are wagging already. Not that they've said anything to him but he's not deaf either. Madge was talking to his mum and dad one night before her and his mum went away to Paris. Something about people talking behind her back. About it being funny her being pregnant after all these years and all that business with her man and all. Plus, Madge said, a lot of folk that work for councils and the so-called labour movement are dead incestuous (she actually used the word incestuous), going back to the days when it was nudge-nudge, wink-wink and hey presto, Bob's your uncle, the job's yours (days which, as far as Madge was concerned, were not only not that long gone but, as far as some folk were concerned, not even gone at all). So some of the people in the Social Work department have partners (or at least friends or relatives) who work for the Housing or the unions. He wondered then if there might even have been a bit of the nudge-nudge,

155

wink-wink, in Madge's (or Stuart's) case but it was all water under the bridge, after all, wasn't it?

So there's folk at Stuart's work that ken folk at ours? his ma said slowly. He was hovering in the kitchen making coffees and he couldn't hear what Madge said but he could just imagine her nodding.

Aye, said Madge when he came ben, there's doubtless folk know her and all.

He didn't know what she meant by that and he wasn't likely to find out because they started changing the subject then. It's funny but, although they all (even his mum now) appear to have accepted his sexuality they are still careful about what they say in front of him. As if they can corrupt him in some way talking about, or even hinting at, sex. Which isn't fair because if they are not going to be open with him it makes it harder for him to be open with them. Like, harder to talk about this new boy he fancies at school – Chris, whose parents moved from Edinburgh, of all places, and is into tennis and stuff. Which is at least one reason why he has started playing tennis at school.

Do they play tennis at this time of year? his mum says and he blushed not because of the tennis but because of Chris and he was wondering if she was fishing, only probably she wasn't.

We play inside if it rains.

Do you need anything for it? his mum says and then he understood all the questions. Of course she was worried about the money. She was embarrassed about going to Paris with Madge when they had no money.

It's all very well Madge saying she'll pay but I can't expect her to pay for everything, and he says, Why not? and she laughed.

Naw, he says to her. They provide racquets and balls and everything. Christ, this is terrible. He cannae say balls these days without blushing. Like a wean, for fuck's sake.

What about shoes?

Naw, you just wear trainers.

You'll need a new pair soon, she says.

I wouldn't mind, he says, looking at his feet. Chris has these fancy new trainers. Goretex lined. Must have cost a packet. Fancy new everything as far as he can see. Although that's nothing to do with fancying him. His folks must be pretty well-off but. Rumour has it he was at a private school. He wouldn't ask but. Not about a thing like that.

We'll get you a pair before I go to Paris, she says.

He sighed. She was right, as usual. If she doesn't come he might get the wrong size. His feet are growing all the time. Sometimes it's hard to tell yourself if something fits. His mum does this funny thing – puts her finger down the back of the shoe to feel if there's a gap or something. He couldn't do it by himself because you have to push your foot as far forward into the shoe as you can without bending your toes. He used to think she was daft and sometimes he still thinks that, but he wouldn't like to go and buy a pair all by himself. A jacket maybe (although she knows all about how to buy a jacket as well) but at least if he gets the wrong size when she's with him (not that he ever has) she cannae blame him.

There is tennis the day. He is smiling as he glances at his fancy new trainers before he packs his shorts and T-shirt into his old school bag. He wouldn't mind a new school bag and a new pair of shorts as well (he has plenty of T-shirts, right enough) but you can't have everything.

After the tennis Chris walks him part of the way home.

You used to live in Edinburgh? he says.

Yup.

Do you miss your friends and that there?

Chris shrugs. Maybe. Some of them.

Miss your old school?

He shrugs again and bites his lip. For a minute Alan thinks he is going to cry or something. He wishes he never spoke.

You won't say anything?

Alan nods, intrigued.

They threw me out. It was a private school.

They threw you out?

They didn't call it expulsion. Mum and dad were asked to take me away. It was so humiliating.

He is astonished. To look at Chris you wouldn't think he was the type to get flung out of school. He is super neat and tidy, he knows all the answers to the questions the teachers ask, he gets involved in extra-curricular activities, for Christ's sake.

Was it smoking? He feels stupid even as he asks. Even the private schools wouldn't throw you out for smoking, surely?

Chris shakes his head.

He shouldn't be so nosey but he can't resist it. Drugs? he whispers. They always fling you out the private schools for doing drugs, even cannabis, even toty wee bits. Everybody knows that.

I'm not interested in drugs, says Chris scornfully. I like to keep fit. Drugs are for mugs, he says, as if he's quoting somebody, his mum or dad or maybe a teacher.

I like to keep fit as well, he says.

They threw me out, Chris says slowly, because I was in love with another boy. They have been walking alongside one another but without looking at each other much.

That's OK, I'm gay as well, he says, stealing a glance now at Chris's face to gauge his reaction.

I thought so, Chris grins.

His face falls a mile. How? How can you tell? His face feels like it is on fire. He had no idea it was so obvious.

It takes one to know one, Chris says, grinning again.

He laughs with relief. Oh, aye, I suppose so. Aye, right enough.

They talk about other things. Music and stuff.

Have you got your own stereo? he asks, trying to imagine what his room must be like.

Yeah, only I usually have to listen with earphones, unless mum and dad are out. Especially my dad. He's a real pain in the arse, my dad.

He giggles. I used to think that about my dad but now I sort of think he's OK. Mostly, anyway.

What does he do?

He's an artist, he says suddenly. He thinks it is the truth, even if a lot of people might not agree with him.

Really? Chris looks interested. What kind?

Oh, erm, he's into murals right now. He doesn't make any money or anything but. He got made redundant from his job, like. Only a friend of his is trying to get him to go into business, with the murals, like.

Really? Chris says. I'd like to meet him sometime.

Aye, well, all right. You can come round for your dinner sometime.

My dad's an accountant. Dead straight. Boring. Do your parents know you're gay?

Aye, they don't mind, either of them. My mum's a social worker, he says, wondering whether that is relevant. He isn't sure. What about yours? he asks.

Hit the roof to start with. Christ. We never even did anything. Just kissed, that was all. I mean, for fuck's sake.

Just kissed. Fuck's sake. He has actually kissed a guy. A boy. Fucking hell. He hopes he doesn't look too shocked. He tries a smile and then realises he didn't have to try. A little shiver of delight goes up his spine. Maybe they will kiss too. *Just kissed.* The thing is, did he want to do more? He tries to imagine kissing Chris. There is a difference between a peck on the cheek and deep kissing. He doesn't really know but he has an idea the kiss Chris gave this boy (or the boy gave him or the mutual kiss) was more than a peck on the cheek. They couldnae fling you out for a peck on the cheek, surely? Even if it was more than that he doesn't think he'd get flung out at his school. Not unless he did it at school and even then. He could just see his mum up complaining about discrimination. She would, too.

He would like to give Chris a peck on the cheek when they part but he wouldn't have the nerve. Even if they were older and weren't at school he doesn't think he'd have the nerve. Not in broad daylight although you see boys wi lassies doing it all the time outside the school. It's not fair. Then he remembers Chris nearly crying when he first mentioned the school to him. He wonders if he still fancies the boy. If he still loves him even, because that is what he said. Although he said *was*, didn't he, past tense? Anyway, he can tell Chris is interested in him. It takes one to know one.

Probably it is a good idea, this business thing, he thinks on the rest of the way home by himself. He thinks he might try and persuade his dad after all. After all, there's a limit to how many murals you can fill the house up with.

Sheila & Gavin

Gavin has been in a funny mood since she got back from Paris. Restless, dissatisfied. It took her a while to realise it was the painting. Maybe it was the way she responded when she came back.

You never said, that's all Gavin. I mean, if you'd just said you were planning a mural in the hall maybe I would have been psychologically prepared.

You don't exactly have to prepare yourself psychologically when you go to an art gallery, Alan pipes in. So why should you have to prepare yourself to look at my dad's stuff? It's better than your bloody Yves Klein any day.

She laughed then. Aye, bloody Yves Klein, although she was hurt too, by Alan. I mean, he'd hardly spoken to her in over a week, apart from the one brief phone call and this is all he has to say to her. Although she could see she'd hurt Gavin. He was just standing up for his da, she supposed. It made a change anyway.

She had thought, stupidly, Gavin would redecorate the hall. Probably because before, whenever she said anything like that, he always tried to please her, surprise her too sometimes. Only this time he went away and pleased himself and she can hardly complain about that, not really, apart from the fact that it's not finished, looks a long way from finished. The thing is, he has never really gone ahead on a folly of his own like this. Joint follies certainly, like the time they ripped out a wall without realising they needed a building warrant and then had to go and put it back again. She can't really complain. The wall doesn't look awful or anything, just unconventional. And she doesn't really see herself as conventional anyway so what is the problem, for fuck's sake?

The problem is only partly that she's not too sure about this stuff in her – their – hall. The problem is partly that she doesn't want to see him disappointed, get let down and then get depressed about it. Because the asthma is not the only health problem Gavin has had in the course of their marriage. He has been depressed before and depression, at least as much as asthma, affects the whole family. She has heard mutterings from both Gavin and Alan about this hall mural being art. Well, it can be a fine line, right enough, and she is no expert, but Gavin is knocking on forty one, for Christ's sake. If he was that bloody talented you'd think it would have shown by now. Fair enough, so the kitchen mural is fine, great. She is not saying he has no talent – that would be unfair. But it is not just about talent, is it? It is about training, about studying for years and years. And to think he turned Madge's offer down. An offer that meant he had nothing to lose, an offer that may not come again unless she can do something about it.

Listen, she said to him, not the night she returned for she didn't want to spoil things, but the day after, after Alan was away to the school and she had masses of things to do at work but still she took half an hour out to have a talk. Listen, Gavin, I hear what you're saying about art and everything, but you have to see it from my point of view as well. We could do with the money. Christmas is coming and Alan needs things all the time. Trainers and stuff. He could do with a new jacket as well.

He never said anything, he muttered.

Naw, well, he doesn't, not any more, does he? He's getting like you. He likes new stuff as much as the next one but he makes do. I mean, Gavin, if he was grown-up and independent, I would think, well, fair enough, but he isn't, is he? He's still a kid. He needs to have a bit of status with his peers. Besides, I like him looking nice and I know he does too. I don't want him going around looking scruffy.

He feels hurt but he can't even explain it. He thought at the start she was happy about Madge's idea for his sake, nothing to do with the money. More about him taking an interest. As Alan said, he can't forever be doing murals in the house, can he? Not enough wall space. Although he could always do them on boards.

He was all enthusiastic about the mural right up until he saw Sheila's face. You would have thought she'd seen a fucking ghost. Of course he sees now he should have left it covered up until it's finished. The trouble with that though is it's going to take ages. He didn't realise when he started it but it's a process, this painting business. Even when he was doing the one in the kitchen he kept wanting to add to it, and then take away. Until he could see the irritation in Sheila's face, then he just got on with it and finished it. He could do that with this one too but he doesn't want to compromise that far. He loves his wife but his work (and he can call it work, at least to himself even if he doesn't dare call it art) is something separate from his relationship with Sheila, although it is linked as well, just as art cannot be totally separated from life.

161

He understands, of course, about the money side of things. Nobody understands about the money side of things better than him. When you are dependent on the state and your wife for your support, when you cannot go to the shop for a loaf or buy your wife or kid a birthday or Christmas present without knowing that the money is coming from either the wife or the state and that a certain amount of metaphorical cap-doffing is part of your life, then you have the most intimate knowledge of how money affects the inner psyche, how the very thought of it eats away at your soul.

He has been able to keep the psyche protected while he lost himself in the mural but no longer. His medical is next week. He got a letter yesterday morning. More than cap-doffing the medical for the right to take money from the state without slaving day and daily, for the right to do your own thing in the house without the state watching your every move. Except his luck has run out. He took a wander down the Job Centre this afternoon just for a look, telling himself it was only for a look. The doctor could just say, Look, you're obviously unfit to work and away he could go, certified free for another six months, or three anyway. Enough to finish the mural. His cough has even come back, probably the result of the painting again or more likely the result of stress, the thought of the bloody examination, folk watching his every move. Only the moment he spotted the advert it was like an omen. Salesperson at Homebase. Paints department. Knowledge of painting and decorating preferred. Giving advice to customers about products. Blah-blah. Only he never went and did anything about it, but now he will. He doesn't want anybody's charity – not the state's, nor Sheila's and, least of all, Madge's. That was the best of it, that Sheila thought Madge was doing him a favour. No, the best of it is that Madge thought she was doing him a favour as well. Not that either of them said so, not in so many words. Well, they wouldn't, would they? And each thought in terms of different kinds of favours. Like Sheila said, Madge was taking an interest and Madge, to do her justice, genuinely was interested. Except the minute Madge saw the hall mural, no matter that it was obviously incomplete, no matter that you shouldn't pass judgment on something unfinished, Madge said it wasn't what she had in mind. He didnae gie a fuck, he wanted to say, because he wasn't doing it for her. He even wanted to say that to Sheila, his own wife, except that that wasn't entirely true, for practically everything he does is bound up with his relationship with Sheila. And the trouble is he did gie a fuck, he gied a great deal of fucks, as it happens, when Madge

162

turned her snotty wee nose up at his mural in the hall. Not because of the money, not a bit of it. Because, when all's said and done, he agrees wi Alan about the money business. He agrees that making money is not what he is about. Not that that makes him an artist. But at least if he is not an artist he is not a fraudster, he is no trickster or charlatan. At least he is not about flogging people something they don't need. What he is after is some kind of truth. And there is no money in that, The only thing he has lied about — and it is only a white lie, a lie by default — is not telling Sheila that Madge is no longer interested. No that she has said as much but he is not daft, he can tell. Madge was all keen on the fruit and flowers and stuff but this abstracty stuff, she says, is not what she had in mind. As if she was a fucking artist herself. That is the trouble with folk wi money. They think they can buy anything.

Madge

It is all very well wanting to meet her but there is the mechanics of it. Some things private investigators can't help you with. It doesn't matter how much money you have, you still have to use your imagination. The private detective found out where she works which, surprise, surprise, is at Stuart's union. Although she shouldn't keep thinking like that, as if he is still present tense.

The detective also found out Karen was married (well, she had asked him about that, right enough) and also the name of the man she was married to and what he did. Not that she particularly cared about those things. Quite the opposite. It was her she wanted to find out about, couldn't the bugger see that? Did he think women were appendages of their husbands or something? What was he wasting her time and money for? She was about to interrupt him but something in his manner stopped her. She began to see he was prevaricating, prevaricating because he was leading up to something. He was just using the hubbie as a lead-in to more difficulty territory.

Any children? she asks and instantly she knows why. She always was a very intuitive person.

She was right. There's something else, he says, after hesitating a mite too long for someone who is supposed to be professional. No children – erm, as yet. Look, you may not want to hear this, or it may be of no interest to you whatsoever, but she's pregnant.

Oh. Oh, Christ. He wanted to break it to me gently, she thinks, because he is thinking what I am thinking. That the baby might be Stuart's. Oh, Christ.

How pregnant? she asks. It is impossible to appear nonchalant. And why should she care what this guy thinks? He is bound to confidentiality, is only doing his job. They will never meet again. Besides, he will hear worse than this day-in and day-out, no doubt. He does investigations for divorce lawyers, pries into the smutty side of people's lives, the side they would never willingly reveal, but revenge, or greed, can work wonders. Like the investigator, she knows a fair bit about the smutty side of life herself. She has done more than a few social work reports for the courts.

Erm, about five or six months, I would say. I don't know exactly.

I see. I suppose you couldn't find out?

He laughs. Short of asking her outright, no. But I would say five or six months is an intelligent guess.

It is now late November. She is five months herself. Not that noticeable. She is tempted to ask the investigator if he has noticed but decides if he hasn't, she doesn't want him to. He knows enough about her as it is. He already knows, for example, about her late husband's affair (he died in the summer, she told him – there was certainly no need to go into what she now thinks of as the sordid details).

I want to get it out of my system, she told him, right at the beginning. That's all. I might go and see her but I want to find out a bit more about her first. I don't even know if she's single, for example.

Before he goes she remembers one more thing.

The husband, she says. Is he home a lot?

Now you mention it, no. He seems to work away a lot. Look, he hesitates. You won't do anything silly?

She laughs suddenly, realising what he means. You mean, do her an injury? Oh, Christ, no. All I'll do her, if anything, is a favour. Let her know what a bastard Stuart was. That she shouldn't be missing him, if she is.

He gives her an odd look as he leaves. No wonder, this is the first time she mentioned what a bastard Stuart was. Except aren't all men who have affairs bastards? This is the first time too, she realises, that she does not really feel any animosity towards this woman. She had thought she would get a kick out of showing off her pregnancy but not now. The knowledge of this Karen woman's prospective family – its cosiness – only accentuates her loneliness. It will be worse, not better, once the baby comes. Sheila is involved in her job, Gavin is into his painting. But barely a few miles away lives this woman who is in a similar situation to her (more similar than she thinks, maybe), who is having her first baby – very possibly her first baby by the same, dead man.

She thought she would have to tread carefully but she is going to have to act like she is walking on glass. It is bad enough thinking you can just go and have a blether with your man's ex (except she wasn't, she is the one who would have been the ex – but no matter, that's all water under the bridge), but if the woman concerned is as pregnant as she is then that is a different kettle of fish altogether. There is no question of lording it over Karen Daly. With two bumps she will have to watch her step. Sheila thought she was mad wanting to meet the woman anyway. Probably she is. It will only lead to heartbreak, Sheila said. But heartbreak is something she got over long ago and this Karen must be a tough nut herself going and stealing someone else's man. Whatever, she will not be saying any more to Sheila or Gavin. Especially not now. Especially now there is another bump to contend with.

Know what day this is? Chris goes, after the tennis.

St. Andrew's day.

Nup. Yeah, well, I know it's St. Andrew's day but what else?

He tries to think but can't. There aren't even any tennis champion-ships on now, are there, so it can't be that?

This is the day it becomes legal for sixteen year olds to have gay sex.

You're kidding?

Why would I be kidding about a thing like that? Anyway, my mum's a lawyer. She knows her stuff.

Really?

That means, one year, four months and, let's see, erm, three days from now I'll be able to have legal sex with another boy. Provided we do it in private, of course. When's your birthday?

May fifth.

Let's see, so you'll have to wait one year......

Five months and five days, Alan finishes for him.

Well, maybe I'll wait that long too, Chris says, without looking at him.

He does not know what Chris means. He does not even know what the law defines as sex. Is it just sex (as in wanking, sucking, even penetration, all that stuff) or does it include kissing because they've done that already? At Chris's house mostly, although last time they did it in his bedroom, when his mum and dad were out. They don't take their clothes off or anything like that but. It was a bit awkward but maybe it will be better next time. It wasn't a long kiss, like you see in the films but it wasn't the peck on the cheek your mother gives you either. On the mouth. Longer than a peck but still closer to it compared with the ones in the films. He has seen his mum and dad kiss like that, although usually when they think no-one can see them. An inbetween kiss. Although maybe they do longer ones (like in the films) when they are absolutely certain no-one can see them, like when they are in bed together, before they have sex. He knows they still have sex because the bed squeaks sometimes. Also because they are not really that old. He reckons they are the sort to make time for it. Not much time though because the two of them are busy people. His dad has started going to these meetings and stuff. Community politics, he calls it. And his mum works into the evening many's the time. They might be broke, but they are still bloody busy.

His dad is out working at the moment. He was at Homebase for a bit but had to give it up because he was coughing so much. Then he got talking to this guy about his painting. The guy said if he was interested there was this job going in this community centre. Pollok, he thinks, or Priesthill. They were looking for somebody to do murals. Voluntary, like.

Voluntary. I don't see why they can't pay you, his mum said. I don't see how the council's that hard up.

I think I'd enjoy it, but, his dad says and she says, Well, I suppose if it's what you want.

Thing is, his dad says, there might be a job eventually, like.

Did he say something? Or was it just a hint?

His dad hesitates. I think it was just a hint. I mean, I think they've applied for funding, like, but I don't know if they've got it.

The usual, his mum says. Just watch you're not being exploited.

Years ago his mum used to do voluntary work. She enjoyed it to start with but then she started moaning about being exploited. That was when she decided to go and do the degree. He doesn't really remember. It's just that his mum still talks about they times. She still moans about people being exploited as well but these days it's usually someone else.

Want to come up? he asks Chris as they reach the place where he usually catches his bus.

Not today. I've got a music lesson. Missed it last week. Mum'll kill me if I miss it again.

Right. So they were kissing in his bedroom when Chris was supposed to be having his piano lesson. Maybe Chris doesn't like his piano lesson that much anyway or maybe he does like it only he likes kissing him better. Still, he wouldn't want to get on the wrong side of Chris's mum and dad, not if they're as straight as he makes out.

When someone calls across the street to him, Hey, you, ya fucking poof and he automatically turns round he realises he has practically given himself away. The boy wasnae even looking at him, he was apparently looking at someone else only he's looking at him now. And he's not on his own, either. There's a wee group of them. He breaks into a sweat as he increases his pace without actually running, without giving the game away altogether.

He is no rush, he decides, for the year and five months and five days to pass. It is all very well for politicians to go and pass laws allowing gay sex for sixteen year olds, but people like him still have to contend with folk at school and that. It turns out the law isn't even in force yet – won't be until the New Year. Not that it'll make any difference to him although Chris says it should help change people's attitudes. He's still not sure about his mum and dad's attitude, never mind Chris's mum or dad's. He has never met them. Even if Chris's mum and dad were OK there are millions of other people who wouldn't be. Plus Chris lives in a posh house in Newlands, even fancier than Madge's place. His folk don't even know who the neighbours are, the houses are that far apart. If word got round that he was gay he can just imagine the looks auld Mr Kennedy doon the stair would give him. No just looks either. Although auld Mr Kennedy, the state o him, couldnae dae you any harm himself he'd have it roon the close, roon the block if he had his way. And then the big yins frae the schemes that go to the same school'd be after him. Waiting for him after the school got oot. They'd hammer him on the way home. It's all very well for folk like Chris who can get the bus frae the school if he wants. He could get the bus too but they'd know where he lives, wouldn't they? Although they could find out where Chris lives too.

He is suddenly fearful for Chris, not just himself. Chris comes from Edinburgh and so is a bit of a softie, a bit ignorant about the ways of some Glasgow folk that would stick the heid on ye as soon as look at ye. He'll not appreciate what an awful risk the two of them are taking, just walking hame frae the school. He cannae wait till the morning. He'll have to phone him the night. Only he'll be away at his piano lesson. Still, maybe he could catch him on his mobile.

Only it's switched off. Right enough. The answering machine comes on but. Christ but, he is not even sure if these things are secure. It goes through to a telephone exchange or something, doesn't it? Still, Chris can read between the lines.

It's me, Alan. I just wanted to warn ye about walking home from school yourself. Just watch yourself and don't say anything if people call you names or that. You're best to just ignore them. Hey, fancy giving us a ring back later?

He hopes the message doesn't sound too stupid. He doesn't usually leave messages on answering machines. Talking to a machine makes him feel like a fucking robot.

His mum and dad are both back long ago and they have had their tea. This is the first time in his life he has waited for the phone to ring.

He could phone Chris back but he feels stupid. What if Chris asks what he's fussing about? He could mention it to his da about the boys in the street but so what? They weren't even calling to him. His da couldn't cope, he'd have to go and speak to his mum and his mum would start making a fuss when it is not the sort of thing to make a fuss about. It is not even against the law, calling someone a poof. It's just verbal abuse (although Chris says his mum says, in theory it could amount to a breach of the peace but that is only in theory. Nae doubt lawyers get carried away with their theories whereas folk like him have to live in the real world, for Christ's sake.) If they don't do anything about racist remarks (not violence now – that is something else) even though incitement to racial hatred is a crime why would they do anything about somebody calling you a poof? If he'd been threatened maybe he would mention it to them. Definitely if he'd been attacked although, fuck's sake, he doesn't want it to get that far. Fuck's sake. No way.

About an hour later the phone rings. He can't get near it for his dad who is back at his mural again.

It's Chris, his dad tells him.

Have people been shouting at you or what?

Not exactly. He tells him what happened. I thought it was me but then I felt so stupid. See the worst bit was them looking and me realising they never meant me at all but because I looked, see, that gave the game away.

I see what you mean, Chris says. Do you think they might recognise you again?

I dunno. I hope not.

Better tell your parents just in case.

Aw, I don't think that's really necessary.

I think you should. Why do you think I moved to Glasgow? Because of the wagging tongues, that's why. I could've gone to a different school in Edinburgh because mum works there, after all. I didn't want to come to Glasgow. There are queer bashers everywhere, I told them. If anything Glasgow's probably worse. That's not the point, dad said. The point is nobody knows in Glasgow. Let's keep it that way. He'd be mad if he thought I even told you.

Why, have you told anyone else?

No, of course not.

Good.

Alan.

Yup?

170

I'm still glad I came to Glasgow.

Are you?

Because I met you.

Me too. I'd better go. He knows his dad is hovering in the background. Wanting to get back to his mural no doubt.

Just remember what I told you about your parents. Night night.

Night night.

His heart is still pounding. Thump thump thump. It's a wonder his dad cannae hear it. *Because I met you.* Fuck, fuck. He's glad he came to Glasgow because of *him*. Fuck, fuck, double fuck. Only he is fucking petrified. In case, Chris said. He should've asked him, in case of what? What the fuck could mum and dad do anyway? His mum is not a lawyer. She can't go getting interdicts and stuff like Chris's mum can. Plus lawyers can do what they like. His mum has to watch where she goes, she says, in case folk recognise her. It's OK for her to go in the town and stuff but she wouldn't want to go walking about Pollok even during the day because there are some folk who think it's her fault they've had their weans taken off them even though it's not her but the sheriff who decides. His mum understands people's problems – she wouldn't go taking people's weans off them even if she could, not unless they couldn't look after them, although there's plenty that can't, she says. Plenty that should never've had them. He's heard her and Madge say so many's the time.

Maybe that's why his mum was so funny when he first told her about being gay, why she wasn't immediately OK, the way his dad was. Because even though she is a woman and was never brought up in a scheme the way his dad was she goes to work in schemes five days a week. Whereas his dad, well, his dad goes to work in a wee world of his imagination. His dad and his art are one thing but real life is quite another. It's like the two extremes, in a way. If he tells his mum about the poof-callers she'll overreact, get all paranoid thinking he's going to get knifed or something whereas if he tells his dad he won't know what to do. He'll be thinking folk like that should go to art therapy or something.

Sheila

She is driving home from work, sitting in traffic. It is the one time of day she has time to think. Although she has been worrying about Alan all day. There is no specific reason for her anxiety, just a vague feeling. She knows something is up but she knows better than to quiz teenagers about their business. She has talked to him about the dangers of unprotected sex and about Aids (or tried to – it was a very one-sided affair, her doing all the talking and him pretending he knew it all already when that is not what it is about, not at all). When he came out with his announcement when they were away on holiday she knew she hadn't done enough just giving him books he was too old for anyway and that didn't recognise the existence of gays. She tried to talk Gavin into speaking to him but Gavin wouldn't do it any better than her. It wasn't so much a matter of wouldn't, it was down to his capabilities, or limitations more like. Men. As Madge says (and who can blame her?) they are not exactly the world's best communicators. It's all subterfuge and countersubterfuge.

Although Madge has been something of a dark horse herself lately. Since Paris she has kept her mouth shut about the mysterious woman in the woodwork. If she didn't know Madge better she'd think she'd decided to forget about her after all. Only Madge is not the type to let bygones be bygones. Not that she would be seeking revenge, for there is no evil in her. Only Madge was always the obsessive type.

The one thing she gets satisfaction out of these days is her job. If it wasn't for her job she doesn't know where she'd be. A steady job with all its challenges and a wee bit of status keeps things in perspective. If ever she has a tendency to look at life with rose-tinted spectacles the job keeps her on course. The job helps her realise her own personal parameters. Whereas Gavin now, Gavin has definitely been day-dreaming since he came back from Nice. All this about being an artist and stuff, all pie-in-the-sky. Not that she would tell him in so many words because folk need their dreams. The folk in the worst parts of some of the worst schemes still need their dreams. Probably they need them more than the rest of us, although, paradoxically, if they spend their lives day-dreaming it is going to be that much harder to rise up out of the mire, is it not? To confront your own personal hell head-on? The fact of Gavin's impoverished background is doubtless one factor in his current attitude as well as his general lack of ambition and, paradoxically, his wild ideas. There is a lack of balance there. Christ knows where he would be without her. Not that she wants to leave him. He is a good, domesticated husband. Cleans the house and makes the dinner every weekday night (usually) although now he is doing this voluntary work there's many's the time he works well into the evening. He's out more evenings than she is these days. And there is still that unfinished Nice mural. He is calling it the Nice mural, for the time being, he says, although when it is finished he hopes he has thought of a more distinctive title. Although it is difficult to think of a title when he is not all that sure what it is really about.

She finds that peculiar, not knowing what something is really about until it is finished. If she was that uncertain in her job people would starve to death. Artists have a privilege in that regard. No-one (apart from themselves, possibly) is going to suffer if they don't finish what they do. Not that she is a Philistine, that she thinks art is not an important part of life but it is not as important as some things, surely? The way Gavin goes on you would think what he does at the community centre is as important as buying your family Christmas presents. Or even putting food into people's stomachs.

She has already been on at him to finish the mural.

The thing is, Sheila, he said, it keeps changing.

You mean, you keep changing your mind?

He shook his head, Not even that, although I keep getting new ideas about it. But the actual place, even. I mean, it was on the news, all these riots over the Summit and everything. I don't even know what it's all about. I feel, like, I have to learn more before I can develop that side of it. I mean, I want to develop the darker side of it.

She gave up. Sometimes Gavin can be really weird. The darker side. For fuck's sake. She can't blame Madge for dropping out of the business idea with him although apparently she is now looking for another business partner. Organic foods or something. A bit different from the murals business. Madge is as bad as Gavin, doesn't know what she wants. Although she hasn't the heart to tell Gavin (assuming Gavin doesn't know already – she can't be sure).

When she gets to the door the feeling of anxiety that has been niggling at her all day resurfaces. Only now it is more than a feeling, this time it has some factual basis. There is no sound coming from the house whereas Alan usually has the stereo on doing his homework. Only the door is unlocked and the lights are all blazing and Alan would

173

never leave the house with the lights blazing never mind the door unlocked.

A low moaning noise suddenly catches her attention. Someone is in the bathroom. She stops dead, suddenly petrified there is a burglar in the flat. Then the sound is recognisably Alan. Alan crying. She pushes open the door and finds him hunched over the sink. His face is bruised and bleeding.

What's happened? Jesus, Alan. She goes to cradle his poor, sore head but he pushes her away.

Don't touch it. It's fucking aching. He starts the moaning-crying noise again.

She has a closer look. One side of his head, just above his ear, is all matted with blood.

Jesus, you might have concussion or something. Come on, I'm, taking you to Casualty. You can tell me on the way about what happened.

He doesn't argue. She scribbles a note for Gavin, telling him Alan has hurt himself and they are away to Casualty at the Royal and will phone later.

So, are you going to tell me? she asks when they are in the car and she has started driving.

I got beat up. What d'you think?

Do you know the boys?

He shakes his head.

Why, then?

What d'you mean, why? How the fuck should I know? How the fuck do I know how these fucking wankers' minds work?

I know, I know, son. She wishes she was not driving. She wants to cuddle him. The last thing he needs is interrogating. It's just the hospital staff will ask you. They have to. It's their job, that's all.

Will we have to go to the police?

Yeah, but not right away. Don't worry about it. Don't worry about anything right now.

She waits in the corridor for what seems like forever for Gavin is still not at home. Flicking through the wee address book she keeps in her bag she realises, stupidly, she does not have the number of the community centre where he works. She is not even sure of the address and she would need that to phone Directory Enquiries, wouldn't she? She doesn't even know what they call the place. It is just the Centre as far as Gavin is concerned. She knows the scheme where it is situated but that is hardly enough. She phones home again and still he is not there. She leaves another message on the answering machine, telling him again she will phone back later. She tries to console herself with the thought that at least Alan is not in any danger, is he? Although they seem to be taking a while. X-rays and all that, she supposes. They will be having to reassure themselves it is not a case of child abuse, too, she suddenly realises. She should have thought of that before, in the kind of work she does. It happens all the time, after all, doesn't it? Although the main culprits are the parents of babies and toddlers there are some parents of older kids, teenagers, too, at the end of their rag, who strike out and even cause broken bones. Even then the kids often try and cover up, think of social work, if not the medical profession, as the real enemy. As alienated as their abusive parents. She suddenly feels pretty alienated herself. She hasn't had a thing to eat or drink since lunchtime, only it won't do to go mentioning that to the young doctor who doubtless works long hours on an empty stomach herself, God help her.

How is he?

I want to keep him in overnight for observation. He appears to have mild concussion although we hope it's not serious.

Can I see him?

Yes, yes, of course.

Only there was some hesitation there, she could swear. She distrusts her. Damn, for all she knows she thinks she beat him up. Or his dad did. Christ, why can't she just be straight with the woman? Why can't she talk about her son like a normal human being? Why should it be a big deal her telling the young doctor here her son is gay? So what if it is up to Alan to say himself? He is still a kid, after all, he cannot always be expected to act in his own best interests.

But it is too late. She can hardly start telling her now, right in the middle of the corridor. In her hurry to keep up with the quick-footed young doctor she almost collides headlong with Gavin who is also walking too fast and who appears to have a young man with him. Someone she has surely seen before?

Chris, Alan's friend, he introduces himself now and the young doctor practically glares at him.

You'll have to wait outside.

Please, Chris says and it is then she realises he has been crying, still is crying.

175

He was worried this might happen, he says. His voice is full of anguish. We both were. It's one thing for people to call you a poof but then it just escalates and before you know where you are they want to kill you.

The doctor looks, if not exactly relieved, as though a puzzle has been resolved. At least she is no longer under suspicion.

Just five minutes, then, the doctor says, smiling.

As the three of them enter the ward it is Chris that Alan turns to. His wee face is all aglow. So this is gay love, she thinks, even before Chris leans forward and kisses him lightly on the cheek that isn't bruised.

Gavin

He has been neglecting his son. For months now, ever since they came back from holiday, all he has been thinking about is himself. Him and his stupid plans. Work of art my fucking arse. All he has ever wanted is here and now, in this city, in this flat. His family is all there ever was to him. Career has never been on the agenda, not till he went away to France and got these big ideas. Sheila has got her head screwed on all right. You cannae work as a social worker without having your head screwed on right enough, for there are plenty of folk in this city who'd screw it off for you. The night Alan landed in the hospital he came straight back to the flat, after they took the boy Chris home, he took out the deep blue emulsion and just painted over the stupid fumblings in the hall he actually had the nerve to think were artistic. He'd already made up his mind at some point on the journey home. A clean sweep, he thought of it as.

Gavin, don't, Sheila said to him but he carried on until it was covered. You could see bits underneath, evidence that something had been there, shadows, but he'd sort it out the next day when it had dried. He wasn't daft enough to try and do two coats before the first one was dry.

All your work, Sheila mumbled but he didn't believe her. No-one but him thought it was any good anyway. No-one understood it. Not Sheila or Alan or young Chris who'd stared at it for ages once. Not Madge who once believed the two of them could make money out of murals (or she could make money out of him, at any rate). Not the guys at the community centre who at least were into art for art's sake, art as a representation of culture, especially Glasgow's culture, of socialism, of poverty, of... of... let's face it, he didn't know exactly what of, because none of us shares an identical view of any of those things, least of all of art.

Why Nice? one guy had says.

Why no? he says back. He was miffed because he felt the guy didn't mean, Why Nice? What he meant was, Why not Glasgow? Why French instead of Scottish?

Other people just try and tell you what to do, what to be. It is no different from when he was a wean. Only the façade is different. He might as well go back to Homebase and sell what people want, or what marketing people make them think they want. He cannot, in the end, compete with good old Paradise Blue vinyl matt emulsion. No-one is going to come and make snidy remarks about the Paradise Blue vinyl matt emulsion. They will not argue about whether it is fucking paradise or not, or at least if they do he will not feel like they are diminishing him as a person. He is too fucking sensitive, always has been. He is too fucking sensitive and too fucking selfish. Alan getting beaten up has taught him a lesson he'll never forget. Christ, the boy could've been fucking murdered.

It's not your fault, dad, Alan says when he came back from the hospital. It's not your fault and it's not mum's fault. The tears were rolling down his cheeks but his son's eyes were dry. It was like he had grown up overnight.

Even the polis were dead nice. In his day the polis thought weans were a nuisance. Even weans beating wan another up but never really merited a charge, no unless it was the next best thing to murder anyway. The polis would gie the weans a good hiding theirselves. No the day but. Weans the day have got rights. The United Nations Convention, the European Convention, the Human Rights Act, all that.

Incredibly, they have got the boys that did it. They are no even getting bail because they were on bail when they did it. Can you believe the luck? he says to Sheila although luck sounds a funny word for it but no if you ever kent anything about the courts in Glasgow. Folk wi good lawyers getting off all the time. Folk afraid to speak out. Well, that could still happen but, as the polis officer explained, corroboration doesnae have to be another witness. These days they can get the DNA off the blood and there's other forensic stuff they can do. No need to let scumbags off scot free.

He actually said scumbags. Meaning not his son who is allowed to be gay (provided he doesnae do anything about it, apart frae the odd wee kiss, till he is sixteen) but the wee shites that beat him up. Wee shites who dinnae ken any better and probably get the same treatment frae their das, no that that is any excuse.

I suppose it'll be all over the papers, once it goes to trial, he says a couple of days later.

Not for under sixteens. He turns at the voice. It is Chris, who has come straight from school to see Alan.

Oh, aye, right. It is like his mind is on go-slow. He is not thinking straight. He is already regretting painting over the mural if only

178

because everybody's been onto him. What did you do that for? All that work you put into it. All that sort of thing. Trying to console him. It only made him feel embarrassed, being the subject of attention when Alan was the one needed attention.

Only just this morning Alan says to him, It's OK, dad. I'm going back to school next week. You go back to work too.

Aye, maybe, he says. Only he is not going to go doing all the hours God sends. Not for the community centre and not for himself either. Although if he needs to keep his hands occupied maybe he could start doing another mural. It was what Sheila had says to him this morning.

Look, Gavin, she says, you could always start over again. Maybe you'll see it more clearly this time.

When he shook his head she says, I liked it better than this – this sea of blue, you know. I'd have liked it better if it was finished but I was too impatient. I promise I'll be more patient the next time. And she gives him a peck on the cheek.

Sheila always brings everything together just when he feels it is all falling apart. It was Sheila phoned the school and arranged to see the headteacher. Arranged for the both of them to come to the school.

He thought he couldn't cope with speaking to a headteacher, unless it was something straightforward, but you don't go and see the head for straightforward things, do you? When he was a wean all you went to the head for was to get the belt.

Aye, times have changed right enough. Although it was Sheila who did all the talking, or nearly all.

Probably we should have told you before, he's gay. I wasn't sure it was important enough but this – this assault has changed my mind. Kids need protection. They need freedom from fear.

Yes, of course, the head says. Yes, absolutely. Erm, although we don't yet know whether the boys have anything to do with the school.

Surely that's not really the point? There's plenty of homophobia around everywhere. I don't think there's any doubt it'll be present in this school the same as anywhere else.

Erm, yes, erm. Well, we don't know that for sure.

For a moment Sheila looks disgusted. Mr McMenemy, she says patiently. I am a social worker. I meet a wide range of people in my job. I know Glasgow although I'm not saying it's worse than anywhere else. People are prejudiced, Mr McMenemy. Prejudice is the thin end of the wedge. Not everyone will go out and beat up a person because he is gay but there are plenty who think nothing of name-calling. Do you not

179

have a policy, Mr McMenemy, to stop that sort of thing? I mean, Mr McMenemy, I know there's an anti-racist policy in the school. We don't tolerate children being the target of racist abuse so why should we tolerate homophobia?

I wasn't aware he had been subjected to, erm, verbal abuse, prior to this incident.

Well, he has. Although it's true he only told me after he was attacked. A few days before the attack he heard these boys calling poof across the road and he wasn't sure if they meant him.

Boys from the school?

I don't know. But surely the point is that he's afraid to be open about his sexuality because he anticipates this sort of abuse?

Yes, yes, quite. I'm afraid we don't have a policy but it's certainly something we should look into.

That was about as far as it got.

You were brilliant, he says to Sheila afterwards.

Thanks, she says. Only I can't see it getting that far.

Maybe we should write to the MP, he says.

That's a great idea. At least, the MSP. That would be more appropriate, since it's an education issue.

Aye, he says. It is years since he wrote a letter to his MP. The time of the Miners' strike, probably. Got him asking questions in parliament about the benefits they werenae getting, the poverty, the way the polis were treating them.

They wrote it together, that very night. The first time in ages they have done something as intellectual as all that together. Because it took a good deal of thinking too. Although it was also a practical exercise.

You were always the contemplative one, Sheila says to him afterwards.

Aye, but you've always had more get-up-and-go, he says back. They laugh. Their first laugh together since It happened.

This time it was Sheila gave him the confidence to act. Although hasn't it always been Sheila? Setting the good example. Lately, till what happened to Alan happened, it has been Painting, Painting, Painting. But, before Painting, there was Life — once upon a time. Although no life that was really worth much before Sheila. Sheila is the only woman there has ever been in his life. No just sexually or as a love relationship. Sheila is the best friend he's ever had. Even his mother he was not really close to. His mother was always too downtrodden.

But he cannae depend on Sheila all his days. He senses that Sheila resents his dependence on her and he cannae blame her. A few days away from the painting and he was losing all his confidence but maybe he doesn't need to give it up altogether. There is such a thing as compromise.

Sheila and Alan and Chris and Madge are all right enough about the painting. He needs the interest or whatever it is. He is no good to anybody without it. He is going to start the day Alan goes back to the school. Part of the skill of being a painter (if not exactly an artist) is about being able to do more than one thing at a time and yet separate out different areas. It is about distinguishing. He can do two things at once. So far all he has done at the community centre is a still life. Fruit and flowers for the café area. He finished it the night Alan got attacked, before he knew. He enjoyed the work, expanded upon what he'd done at home only he had more freedom at the community centre, he could do it as big as he liked. It was brilliant being able to do these huge oranges and apples and then sunflowers.

Why sunflowers? one guy says to him.

Why no? he says back because he was busy and wanted to get on with the job but he knew why. Symbolic. Bringing a bit of joy and happiness. He was right too. He was just about halfway through the sunflowers when this kid comes in after school and just gawps.

Jesus, they're brilliant. They look real, he goes.

How can they be real? his mate says. They're gigantic, for fuck's sake.

They still look real, the wee lad insisted and he turned round and smiled at the kid then. The kid smiled back but the other boy just shrugged. You're daft, he says. He wondered if the boy meant he was daft as well, painting a thing like that.

He was pleased to be able to go back to the still life in a way, because he wasn't sure if he could do it again. He did it better the second time round. Only he wants to try something completely different. He was talking to one of the guys at the centre the other day about Glasgow and its history and stuff. The socialism and everything. Red Clydesiders, all that. Only he doesn't want to be partisan. It is not that he is not a socialist – of course he is – but there are different kinds. Whatever he does has to have some personal meaning for him, though people will doubtless make their own interpretations, as they always do. There will be no money in it which makes it easier in a way because then folk will not be able to dictate, or at least not as much (because folk will always dictate, come what may, especially some political types, the ones who think they are God's gift and all that).

The only thing is he will have to plan this one better. He can do that at home, while he is starting on another mural. Although, on second thoughts, he will have to plan this one too. No more dabbing at the wall, seeking inspiration while wielding the paintbrush. Although probably he will still do that. But he needs to have a wee bit more of a clue too before he starts. Maybe what he could do is buy some hardboard from the DIY store. He can get it when Sheila comes home for it will be too heavy to carry. If he paints the mural onto hardboard first he will always be able to move it. That would be an idea. He could do the same at the community centre. And he will look up books. Not just art books, but books about Glasgow. About what it represents to different people. The Clyde, the ships is maybe a bit obvious but it will not all be obvious or easy for everybody. Because this will be something not just for him but for Glasgow people who are as different as chalk and cheese, when it comes down to it, although they all share the same skyline. Even if it is mainly for himself, your ordinary person in the street should be able to understand it, or at least some of it. He does not want people to come up and raise their arms in the air in exasperation. Their eyebrows maybe and they can slag it all they like. But he wants to make them think. He wants to see a glimmer of recognition there.

She is sitting in the queue in the maternity department at the Western General. She is as keen (keen – Christ, that doesn't sound right but what is she if she isn't keen?), aye, well, as happy, then, as she ever has been to have this baby that jogs about inside her like billy-o the whole long day, but that doesn't mean she enjoys waiting in a queue. Apart from the magazines to read, and that she gets to sit rather than stand (well, they could hardly make you stand at thirty weeks now, could they?) it is no different, really, from queuing up at the supermarket. Except that it is bloody worse because the wait is longer. Except for the Christmas rush. God, imagine comparing the maternity wing with the Christmas rush. Except probably it was a wee bit like that this time last year what with all the millennium babies. Or was that just a bit of a myth? She can hardly remember that far back. It is like half a lifetime has happened since then.

It is all for the best, she tells herself, has been telling herself for months now. The baby (of course) is all for the best. The fact that Stuart is not here is all for the best (she prefers to think of him as not here when she thinks that – it is not quite the same as being glad he is dead, after all, even if she is. Well, if she wasn't so well-off she mightn't be so glad but she is, isn't she? She couldn't not be when she is four hundred grand the richer, not counting the mortgage getting paid off and all).

The richer. It makes her think of her marriage vows. For richer, for poorer. Except the better-off they became the more her and Stuart got alienated from one another. Now if she could've had the old Stuart back, the one she fell in love with, that would be a different story. After all, she has not changed really, has she? She is basically the same person Stuart married.

She looks around her. Some of the mothers-to-be are just young lassies, barely out the school. The rest in their twenties and thirties. She must be the oldest of the bunch. They made quite a big deal out of it at the ante-natal clinic to begin with, but not now. It is not that rare a thing after all, having a baby at forty two, although there is more of a health risk, so she is definitely having it in the hospital.

The main thing is not your age, one doctor said to her – a young Asian woman. It is your present state of health. Healthy older women should have fewer complications than unhealthy younger ones. You don't smoke, do you?

They have been quite sympathetic, the hospital staff. The whole lot of them, for she usually sees different folk every time she goes. Especially sympathetic because she is a widow. At the first appointment she explained her husband had died in an accident on holiday, not long after the baby was conceived.

Aye, she's had plenty of sympathy. She is up to her ears in sympathy. The trouble with the sympathy business is that you cannot always tell how sincere it is. It makes her harden her heart, so it does, when she is not a hard sort of person. Not with the hospital folk for they were just doing their professional duty which was fair enough. She's been in the sympathy business long enough herself. Only at work there are a number of possible explanations:

A. Folk are genuinely sympathetic because she has lost her man. Sympathetic both in the sense that they pity her (and here she is not proud for maybe a wee bit pity has its place — better other folk pitying ye than feeling sorry for yourself) and/or in the sense that it could have been one o them i.e. you never know when your man's goinae go and get munched up by a bloody great man o' war that just happened to get into a sea it shouldn't have been anywhere near. Oh, aye, it could happen to anybody so it could.

B. Now, what was B? Oh, aye, B, is that her colleagues are merely extending their professional attitude to their colleague in her hour of need. That, regardless of appearances and nasty rumours about the deceased having it off with his assistant (well, rumours being rumours, or rather rumours of rumours and what is the difference anyway?) that Madge, despite her new-found wealth and what for anybody else would be a stroke of unbelieveable bloody luck, is entitled to the professional shoulder to cry on, is quite as deserving of professional sympathy as any of her clients whose men are in the jail at Christmas (right enough, some o them are maybe better off with their men in jail at Christmas, or Hogmanay). Women who have been battered to fuck countless times in the past and will doubtless carry on getting battered to fuck for the forseeable future, women whose weans have been taken off them, women who are up to high dough wi half the loan sharks in Glasgow. Oh, aye, sure, compared wi them their colleague Madge who is rolling in it and is free of that dirty old fucker for good and always, nae fucking strings attached is indeed deserving of professional sympathy. My arse.

C. Well, C is that maybe the buggers really are sympathetic not because she has lost her man (her man being no great loss to anybody, after all – quite the reverse) but because, well, because of all the talk. It seems half the social work department knew Stuart screwed around (when she didn't – although fuck knows how she could've been so bloody naive).

If she could take her pick she'd go for option A but it not being in her power to choose she senses, deep in her heart, the best she can bloody well expect is option B. Only that is no exactly bloody likely either. Option C is definitely the most likely explanation.

Two bloody hours.

Terribly long wait, the woman beside her goes. Well-dressed middle-class type. Safe to talk to. She was a wee bit scared, to tell the truth, to go talking to folk in case she discovered afterwards they were clients. Even if they weren't clients now they could come marching into the office next week. Sometimes folk got it wrong, thinking because the DSS gave them fuck all they could just go down the social work and they'd sort it out. They thought it was what you do when you have a baby. Making an appointment wi the social work is as essential for some folk as rich people getting their kids' names down for private school or financial planning when they are still in the womb. The folk the government like to call socially excluded (when they aren't fraudsters or scroungers) are just as likely to make provision for their weans only of a different order. Or maybe they just wanted to take it out on someone. Unwanted baby, boyfriend who'd fucked off at the nearest opportunity, parents up to high dough wi their weans' exploits, sometimes another baby on the way there too. She has seen it all. It puts her off meeting people except in the most circumscribed of circumstances. But this woman here. Smartly dressed – Next gear, Debenhams, Frasers, the like – now she's no going to turn up as a client the morrow (she is no in the morrow for she is on maternity leave but what about when she returns to work since the self-employment plan has got nowhere yet?)

Yeah, she turns and smiles. So have you got long to go?

I'm thirty weeks. I'm due at the end of March.

I'm the first of April. Isn't it awful?

Maybe I'll see you in the ward then.

They both laugh. Two comfortable middle class women who have nothing to fear (do they?) from an impending birth. Only this woman is only thirtyish.

185

Is it your first?

The woman nods. I've bought masses of books and everything but it's still a great mystery really.

I know, Madge nods. It's my first as well. She nearly tells the woman they were trying for years. Fucking decades, practically. Once she was open with strangers, even with intimate information like that but something stops her.

Do you go to the classes? the woman asks her.

I'm going to start. I've just started maternity leave, she explains. Do you go yourself?

Yes, although I also go to the NCT ones. I'm trying to make up my mind but they're both good really.

Exercises and all that?

Oh, yes. It's really good, they say, for when you go into labour. Good preparation.

I suppose they like the dads to come too?

Well, it's not compulsory. The woman is hesitant. It's a matter of personal choice, I suppose.

Not in my case, Madge shakes her head. My husband died last summer. An accident.

How awful. I'm so sorry.

It's OK. I'm coping.

She is lying. She is doing better than that but she can hardly turn round and tell this total stranger what a bastard he was and how she is better off in more ways than one without him.

I'm separated myself, the woman says.

She is shocked. I'm sorry, she says, although it sounds inadequate, possibly inappropriate. Are you supposed to offer your condolences when someone is separated? She might have thrown him out, of course.

Oh, don't worry about me, the woman says. I've got a good job. I'm coping as well.

What is it you do?

I work for a trade union. Management. I can get up to nine months maternity leave, half of it paid. She laughs now. Good pay and conditions. What do you do yourself?

I'm a social worker.

For a moment she thinks the woman is about to introduce herself. Then she doesn't need to. The receptionist is calling out, Karen Daly.

The woman gets up. That's me. See you again, maybe.

Right, aye, bye. She is still working out the implications even as she speaks. Works for a trade union. She wishes she asked which one but maybe she didn't really want to know. For months and months she wanted to know about Stuart's affair (horrible, horrible word but not as bad as mistress, surely?) but slowly, gradually, the desire to know dwindled. All for the best. She kept hearing her mother's words. All for the best. What you don't know doesn't do you any harm. Only now she does want to know. She knows too much already not to know any more. Karen Daly is not just pregnant but she has separated from her man. There could be a million and one reasons why, but it is as likely (or more likely) to be because of Him. The affair. She doesn't care. She doesn't care one way or the other whether Karen Daly and her man have split up because revenge is not in her. A relief in a way because she couldn't be certain, could she, until she met this woman in the flesh? Not revenge then but what was a curiosity that was all but gone is now firing up again. She will fucking explode if she doesn't find out whether Karen is having Stuart's baby, or her husband's.

After the appointment she goes straight round to Sheila and Gavin's.

Look, Madge, you'll have to calm down, Sheila says to her. The thing is, Madge, no matter what she tells you, you'll never know whether she's lying or not.

She shouldn't have gone, right enough, they've have had enough on their plate lately what with all that bother with young Alan. Only there was no-one else she could turn to. Jesus, did they all know at work too? If they knew so much they must know about Karen and so they must know she's pregnant. You don't need a degree to put two and two together. The thing is, is Sheila trying to put her off because she has an idea herself (has she even heard something?) Is it bleeding obvious or what? Is she just too stupid to see what's right in front of her nose?

There's no sense torturing yourself, Madge, Gavin says.

But maybe all she has to do is ask. Not straightaway. Get to know her first, Maybe she could find out what supermarket she shops in. The investigator guy could do that for her, at least. See where else she goes. And the NCT class. She doesn't even need an investigator to do that for her. She can find out about that herself.

There is another way she can find out, she realises, on her way home in the car. She does not even have to ask. The woman – Karen – will have the choice about whether to put her husband's name on the child's birth certificate or to leave it blank (but not, like her, to include the name of a dead father, since he wasn't her husband). She could still be lying even if she does put down her husband as the father. For that

187

matter the two of them could be back together by the time the baby is born and the husband even could be the one to go down and register the child's birth. Although, considering Karen's attitude, she somehow does not think that is very likely.

Already she is plotting. She cannot wait forever for this important information. It would be a little odd to go down and ask for a copy of the child's birth certificate too soon after the birth. She has no wish to pretend she is Karen – that would be going too far. And yet the other scenario that is dawning on her could end up getting her the sack. What she could do, once she is back at work (or Sheila could do it for her, except she doesn't know if she has the nerve to ask Sheila, and would Sheila really do it?) is to write to the registrar and request a copy of the child's birth certificate. Social work departments have an obviously legitimate reason for doing that sort of thing. No questions asked. Unless by some awful coincidence Karen happened to know the folk there.

She cannae do it. She is just being stupid. She will just have to go and ask the woman. Anybody can lie on a child's birth certificate. They do it to protect the child. She cannae blame them. She would probably do it herself. At least if she asks the woman – Karen – face to face, straight out, even if she doesn't get a straight answer (and she doesn't really expect one, does she?) then you can tell a lot by the expression on a person's face. Faces give people away. Especially if she takes her unawares and just comes out with it. Which means Karen mustnae suspect a thing.

Only maybe she suspects already. She has every reason to, now she knows her man died in an accident in the summer. She knows she is a social worker. She'll maybe have put two and two together.

But Karen doesn't know her name. She could swear blind Karen wasn't at his funeral. Karen doesn't know what Stuart's wife looks like. Isn't that how women who have affairs behave – pretend the wife doesn't really exist (although how would she know)? And as for Stuart (the bastard), she can't imagine him talking about her to this Karen. Telling her his wife's a social worker. Now why the fuck would she want to know that?

She suddenly wants to cry. To think that bastard could carry on annoying her even after death. The awful thought has come to her that, if Karen really is having Stuart's child, the child might be entitled to a share of Stuart's money. Not the insurance, for that is a separate matter, but what about the rest? Should she even go to a lawyer?

The phone is ringing. Thank Christ for the phone to break into her crazy thoughts. Anybody, even a double glazing salesperson would be welcome.

Hi, it's Alan.

Hallo, Alan, how're you doing?

Fine. Er, I was wondering how you were.

Oh, fine, fine.

I was thinking about coming round to see you sometime.

Oh, great. Do you know, Alan, I could just do with a – a visitor. I'd love to see you.

Can I bring a pal as well?

Yeah, yeah, of course you can. Who's the pal?

Chris. From school.

Right. Would you like to come for your tea sometime this week?

Could we come tomorrow?

Aye, of course you can. We'll get fish and chips, will we? Do you still like fish and chips?

Aye, brilliant. You're a pal, Madge.

As she puts the phone down she vaguely wonders whether he has fallen out with one, or both, of his parents. Gavin has been a bit neurotic lately. So has Sheila for that matter (Christ, she's one to talk). Then it dawns on her. Sheila mentioned something about this Chris lad. How she had a notion he was gay. She has been noticing more things, she says, not just after Alan made his own announcement but after he got beat up, the poor soul. At least they've got the wee bastards that did it. Not that wee either, by the sounds of it. They'll probably wind up getting probation or something. Get palmed off onto the social work. As if they dinnae have enough to deal wi. Right enough but what use would prison or the Young Offenders be? Just harden their prejudices. Turn muggers into murderers.

She's looking forward to the two of them coming round now. It has been lonely being off work, even though there's the baby to look forward to and everything. Since meeting that Karen her own baby has been at the back, instead of the forefront, of her mind. It was Alan who reminded her. He is still a kid, after all. Still needs looking after. And she will need to get out once in a while after the baby's born, so maybe he could babysit. Although they're supposed to be sixteen, right enough.

The baby is kicking her in the stomach again, trying to assert itself. For the first time she wonders if it will be a boy or a girl. She doesn't even know what she wants. Although she is a bit worried that if it's a boy he'll turn out looking like Stuart, turn into Stuart even. Imagine going through all that agony only to end up with another Stuart. Or maybe she will have the girl and Karen will have a wee Stuart. Another Stuart to haunt her, take his revenge. Christ, who is she to talk about folk being neurotic? She is talking about an innocent wee baby. Paranoid is what she is. Paranoid as fuck. Fuck.

Sheila

I'd like to come as well, Alan said last night when they were talking about it.

You can come after school and have a look. Can't he, Gavin? You can't go taking time off school.

It's my da's big day, he says.

For a minute she thought he was going to start the way he used to, before the holiday in Nice. If he starts again, she said to herself, I'm going to see about Anger Management classes or something.

How would you do that? Gavin asked her when she mentioned the idea, out loud, early last summer.

The GP makes a referral to a psychiatrist, she explained. She knew enough about it. Enough of her clients had had referrals. Christ only knew what the waiting list was like, right enough. What are folk supposed to do in the meantime? Murder their families? Well, some do, of course.

Och, come on, Sheila. That's going a bit far, isn't it?

No, I don't think so, Gavin.

She could've, should've really, said a lot more but they weren't exactly communicating that well then, were they? They were all pretty uptight at the time. That was one of the things she worried about after Alan was attacked, that he would just lose it, go over the edge. Trauma can have all sorts of psychological implications. It is well-documented. Only it never happened (or hasn't, yet). Then there is still the trial to come. He could still crack under the pressure. But she doesn't think somehow that he will. He has Chris, of course. She hopes that Chris will be around long-term. And that Alan will cope when he isn't. A special friendship is what we all need (she cannot quite think of it as a relationship although she doesn't know if that is how Alan thinks of it).

Only Alan just shrugged when she told him straight he had to go to school. Thank Christ. Before he left this morning he even grinned and thumped Gavin on the shoulder.

All the best dad. Have some champagne on me, eh?

Gavin is incredibly nervous. He always has been, of course. She minds the day of their wedding. Folk told her afterwards he was at the church half an hour early. Half a bloody hour. Afraid to do the wrong thing but not in the fawning, deferential sense. No worried about getting a showing up himself. Afraid to do wrong by her.

It would be all too easy to be dismissive of the event as a wee parochial thing, a wee something folk in community centres do to justify the existence of their jobs. But some folk have no life at all without places like these to go to. The pensioners' lunch club, youth clubs, playgroups and playschemes, Keep Fit, Welfare Rights. The middle classes go to private gyms and have their nannies and nurseries, their kids go to music lessons and swimming clubs and what-have-you. When you live in a block of four with green stuff growing under your bed and all your money goes on your electric and the loan sharks, a place like this is manna sent from heaven. Sometimes quite literally because they have a good wee community café going. When your cooker's on its last legs and the Social won't cough up for another one and you can't afford the repayments at least you can maybe afford 50p for a bowl of good home-made soup your mother never taught you to make, because she was always up to high dough as well trying to make ends meet with wee weans, even not so wee ones, the same as you are. Only weans are worse these days, never satisfied, always wanting something, so it is worse overall.

There is quite a crowd gathered. The local councillor – a woman whose name she cannot remember, unfortunately and it is too late to ask Gavin – and the management committee Gavin is introducing her to, but lots of other folk are here too. When the councillor pulls the wee cord that draws back the curtain there is an audible intake of breath. And no bloody wonder. She is no art critic but it looks absolutely fantastic. It makes her want to cry.

The councillor, too, is genuinely moved.

I just want to thank Mr Taylor – Gavin here – for this incredible – this beautiful – work of art. Gavin, it is really wonderful. Not that any of us could begin to take it in all at once. Look, I'll just hand over to Gavin here. Gavin.

There is tremendous applause as the councillor makes room for Gavin. Even though she admires the painting so much (and, as the councillor says, cannot yet begin to take it all in, for it is sort of chaotic too) surely the applause is really for Gavin rather than the painting?

It is not exactly a podium – just a wee makeshift sort of stage constructed out of what looks like pallets – but it seems just right for this sort of thing. Not that she has ever been to anything like this. She has been to various Open Days, Community Fairs, fun gatherings with amusements for the kids, workshops for the adults, stuff like that, but this is different. Maybe she didn't really think before about art being for ordinary folk in schemes. Maybe she does understand Gavin's art a wee bit better (but only a wee bit).

Gavin seems at home, anyhow, more at peace with himself. Slowly, methodically, he points at all the different areas of the painting. She has never heard him speak in public like this, least of all discuss his art. She is more than surprised – awed even – but also a little envious. Is she such a poor listener he can explain better to folk here what it is all about?

He is pointing out the People's Palace (still his favourite museum), the Gallery of Modern Art, the folk with their banners and the ship in the background. Folk will like the banners anyway, even if they think the ship is too wee. It looks like more of a boat than a ship. And the Clyde. Now, there is definitely something peculiar about the Clyde although she can't say exactly what it is. And there is something near the water that looks suspiciously like a palm tree.

I'm going to call it *Sunflowers and Beach, Glasgow*, Gavin continues. Or maybe *Sunflowers, Palm Tree and Beach, Glasgow*. You'll all ken well enough without me telling you that you cannae grow sunflowers outside in Glasgow – no unless you're very lucky anyway – and, even if you did manage them, you couldnae grow palm trees unless they're in the Botanic gardens. Aye, there's nae palm trees and definitely nae beach in Glasgow. Plenty water but nae beach.

There are a few laughs, but not a lot. They are anxiously waiting for Gavin's interpretation of the big picture in front of them, afraid to decide what they think of it. Gavin doesn't seem surprised. Maybe that is as it should be. For once folk not rushing in and making up their minds.

Naw, I picked the sunflowers because I'm a fan of Van Gogh, to tell you the truth. Unlike some of the folk whose work I've seen, Van Gogh hardly made a penny frae his works, even though there's other folk making millions these days. Sold his paintings just to get bed and board.

There is, however, a beach in Nice, Gavin goes on to say. A bloody beautiful beach that's miles long. Although I daresay some folk would turn their noses up because there's nae sand, only pebbles. No as good as Largs, I can hear some folk say. Aye, well, I suppose it depends on what you're after because the water's warmer in the bay at Nice.

She feels the colour rising in her cheeks. Whereas a moment ago she was as proud as punch of this man, now she worries he is making a fool of himself. Why couldn't he have discussed his speech with her? She didn't even know he was going to make a speech. The comparisons with Van Gogh and Nice are, Jesus, a bit spurious to say the least (aren't they?). The best (or worst) of it is that he is (for once) so bloody confident, so bloody sure of himself. And, Christ Almighty, the folk here are beginning to fall under his spell. You could hear a pin drop, the place is that quiet. As long as there aren't any art critic type people here who will slag him to bits in the paper the morra. Besides which maybe she is anxious about what Gavin is going to say about Nice. She suddenly thinks about Stuart. Stuart drowning.

Yous'll maybe be wondering what in the name has Nice tae dae wi Glasgow, Well, plenty, probably. Like they're baith beautiful cities and all that. But I can only tell you what the connection means to me, a Glaswegian. Nice inspired me to start painting, that's all I can say. And Glasgow continues to inspire me.

So the sunflowers are the wee bit of light in the darkness, Gavin is saying as if he had been doing public speaking for years. I mean, let's face it, Glasgow is not all sweetness and light. It's no that long ago rickets was rife. There's folk among us'll remember rickets in Glasgow. And we still have the highest death rate frae heart disease in the country. There's things we cannae boast aboot. I mean, it can be what you want it to be. So can the beach. The beach can be Doon the Watter, or it can be Nice or anywhere you remember having a lovely holiday because our past is part of our present. The beach is pleasure and leisure and all that. Liberation. The beach is symbolic. I even put the mountains in at the back. Ben Lomond or the Alps. Take your pick. We are only limited by our imagination. And art is there to help our imaginations.

Whit aboot the banner? somebody is saying. The pink banner. I mean, Gavin, should it no have been red?

She can see the flush rising on his cheeks.

It could have been red, he says slowly. Of course it could. But I wanted it pink because this is a painting for the twenty first century. I'm no saying Socialism's dead, Jim, nothing like that. He hesitates and it is only at the last moment that his voice goes high and thin.

It's maybe obvious even if you cannae read the writing on the banner, he says. It says GLASGAY for those of you who cannae see it frae the back there. It's an attempt to be inclusive, if you like. That's all it is.

As he steps down she realises the effort it must have taken to speak the way he did, that confidence can be a short-lived thing, that maybe it is all ebbed away already. He looks embarrassed. Jesus, he whispers to her. They'll be thinking I'm half-cut. I don't know what came over me.

They're all applauding although she doesn't think the applause is maybe quite as loud as it was before he started the speech. No matter. As long as they are still applauding. She would applaud too but she has her arm round him, hugging him. She would carry on hugging him but the mobile in her pocket is vibrating away. She turned the ringer off but she suddenly remembers Madge who is overdue and not very well.

You were brilliant, she says. The painting is brilliant.

It's Madge. She lifts the mobile to her ear and is relieved that the councillor has come over to speak to him so she can head off out into the corridor to talk to her in peace.

I've been having labour pains – at least I think it's labour pains – since the small hours. I didn't want to disturb you only my waters've just broke. How did it go?

Och, very well. Very well. He's just finished his speech. Do you want me to come and take you to the hospital?

Och, no. I can get a taxi. No, I just wanted to let you know, that's all.

Aye, well, all the best, Madge. I'll phone the hospital later on to see how you're doing.

Aye. I could maybe phone you anyway. If I'm up to it, that is.

Back in the hall there is music and dancing. She can hardly believe all this has been laid on in honour of the painting – in Gavin's honour. She racks her brain to try and remember if Gavin said something about an opening, anything else but she can't be sure. Anyway, Gavin was the only one (she thinks) giving a speech so there can't have been anything else, can there? Maybe the wee shindig is their way of saying thankyou to Gavin who has, after all, done a full-time job for sweet FA. House painters, like he was before, get a better bloody deal than that. And if they wanted to do things properly they could have had the bloody do in the evening when Alan could've come. There's a wee group of kids doing Scottish dancing. If they could get the time off the school so could Alan. Shit.

She is back to feeling dissatisfied again. She knows no-one here (maybe that is for the best. Maybe some of them are social work clients, after all). She should've offered Madge a lift to the hospital. It would've got her out of this. Although one reason why she didnae offer Madge the lift is because she had this fear – still has it – that Madge was going to ask her to stay with her, help at the delivery. No way, no fucking way. They are not that bloody close. Although you hear about sisters, daughters even, doing it sometimes. It's no fun going into a delivery room on your ownio. At least she had Gavin. Not that he was a helluva lot of use if she remembers correctly. Weeping like a wean.

Absurdly, she feels out of her depth. And what is all this stuff about Glasgay, for fuck's sake? Gavin isnae going to turn round and tell people about his own son, is he? He wouldnae be that daft, would he? Maybe it's just as well she stayed if she can get him to keep his big gob shut. Where is the bugger anyway? She turns as she feels pressure on her arm. Gavin.

I want you to meet the local councillor, he says to her.

A sense of normality begins to return as she begins to engage the woman (or the woman engages her) in the importance of community spirit, in bringing art to the people. A lot of what they say is jargon, she knows — but it is a world familiar to her (she uses similar jargon on a daily basis in her job, after all). She senses, too, the councillor is relieved to be talking to a fellow-professional. It lends an air of normality to the business not just for her, then. That is the trouble with arty types like Gavin, you don't know where you are with them, you don't know where to place them. When the councillor starts talking about funding for community art projects she doesn't pursue the subject. For all she knows Gavin has been on about it already (although she doubts that). Anyway, after what he said the day, it seems Gavin can fight his own battles.

As the councillor moves on and she blends into the company at last, chatting now to a woman her own age who says she's on the management committee, she thinks again about what Gavin said about being inclusive. It is more than jargon, that word. It is government-speak. It is definitely not the sort of word Gavin would use. A lie then. A fib to avoid the real explanation for the Glasgay. A personal thing then, a tribute even, is what he meant. It is a nice touch. She looks over at the painting again. It will take a while to get into, right enough — there is that much of it — but she thinks maybe the pink banner with the folk — young and old — holding onto it is her favourite bit. She wonders what Alan will think when he sees it.

Madge

She is staying in the hospital that bit longer than most folk not just, she suspects, because she had a Caesarian, but because she is that wee bit older than your average new mother. She doesn't mind. It gives her a bit of time really, to think through not just how she is going to spend the next few weeks – getting all the baby stuff she should have bought months ago – but the next months, years even, as well. Like, is she going to go back to work? It makes her realise how little she has thought it all through, her future, the baby's future. The last eight months (och, no, let's face it, the last donkeys' years) have been a sort of blind panic. One day at a time. It was bloody murder living wi Stuart and then it was great being pregnant, only Karen was pregnant too, and then there was all this paranoia about Stuart's ghost when she doesn't even believe in ghosts.

She has been winding down since the birth. She has had to learn everything from scratch, the way all new mothers do, but that suits her. A new beginning. Time to let go of the old. She had all but forgotten Karen Daly when, two days after she was delivered (delivered! Jesus, the words these health care people use!) who gets wheeled into the ward but Herself.

It was like Providence (or the Second Coming). It would have been crazy not to go and have a look. Thank fuck, thank fuck, she muttered to herself when she stopped by the bed to say hello and Karen told her it was a she. She could have danced, despite the stitches. Only afterwards she lay in bed, feeling suddenly upset, realising she still didn't know. This morning the knowledge was irrelevant and then suddenly it was important again. Only she can hardly go and ask a woman just out the delivery ward if her baby is her husband's or someone else's. She'd be liable to smack her one in the face or something.

Visiting time and she had to tell Sheila, who came alone this time.

Sheila couldn't resist a look herself. The next bay down, she said. In the corner by the window.

In the corner, by the window, you said, Sheila repeats, when she comes back.

Aye, that's right.

There's a man with her. From the way they're sitting I'd say he was her husband.

Oh.

Maybe they're back together.

So they are. Karen herself came to tell her that evening.

I feel a bit embarrassed about telling you we were separated, she says, almost nonchalantly. You won't say anything to anyone, will you?

She shakes her head. Actually, maybe there's something you can do for me?

Oh?

She takes a deep breath. It is now or never. Providence and all that.

I was married to Stuart McCracken, she says carefully, watching Karen's face as she says it.

Ah, says Karen, a dark horse if ever there was one. You know, I had an idea. There is a ghost of a smile on her face.

Did you? She does not know whether to believe her.

Och, just when you mentioned the accident, you know, I put two and two together. Not that he told me, I mean. I had no idea till you turned up at the ante-natal.

We thought we couldn't have kids.

Oh. He never told me. He never really said much about a lot of things. I suppose I didn't really know him that well.

Apart from in the biblical sense, you mean, Madge says, trying to sound sharp but only succeeding, she reckons, in sounding a wee bit ridiculous.

Karen flushes, to give her her due. Did he talk about me?

Madge is incredulous. Are you kidding? I didn't even know you existed till last summer.

You know I finished with him? She is practically haughty.

No, I didn't know.

You thought he finished with me? She is incredulous. Is that what he told you?

You don't understand, Madge says slowly. I never knew you finished with him because I never even knew he was having an affair until my friend told me.

Oh, I see. Erm, does your friend work at the union or what?

She shakes her head. She's a social worker.

Karen frowns. Christ, I know people talk but I didn't realise it was that bad.

Madge shakes her head. My friend only knew because Stuart told her. He never told me. I mean, he might have got round to it or he might not but he drowned. Look, there's something I've been wanting to ask you.

She doesn't want to ask it, of course. It is more of a necessity, a purging of the past.

That's my baby crying, I've got to go.

Madge follows her back to her bed although her own wee mite is beginning to stir. In here the one wakes the other. Funny, she minds her mum saying something of the sort about when she was born.

She waits until Karen has the baby settled before she speaks again.

Stuart and I wanted a baby for years. Eighteen years. You think the longing goes but it doesn't really. You only bury it under other things but it always resurfaces. We stopped talking about it, stopped trying, eventually.

He never told me you were pregnant, Karen repeats. I'm glad I finished with him. Even though he's dead I would feel it was on my conscience. Married men are one thing but married men with kids are something else.

Madge smiles to herself. This is a new one on her. A new kind of morality. She can just imagine repeating this conversation to Sheila and Gavin. The nerve of the woman.

I just can't stand that kind of deceit.

It is Madge's turn to be incredulous. You don't think, she says, stopping for breath, that having an affair with a married man is deceitful?

Maybe, but not every couple takes monogamy for granted. I mean, Stuart had loads of affairs, didn't he? Karen says, almost absently, as if she is not meaning to be cruel. I mean, it's not as if I was the first. Just because he went on about the two of us living together I wasn't fooled for one minute. Not one minute. I mean, they all say that, don't they, that they'll leave their wives?

Madge is nearly in tears. I don't believe you. You're just making that up – about the other women.

She is trying to sort out in her head which is worse – the other women or the fact that he was going to leave her. If he was going to leave her.

Karen bites her lip. I'm sorry. I thought you must have known. I still can't get over you not knowing about me. Although the – affair – was pretty short-lived, I suppose. I suppose that's why I finished with him. I mean, it would have happened sooner rather than later anyway but I suppose I knew it couldn't go on after I got pregnant. You know, he thought – he actually had the nerve to think it might... She stops in mid-sentence.

What? Although she knows fine what.

Karen stares at her now. Oh, Jesus, Jesus, don't tell me you thought it too. Christ, of course she isn't Stuart's. Of course not. Christ.

How can you be so sure?

Because we had protected sex, of course. I don't go around having unprotected sex, you know.

Except with your husband.

Absolutely.

If she is lying the woman is bloody good at it. This is as much as she is ever going to get out of her. Her wee Moira is crying. She goes to see to her without another word to the woman.

So, after the bitch finished with Stuart (assuming she isn't lying, only you can't trust folk like that) then maybe Stuart wasn't going to leave her after all. If he was going to leave her because this is the first she's heard of it. Even if he was maybe he changed his mind. Or maybe Karen just changed it for him. Either way she has no regrets, not for a minute. Because if the bastard had plenty fish in the sea as Karen made out (and she's pretty bloody sure she wasn't lying there – she could tell by the look on her face) then he wasnae worth the fucking candle. Her and wee Moira are better off without him and she doesnae just mean the money. And for all she knows Glasgow – Scotland even (even fucking Britain since he was always travelling here, there and everywhere) could be full of Stuart's bastards since he wasn't so fucking infertile after all but they cannae fucking prove it and they sure as hell arenae getting a bloody penny off of her.

She is going back to her own name and so is wee Moira. The only place Stuart McCracken's name is going to survive will be on the birth certificate. Only one thing remains, one thing she wants – no, needs to ask Sheila.

See when Stuart told you he was having an affair, Madge whispers to her when she drops in the day before Madge is due to go home, to see if she needs anything.

Aye, she says, although she doesn't see, not at all.

Well, how exactly did he put it?

She doesn't want to put words into Sheila's mouth.

Look, I don't remember the exact words, Madge.

That's not what I meant. Look, did he tell you he was going to leave me?

Sheila flushes. Christ, Madge, I'm sorry, I don't exactly remember. I was just that shocked when he mentioned this other woman.

It is Madge's turn to flush now. With anger.

Oh, come on now, Sheila, I'm supposed to be your best friend and you're saying you don't remember – like you never *noticed* – whether he was going to leave me.

I thought you wanted to put the past behind you, Sheila says miserably. What does it matter now? Look, I only stopped to speak to him because I'd noticed him coming out of this sex shop and he saw I noticed him. So we went for a coffee, a drink. I had a drink with him.

Go on.

He wanted to explain, he said, about what he was doing in the sex shop. Explain that he wasn't getting anything for you two. We're no longer an item, me and Madge. That was what he said. Those were near enough his exact words.

I see. That seems pretty clear.

I was so confused for ages. I was really raging inside. I mean, he only told me this after we had our drinks and our sandwiches or I would never've sat there with him. I was so disgusted.

He wanted you to tell me, Madge says slowly, as the words form a picture in her head.

No, he didn't, Madge. That's the thing. He said he'd tell you himself. He just didn't want me getting wrong ideas – about the sex shop.

He probably thought you'd tell me just the same.

I doubt it.

Och, well, either way you're right about it not making any difference,

Madge sighs.

I suppose you know she's gone?

Is she? I never bothered to look. Och, good luck to her is all I can say. I wonder if she has him on her conscience.

What do you mean?

She says she finished with him. I don't know when exactly but I presume it was after he met you.

You mean, she might've driven him to it? I thought it didn't look like suicide because of the way he was dressed and everything?

Doesnae prove a thing but, the way he was dressed. Naw, I'm just lucky a bloody great man o' war took the wrong turning.

Sheila half-laughs, not sure if Madge is joking.

It's the first time I've said as much, isn't it? Madge smiles.

Sheila smiles back. She doesn't think it is, although she wasn't maybe as blunt before. Och, Christ, who can blame you? she says, still a wee bit shocked. She just hopes her face doesn't show it.

Gavin

She brought it up the first day he went to see her, after she was out the hospital. Offering to babysit, like. Alan had offered as well but she might be worried he was a bit young. A bit useless too, he reckoned, although he wouldn't say that. Not even to Madge. Maybe especially not to Madge in case it got back to Alan.

I'm not going back to social work, she says.

What will you do then?

I'm definitely going into business. She pauses, expectantly.

I thought the organic food thing fell through?

Och, I was never that keen on that anyway, she says dismissively. I still like the idea of the murals, Gavin. I just need a partner. And she gives him this long, hard look.

Aye, well, Madge, he says.

You could still do your more arty stuff at the community centre or at home or wherever. This needn't even be full-time. If you got fed up with it you could always leave. I could make you an employee if you want. Then you'd be guaranteed a salary.

Aye, well, he says again because he was just gob-smacked.

I've started drawing up this business plan, she says. Only I need your advice about supplies and so on. We could start small. Just doing offices, stuff like that. I know a guy who's interested already.

Give us a couple of days to think about it, Madge, he says.

She looks surprised. I was going to suggest a couple of weeks.

He isn't doing anything at the community centre these days. Now they have their mural he doesn't seem to be needed anymore. Until somebody comes up with some bright idea. He suggested brightening up the corridors but he got the impression folk weren't exactly keen. Whenever he goes up the place – which isnae that often these days – he sees ones passing, looking at it, no exactly saying they dinnae like it but puzzled, like. He isn't exactly a crowd-pleaser, never was, still it's disappointing but. Everybody isnae like the wee laddie that day about the sunflowers.

We're thinking about getting the kids at the summer playscheme to do their own mural, someone said.

Fair enough. Great idea, he said. He meant it too. Hopefully the wee sunflowers laddie would get in there, dae his bit. He was probably the reason he put the sunflowers in the Glasgow mural, as much as Nice or Van Gogh or any other reason.

He has plenty to occupy him, anyway. He is working on a painting at home. A portrait of Sheila. He never tried his hand at a portrait before. To start with he was petrified she wouldn't like it, would hate it. Don't people always like to be flattered? Plus lately he doesn't think Sheila is all that happy with getting older, getting lines under the eyes, even her jaw drooping that wee bit. He cannae deny those parts of her. He loves them every bit as much as the rest of her. A camera could lie better than he could.

He didn't let her see it at first. He was afraid her opinion would influence him, maybe make him drop the project altogether. The more he got into it the harder it would be to leave it. As the painting developed he felt he knew his wife better and better. He began to see facets of her personality that had never struck him before. He got into the depth of it, the way he had got into the depth of *Sunflowers and Beach, Glasgow*. Maybe it was the title annoyed folk for he had insisted on naming it himself. How could he own it otherwise?

It was Alan persuaded him, if in the end he needed persuading.

You'd be doing Madge a favour, he says. Never mind the money. It'd be an experiment for you, a chance to go out and meet people.

Aye, you're right, he says at last. He was thinking, but didn't say, that an artist needs to go outside his own environment, even to recognise where he is coming from. He has never been near middle class people in his life. Not unless you call Madge middle class. Christ, some folk would even call Sheila middle class only he thinks different. The two of them (Stuart as well, now he minds) were born into working class families but class, he feels, is something you carry with you all your born days. He was talking about this to Sheila one day and she said she had spoken to a colleague about the subject shortly afterwards. The colleague went one further (which him and Sheila both agreed was ridiculous), trying to make out that you always pass your class onto your children. An absurdity, when you think about it, for how then would there ever be any movement between the classes? Social status would be fixed forever and a day.

Pure mental, Alan, who was listening, agreed. He and Sheila laughed. Alan being a good example of a mixture, he reckons. He wouldn't bother going too far into the exact quantities, the proportions, class analysis being something of an inexact science.

Don't get me wrong, Alan says. I think you should do what your heart tells you and all that. But see after that guy made the comment about the pink banner, like, you have to admit there's numpties everywhere.

I ken that, son, I ken that, he says but Alan had a point. Maybe he thought there was less of them in community centre-type places and maybe he is wrong. It was Sheila told Alan about what Jimmy said about the pink banner. To tell the truth, he wouldn't have repeated it to him, maybe in case Alan flew off the handle but also there was the loyalty streak in him. His ain people, all that. He might have come from Easterhouse whereas the community centre is in the south side but they are still his ain people. But then, right enough, look at his da. Imagine showing him a painting like that, fuck's sake. Only Sheila mentioned it because, well, presumably Sheila has a different view about loyalty. That and presumably also now she trusts Alan not to fly off the handle all the time.

He didn't have to ask Alan what he thought of *Sunflowers and Beach, Glasgow*. Him and Chris just went along themselves for a look.

Purely belter! Alan goes, grinning all over his face. It was an expression the two of them had picked up from this film they had seen. Chris was grinning too.

What bit did you like best? Expecting him to say, The banner, of course.

The beach, Alan says.

Me, too. The beach, Chris goes.

Imagine having a beach in Glasgow. It's brilliant! Alan says.

Aye, purely belter! Chris goes and the two of them go away shrieking.

What about the banner? he asked Alan afterwards, when Chris was away and he had calmed down.

What banner? Alan asked. It was then he explained and then Sheila came in and told him about Jim. Then the next day Alan and Chris headed off for another look.

Maybe a lot of folk dinnae even notice the banner then, he thinks. Especially the first time round. It's hard to see the mural as others see it. As Sheila pointed out, it's hard to take it all in at once.

Now that's not a criticism, Gavin, she emphasised. If anything, it's a compliment.

He smiled then. He kent she meant it that way. Anyway, he will have to learn to take (constructive) criticism if he is going to do murals, never mind be an artist.

What are you up to the day? Sheila asked him a couple of days after Madge had brought up the murals project again. A second chance, or maybe a last one. He had broached the subject that night wi Sheila but Sheila wasnae getting involved.

You do what you think is best, Gavin, she goes. To tell you the truth I'm out of my depth anyway.

Away o that, Sheila, he says. Only he cannae expect her to be into everything he is, right enough. Pity, he says, wi just the ghost of a smile on his lips, an art critic for a wife could be a bonus in this line o business.

She gave him a friendly shove then. Away, you, but he didn't think she assumed, even then, he was going to go ahead wi it.

I'm away for a walk. It's a lovely day. Maybe she had forgot what they were talking about two nights ago. Maybe it was as well not to mention it. Maybe Madge had changed her mind already. Maybe it was just post-natal hormones or something that had got her rushing around like a mad thing when she had a wee wean to take care of.

I don't suppose you'll be going anywhere near Madge's? It's just that I've got the wean some more stuff. I'm terrible. I cannae pass a baby shop these days.

Aye, all right. Just give us the stuff, he says.

Good luck wi the new project, she whispered after he kissed her goodbye. She said it that quiet he was beginning to think he'd imagined it.

He feels lucky, right enough, as he wanders out into the street later that morning carrying not just the baby stuff but a big bag containing a calculator and a notebook as well as a large sketch pad. Madge will expect him to be organised. He has already made a number of sketches in the pad. You have to start somewhere.

He is pleased to find the sun is shining. As he sets off he starts to hum to himself, singing the words inside his head, *C'était une Histoire d'Amour*.

For a full list of our publications please write to

Dewi Lewis Publishing
8 Broomfield Road
Heaton Moor
Stockport SK4 4ND

You can also visit our web site at

www.dewilewispublishing.com